THE DEAD ONE PROTRUDES

By DON THOMPSON

Copyright 2018 ©

ISBN – 13: 978-0-9897196-1-2

TABLE OF CONTENTS

1 AMERICA IS GREAT AGAIN 1

2 THE OPENING ACT 3

3 CONFLICT MANAGEMENT 12

4 THE DEAL 21

5 THE DEAD ONE PROTRUDES 31

6 IT WAS WHITEMAN 36

7 MORE STIFFS 41

8 MORE NEWS FROM GOOFYTOWN 47

9 THE COPS AGAIN 56

10 MORE OF THE CONFLICTS COMMITTEE 66

11 TO BUY OR NOT TO BUY, THAT IS THE QUESTION 74

12 THE ESTATE PLAN 83

13 CHICAGO ART PANEL COMPANY 96

14 MORE NEWS 101

15 ESTATE ADMINISTRATION 108

16 THE GOLD COAST ASSOCIATION 117

17 WIGGY REPORTS 130

18 PANSY'S PARTY 135

19 SEAN AND THE COPS 150

20 ASSOCIATE MATTERS 157

21 THE FUZZ BALLS AGAIN 168

22 MORE OF THE PRACTICE OF LAW 188

23 WORLD AND LOCAL AFFAIRS ARE BUTT CRAZY 193

24 ASS PISS MEETING	200
25 HUMP DELUXE GOES DOWN	206
26 THE RING	208
27 MORE OF THE COPS	215
28 FIRE!	220
29 FIRM PARTY AT THE SQUASH CLUB	228
30 NEWS OF THE WORLD	263

WARNING!

Do not let your parents catch you reading this book.

THE DEAD ONE PROTRUDES

1 AMERICA IS GREAT AGAIN

It is summer 2017 in dear and delightful Chicago. To everyone' surprise, Sillary Flinton won the election, even though Ronald Hump and his Vice Presidential candidate, Akhmed Faruqe, won the popular vote. America is great again! Very, very, very great! At what is as yet an unanswered question.

Hump had been talking about building a wall between the U.S. and Mexico and having Mexico pay for it which was ridiculous, but popular, so Flinton had come up with her own wall promise. After consulting with her soon to be Vice President, her husband Will, she realized that a wall between the U.S. and Mexico would hinder our invasion so she promised to build walled off safe communities. The idea was to make them safe from criminals and murderers by building a wall around them, limiting access to those with proper credentials, monitoring all communications and subjecting them to constant electronic surveillance. The basic idea was that for true security we have to lock up the law abiding people so the crooks and terrorists can't get at them. Flinton proposed experimenting with two versions. One was to be in an urban area and one was to be in a secret location. The principle behind the secret location was that if the evil enemies of America can't find us, they can't kill us. Flinton had also started talking against Mexican immigrants because this was so popular for Hump.

After Flinton revealed her plans for walled secure communities during the campaign the rest of the world expressed their approval for the idea and when this was revealed Hump's lead disappeared. What the

THE DEAD ONE PROTRUDES

press did not reveal was that the rest of the world was in favor of some kind of wall all around the U.S. keeping us in, not them out. Mexico and Canada were especially in favor of the idea.

THE DEAD ONE PROTRUDES

2 THE OPENING ACT

Fenton, Pettigrew & Cohenstein was one of Chicago's most prestigious law firms. It was an amalgam of an old line, snobby, anti-Semitic law firm that was not doing so well anymore and an up and coming firm headed by Zenon Cohenstein. Fenton, Pettigrew was still headed by one of the anti-Semitic snobs, namely Graybourne St. Charles. He had basically inherited his position and kept it because he also inherited the firm's biggest client, The Swifton Bank, one of the largest in the world. The firm occupied floors 40 to 55 in The Bank's building, known as One Swifton Plaza, in the center of Chicago's downtown. The firm's only other U.S. locations were a suburban office in Highland Park, known as the Lake County office, and one in New York. It had offices outside the country in Mexico City, Shanghai, Hong Kong, Singapore and Mumbai. There were 60 equity partners and 200 other partners. Equity partners actually owned the firm and got the profits. The other partners were basically employees who got a share of the profits determined by the equity partners, although their compensation scheme was whatever the equity partners wanted to make it. The other lawyers were the younger ones called associates and were usually paid a set salary and a bonus at the end of the year. In total there were 630 lawyers. The firm basically had big rich clients and did big money deals and litigation. The equity partners had some of the highest lawyer incomes in the country and most people working there were, in their own estimation, quite superior.

One of the equity partners who worked there was not regarded as one of the leading lights of the legal world or even regarded at all since he rarely attracted anyone's notice. He was Bumper Lohman who was

THE DEAD ONE PROTRUDES

perhaps the world's biggest nobody. Hardly anyone knew he existed. He was a simple old guy who talked in nouns and verbs with very little in the way of adjectives and adverbs. As such, hardly anyone could believe that he was a lawyer. On the other hand hardly anyone had to figure out whether he was or was not a lawyer because hardly anyone was aware of his presence, due to the brevity of his statements. He usually said whatever he had to say before everyone else in the place had finished scrapping their chairs around and coughing and trying to hide their farts in the process of getting settled. As a matter of fact, the last time he had addressed a group of the firm's associates there were constant shouts of "Can't hear you!" as he spoke. What he had to say ended quickly so the associates were still shouting at him to speak up. He merely shouted back, "So shut up and listen!" and repeated what he had said whereupon there was a steady, low, murmuring of, "What did he say?" throughout the room. Who can understand something without first being told that they are going to be told something that will elevate them to an ecstatic Heaven on earth and then being told what they are going to be told and then being told and then being told what they have been told? Sometimes you have to give them a treat first to get their attention and a treat for a reward at the end.

Lohman was the Managing Partner. He was not the Chairman, the big boss. That was St. Charles. He was not the Vice Chairman who was Cohenstein. He was just the guy to take care of things. When something not involving a star role needed doing suddenly everyone knew he existed. A large law firm is a loony bin and not only the basics of running a business, but constant emergencies needed attention. Lohman and his people did that. The big important stuff was handled by the Management Committee consisting of nine equity partners owning over fifty percent of the interests in the firm. Oddly enough,

THE DEAD ONE PROTRUDES

Lohman was one, although he was the one on the Committee who owned the least and earned the least.

Matters of importance involving St. Charles and Cohenstein were usually handled in St. Charles' conference room on the 55th floor. However on this wonderful Thursday, June 8th, it was being worked on so the emergency of the day was going to be held on short notice in Lohman's conference room on the 44th floor. St. Charles and Cohenstein had arrived and Lohman's secretary, who refused to be called a personal assistant, had left the outer office to take something to the Business Office that Lohman wanted explained.

"Bumper," said St. Charles, "there is a matter of great urgency. We must have a meeting of the Management Committee immediately. Matters involving conflicts of interest and the most highly placed persons have arisen."

Lohman said, "What about the Conflicts Committee? Remember that we have a committee to look into conflicts of interest. And the Business Office is supposed to screen them to begin with and refer any questions to me."

Cohenstein said, "We know that, but this is big stuff."

"Like what?" asked Lohman.

"Like Flinton and Hump," said Cohenstein, "and one of our clients."

St. Charles said, "It's that wall business. They want to build some sort of wall here in Chicago and the only concrete contractor who can handle a job like that is our client - - -." He looked at Cohenstein.

Cohenstein said, "Yeah Bumper, that - who is that concrete company?"

THE DEAD ONE PROTRUDES

"Whiteman Materials," said Lohman. "They are our client."

"Yeah, them," said Cohenstein. "That Hump guy wants to be the concrete contractor for the wall and who would he get it from - our client. So there is a rumor he also wants to build it on land he owns or controls or can get his hands on and The Bank is talking about financing some of it for him."

"Exactly," said St. Charles. "We have to figure out how to maneuver through all this without representing conflicting interests."

Cohenstein, who could sell heaters in Hell, added, "And we want the business and boy, could we get some good PR out of this!"

Lohman saw nothing new in this. Trying to get nine busy lawyers in one place at one time on short notice is not easy. However, he was called upon to do it quite frequently. In this case though, they added some people to the pot. "Get the Whiteman lawyer here too and get Bungus," said St. Charles. "Who is the Whiteman lawyer anyway?"

"Shannon McClurg," said Lohman.

Bungus was Bungus LaRue who was the firm's "Governmental Affairs" partner. He was formerly a congressman and now operated as a lobbyist and fixer in the ways that are currently legal. What else he did the firm was not too eager to know and he was not usually asked to explain most of the things he was up to. "Don't ask - don't tell" is a useful device in many areas. Remember when Will Flinton was President and he imposed the doctrine on the armed services? He thought as Commander in Chief he should benefit from the rule.

THE DEAD ONE PROTRUDES

Lohman told St. Charles he would arrange everything and St. Charles and Cohenstein were getting ready to leave. St. Charles never asked anyone he expected to grovel in front of him if they were busy or otherwise occupied or if what he wanted could be done and he never thanked them for their efforts and today was not an exception to the rule. Just as Cohenstein was saying, "Thanks Bumper," a young lawyer in the firm and one of his clients bust in. Lohman had made an appointment with them and he had not been able to call it off or postpone it on the short notice he had from St. Charles and Cohenstein.

The young lawyer was John Sweeney who had a seemingly magical ability to attract show business, entertainment and internet clients. This ability translated into high and rapidly growing billings and he had just been made a partner as a result. Lohman had been the name partner on his matters while he was an associate, but Sweeney did all the work. As a partner he still wanted Lohman consulting on his matters and some of the clients did too and he and one of his clients were coming in for that purpose. The client was Trisha DeLang, the world's hottest pop star. Sweeney was an Oh Wow, Hey Duder. Trisha was the biggest potty mouth in the trade. Since Lohman's secretary was not at her post they just went on in to the conference room when they heard voices coming from there.

Sweeney said, "Hey Bumps!" He saw St. Charles and Cohenstein and waived at them and said, "Dudes!"

Trisha had been humming and bopping about as she came in and suddenly she said to everyone, "My new song - get this--." She broke out in a song and complimentary body movements:

THE DEAD ONE PROTRUDES

"Humpy Dumpy built a great wall
Humpy Dumpy sat on his wall
Humpy Dumpy fell off his wall
Shit - on the wrong side of his wall.

Humpy Dumpy stranded was he
Not on the U.S. side was he
He had no passport - oh tee
Stranded in Mexico was he

Humpy Dumpy tried to get back
Please he said, give me some slack
I'm a citizen coming back
To my home in the old outback

The States' guard was taken aback
Thought Humpy was an old wetback
So Humpy had a new, different life
Making cheap for the U.S. fleet.

Humpy - wall
Dumpy - fall
We all do the fall
When we build a wall

Ew -ew-ew -oh-oh-oh
Ew-e-ah-building a wall
Down-down-down - de-do-do
Fallin' down oh from the wall."

THE DEAD ONE PROTRUDES

Trisha finished with throwing her arms up in the air and shouting, "Fuck ass!" Sweeney grabbed her and hugged her.

St. Charles had trouble keeping his undies clean. "What did she say?"

Sweeney said, "Fuk a say."

"What is that?" asked St. Charles.

"It's common Spanish slang," said Sweeney. "It's an expression of ebullient exuberance. It means, 'Hey you! Say!' Her Spanish isn't very good."

St. Charles was too confused to do anything except go into his pause mode. Cohenstein started clapping.

Trisha said, "I was gonna do -," and she broke out in song again:

> "Humpy fit the battle of Mexico,
> of Mexico, Mexico
> Humpy fit the battle of Mexico
> and the wall came tumblin' down."

After a pause Cohenstein said, "Oh, I get it. Jericho - that's it. For a moment there it just passed over my head."

"Is that where the term 'Passover' came from," asked Sweeney?

Cohenstein chuckled and then came over to St. Charles and lifted him up from his chair and said, "Let's go, we have work to do and so do they I hope."

"What work?" asked St. Charles. He did not really understand the word as applied to himself. Applied to others he understood it, but himself?

THE DEAD ONE PROTRUDES

Work? He had people to do that for him. He got up and he and Cohenstein left.

Sweeney and Trisha got seated and so did Lohman. Sweeney said to Lohman, "We wanted to run it by you. Maybe the words should be toned down. What do you think, Bumps?"

Lohman said, "Toned down? That's a strange idea coming from you. I'm not the one to ask anyway. Ask Trisha's agent and some of your show business contacts. These days you can get away with anything. And see if you can get ahold of Bungus. See what he says about the obvious reference to Hump."

Trisha said, "Whatever I do, I want to keep the tune - the music." She leaned over and kissed Sweeney.

Now Sweeney was a good looking young guy who would tell you that, "All the girls like Sweeney weeney." But lawyers who get into their clients get into trouble. Lohman decided to get explicit. "Are you two romantically involved?"

Sweeney said, "Not since I've been her lawyer. Anyway she doesn't like the same guy all the time. She even wants to do Sean - or wanted to." Sean was Sean Featherbottom, a rather obviously gay young associate who often worked with Sweeney. "I had to tell her he's gay."

Lohman remarked, "You had to tell her?" He looked at Trisha and asked, "You didn't know?"

Trisha merely said, "He's cute."

Sweeney said, "Remember when he wasn't even dealing with it himself? That's when she wanted to do him."

THE DEAD ONE PROTRUDES

"What do you mean he wasn't dealing with it?" asked Lohman.

Sweeney said, "He was a closet case - hiding it from himself. That's an old term. It has two meanings. One is hiding it from everyone else and one is hiding it from yourself. Sean was hiding it from himself."

Lohman remembered back to a dramatic scene at a firm party when the cops bust in to arrest Sean for the murder of one of the firm's top partners, which Lohman explained had been done by another partner, and he "Came out." "Oh, I remember," he said. "I think I'd better check my closets when I get home."

THE DEAD ONE PROTRUDES

3 CONFLICT MANAGEMENT

The Management Committee consisted of St. Charles, Cohenstein, Lohman, Alan Allen who specialized in Municipal Securities, John Feepot, head of Corporate, Gooster Fileform, head of Securities, Pincus Ruhlman, with a diversified practice, Jeffrey Wax, head of Tax, and Peer Freebornstein, head of Litigation. It usually met on the first Tuesday of the month, but it was sometimes rescheduled. This time Lohman had managed to get them all present for a rescheduled meeting on June 13th. The meetings were usually held in St. Charles' conference room and by this time the work on it had been completed so that is where it was to be held.

These meetings proceeded in a set way. St. Charles was never there while the others arrived. Only after his secretary told him everyone else was there did he deign to come in. When all the other Committee members were there, as well as Shannon McClurg and Bungus LaRue, St. Charles came in and greeted the group and then turned the script over to Lohman who would lead everyone through the meeting. Lohman told those present that there was a special conflicts of interest matter they had to review and then quickly got them through the other items on the agenda which were few. Then he directed their attention to the conflicts matter.

The firm had a Conflicts Committee to consider conflicts of interest. Law firms are not allowed to represent conflicting interests. For instance they cannot represent both a buyer and seller in the same transaction. Some conflicts can be waived by the clients and some cannot. The Business Office of the firm, headed by Geeley McDade, the Business Manager, usually did a search of the firm's records on any

THE DEAD ONE PROTRUDES

new matter to look for potential conflicts. The lawyers of the firm taking on new matters were also supposed to do a check. All potential new matters were also circulated to all other lawyers in the firm to see if they knew of any conflicts. Any potential conflicts were brought to Lohman's attention and if there were any questions, the Conflicts Committee was called upon to resolve them.

Lohman had asked the Conflicts Committee members to be present at the Management Committee meeting. The members of the Conflicts Committee were Lohman and Ruhlman, Geeley McDade, Joe DiBello, a younger partner, and John Sweeney.

One conflict in the firm, although not one called a conflict of interest between clients, was between St. Charles and Ruhlman. St. Charles kept his cat, Pussy, in his office. Ruhlman brought his rottweiler to the office with him and took it, or it followed him, around. The rottweiler was usually at the Conflicts Committee meetings, which were held in Lohman's conference room, but the dog was not welcome anywhere near the St. Charles offices. So, no rottweiler.

Lohman had done his homework for the meeting. He explained the background of Hump and Flinton running for President and Flinton having taken up some of Hump's popular campaign points, including building a wall. At this point Sweeney said very audibly to the person next to him, "They were running for President? I thought they were running for Turd Of The Year or something like that." It was fortunate that St. Charles, as usual, was not paying too much attention.

Lohman continued. "So, President Flinton wants to build this walled community here to test out her security ideas. Also Hump wants to be the contractor building the wall and the community on top of the fact

THE DEAD ONE PROTRUDES

that he wants it to be built on land he has an option to buy. It's the old U.S. Steel South Works plant that has been sitting there abandoned on the South lakefront for some years. I think it is over 400 acres in size. Everyone has been talking about developing it, but so far nothing has happened. The only concrete contractor big enough to handle the job is one of our clients, Whiteman Materials, Inc. Shannon here represents them." Lohman motioned towards Shannon McClurg.

"Hump is also saying he wants to be the concrete contractor. With what, I don't know. He has no plant. He would have to get the concrete from Whiteman and Whiteman would have to be a subcontractor. Whiteman would do the job, but the paperwork would say Whiteman was selling to Hump who would be selling to the general contractor for the job. And that general contractor would be some company set up by Hump. In effect he would just get a cut of the concrete money without doing anything. Now you should know that Hump owns a cement company in Mexico. It is one of the largest in the world and it is the major supplier of cement to Whiteman. Cement is one of the major components in concrete."

Lohman went on. "Avon Whiteman is the owner of Whiteman Materials. He has lent money to Hump and Flinton for their foundations in the early stages of their campaigns and his company also lent them money which he was trying to collect. However, he has been missing for a few years and the company is being run by his wife and the collection attempts have ceased. Naturally Hump owes a lot of other money. In fact, I hear jokes saying that when we hear he is a billionaire it is his debt that is being referred to. At least I think they are jokes. One holder of his debt is The Bank, another one of our clients. That debt is past due and they are negotiating an extension. These

THE DEAD ONE PROTRUDES

negotiations also involve a new loan. Hump wants to get the money to do the project from The Bank. On top of this Hump wants to exclude those of Mexican ancestry and origin from the labor force on the project. Now, The Bank may want to lend more money to Hump only if it could securitize the loan. That is, sell interests in the loan to investors. That way it could make the loan and then sell it and get rid of it. It would need us as outside counsel for a lot of this."

Lohman then added, "I forgot something. I just learned this morning that Hump has already formed a company to be the contractor and he is trying to get a loan from The Bank for that company too."

At this stage LaRue, the Governmental Affairs guy, injected, "That Hump bills himself as one of the world's multi-billionaires and a big deal real estate developer and owner. A lot of people in Washington think he ran for office just to stave off his creditors and get more bargaining power with them. The word is that his foundation raised more than five hundred million while he was running and then invested it through intermediaries in debt issued by shill companies that then used the money to buy debt from his other companies. In other words the money was contributed to the foundation so it didn't have to be paid back. Then the foundation paid off a lot of Hump's debt with it. Supposedly the foundation shows it as investments in the shill companies on its books and will write it off some day as a loss when the debt isn't paid off. But who cares? The foundation never had the money to begin with. It is the contributors to the foundation who are out the money and they don't expect gifts to be repaid. At least in money if you know what I mean."

LaRue continued. "That stuff about Mexicans not working on the project is hokum. His hotels and other businesses employ a lot of

THE DEAD ONE PROTRUDES

Mexicans and a lot are illegal immigrants, but with him it's all about attention getting - the one thing he's competent at. Anyway, no one knows what is going on in D.C. now. Everything is up for grabs. You should remember that, despite their jabs at each other, Hump and Flinton are old friends and one of the D.C. rumors is that he lost to her on purpose and that he only ran to improve his bargaining position with his creditors. And the Mayor, that Toby Rich guy who left politics for a year and magically made twenty five million dollars. He's in bed with them too. He wants to get the wall here because it's a big boondoggle for everyone and so he can tell the voters how many jobs he created."

St. Charles exclaimed, "Hump's a very astute businessman! How many people do we know who can be a billionaire with someone else's money?"

"Right," added Lohman. "Hump's a business wizard. How many people do we know who can go bankrupt running a gambling casino? That takes real skill. And his debt. Debt is an asset. Most of the money in the world is invested in debt like government and corporate bonds."

"Just so," exclaimed St. Charles. "The more debt we have the richer we are."

"In money, yes," said Lohman. "In seed corn, no. At least when the borrower uses the money to buy seed and eats it instead of planting it."

St. Charles just sat there with a confused look on his face, not understanding how the conversation had turned to agricultural subjects. Lohman just thought to himself that he was lucky St. Charles did not catch on to his disguised criticism of the expressed wisdom of the great leader.

Lohman then tried to get everyone's attention directed back to the problem at hand. He called on McClurg to explain more about the concrete company. McClurg explained that Whiteman was the biggest concrete company in the Midwest and besides supplying the concrete for construction projects, sold cement to other contractors, both in bulk and bagged cement for smaller jobs. It had plants all over the Midwest, but its major plant was in Chicago on the Calumet River which entered Lake Michigan on the south side of Chicago. He explained how the city had long ago made a decision to transfer all its industrial river traffic to that river instead of the Chicago River, which wrapped around downtown Chicago, because all the traffic on the river required so many bridge openings that it was hard to get to the north and west sides of the city. Even so, Whiteman still had several plants on the Chicago River which, until recently, were supplied by big ships using the River. Now all cement went to the Calumet River site and was distributed to the other locations from there by rail and truck.

McClurg explained that almost all the cement currently came from a cement company called Humpy Cement located on the east coast of Mexico. He explained that he had been told that Hump owns the company. The cement is shipped in bulk and in bags from there. Mostly the bags weigh about 94 pounds, although there are all different sizes. They are mostly used by small contractors who come in to buy them. Most of the cement is the bulk, unpackaged kind. The ships sail from the east coast of Mexico and go east around the U.S. and north up to Canada where they enter the St. Lawrence Seaway. Then they come into the Great Lakes and come to Chicago and down

THE DEAD ONE PROTRUDES

the Calumet River to the plant. He said that he has heard that Hump and Flinton together own the shipping company that delivers the cement and hide their ownership in a Cayman Islands trust company, but he wondered how that could be true. At any rate he said he did not actually know.

McClurg continued on to explain that the cement is actually sold to Whiteman Materials by a U.S. subsidiary of the Mexican company called Humpy Materials, Inc. This was set up by a lawyer named Sam Meacham of Finebaum & Akhbar. When McClurg explained this some of those present made unfavorable remarks. McClurg said, "I know, I know. I have trouble with him too. Whenever we have trouble with the cement supply we have to deal with him. He's, well - , a shyster. By the way, I heard that he set up the contracting company Hump wants to use for the wall project."

At this stage St. Charles asked, "What is a shyster?"

"A low life lawyer," said Cohenstein.

"What's that?" asked St. Charles.

Cohenstein remembered who he was talking to and added, "He's not up to our standards."

St. Charles gave a sigh of recognition and said, "I see, I see."

McClurg then explained that, with regard to business matters, Whiteman dealt with the U.S. manager of Humpy, Jared Bannon, who seemed not to be much of a trouble maker. Whiteman did not deal directly with Hump himself or anyone at the Mexican company.

THE DEAD ONE PROTRUDES

He then went on to explain that the owner of Whiteman Materials was Avon Whiteman who had been missing since late 2014. One evening everyone was expecting him to show up at the main plant and he never did. He was last seen at his mansion on the North Side in the city's Gold Coast neighborhood. The mansion had been built long ago by a prominent lawyer and then eventually wound up being owned by Nudie Magazine's owner who used it for many publicity events and named it the Nudie Mansion.

Since the whereabouts of Whiteman were unknown and the affairs of the company had to be dealt with his wife, Trulia Whiteman, was appointed by the Probate Court as an administrator to run the company and all his other financial affairs until Whiteman was found or determined to be dead. Whiteman's son from a prior marriage, Eddie Whiteman, also worked at the company and it was he who handled most of the day to day details. "By the way," McClurg remarked, "just so you know - this is a racially mixed situation so keep that in mind when saying anything here. You have to avoid saying things that can be construed the wrong way. Whiteman is a black guy and his wife is white. Then they have a butler named Blackman who happens to be white. I think his first name is Snively."

McClurg explained how Whiteman Materials was the leading concrete contractor in the Midwest and was constantly expanding. It did most of the major public projects and a large share of the large private projects. This requires a lot of what might be called relationship work with government officials and schmoozing of the private contractors and Trulia was good at that. McClurg explained that other than that she was not too brilliant and that is where the kid came in. He knew what he was doing and was competent at running the company,

THE DEAD ONE PROTRUDES

although he took orders from the wife and did not handle the financial matters. McClurg then explained that, like all companies involved in public works, Whiteman Materials used minority contractors. For this purpose the wife had her own company that served as the female owned company. The kid had one for an African-American sub and Whiteman's chef and maid, who were married, owned a Hispanic sub.

There followed some discussion among those present and ultimately it was decided that the Conflicts Committee would have to do a lot more work on the matter and the meeting ended. Cohenstein and St. Charles were conferring further as everyone was leaving. St. Charles said, "I've never met that Hump fellow. Until recently I thought he was a member of the European nobility. Someone told me he was the Duke of Orange."

"I think they were joking," said Lohman. "Remember seeing him on tv and how he looks a little orange."

"Oh," said St. Charles.

Cohenstein said, "I think somebody should put a 'Baby On Board' sign on his forehead. But maybe not. I think he's got asteroids in his head."

St. Charles asked, "What? What? Asteroids? What is that?"

"That thing you go to the ass doctor for," said Cohenstein.

"A proctologist?" asked St. Charles.

"Yeah," said Cohenstein. "One of them."

"You mean hemorrhoids," said Lohman.

"Yeah," said Cohenstein. "That's it. He's got 'em upstairs."

THE DEAD ONE PROTRUDES

4 THE DEAL

McClurg had earlier talked to Lohman about Whiteman Materials wanting to renew its line of credit and also exploring a deal to buy another company. This he would usually do to get the matter cleared and to get people assigned to the work. In addition he usually wanted Lohman to work on the Whiteman deals because Lohman knew Avon Whiteman personally from having gone to college with him and living in the same neighborhood and going to the same church. Also McClurg was mostly a sales partner who needed a lot of help on legal matters. At college Lohman and Whiteman were in the same fraternity - one of the few at the time that accepted blacks. The fraternity had something called a "white clause", but the local at their college just did not tell the headquarters about the race of the members. The local accepted Jews too, although at the swearing in ceremony when the recruits (called pledges) were sworn in to become members everyone had to swear that they were a white Christian. At this ceremony they had white hoods over their heads. Needless to say the headquarters of this fraternity were in the South. At the first ceremony Lohman attended after he himself became a member there were two blacks and five Jews among those being sworn in. They had been given the script in advance so they knew what they had to say. One who was sitting next to Lohman leaned over to him and said, "I can't say that."

Lohman leaned back and said, "You have a hood over your head. No one can tell if you are saying it or not."

Times have changed, but they were only starting to change then. We no longer have black guys hiding under the white hoods so these days

THE DEAD ONE PROTRUDES

when someone black refers to being "in the hood" it means something else. Anyhow, Lohman was usually in on the big Whiteman matters.

Lohman and McClurg had already gone over the matter before and had discussed who they wanted working on it. Lohman, being the Managing Partner, could usually get whoever he wanted to work on a matter, provided they were not too busy on something else. This time he got his preferred cast of John Sweeney, Sean Featherbottom, a junior partner named Joe DiBello, and an associate named Tambola Cook who was a little weird, but somewhat of a genius at finding and interpreting the law. Lohman got all these people together in his conference room, together with himself, McClurg and the lead outside accountant for the company on Friday, June 16th, early in the morning.

The company Whiteman was considering buying was another concrete company which had a large share of the market on the West Coast. Investment bankers for that company were looking for buyers and Whiteman was one of the prospects it was being offered to. Naturally it was being offered not directly to Whiteman, but through another investment banking firm which purportedly was representing Whiteman. In deals at this level everyone was usually just trying to make the investment bankers happy because they were all playing the referral game. That is, they all wanted to get business from each other by having the other refer clients to them. The investment bankers were a huge source of business and all the law firms and accounting firms wanted to get business from them so the object was to keep the investment bankers happy and get more clients referred from them. In other words, the lawyers and accountants were primarily trying to keep the investment bankers happy. The primary concern was to get the deals closed so the investment bankers could get paid. Lohman and

THE DEAD ONE PROTRUDES

McClurg were not part of this game. They did want to keep the investment bankers happy, but they were more interested in their clients' needs than getting business from the investment bankers. That's why they had regular, continuing clients and did not need the new business all the time.

Initially Lohman and McClurg wanted to evaluate the company being offered and to review its financial materials to determine what kind of offer, if any, Whiteman wanted to make. This offer would be made through their investment banker so Lohman and McClurg wanted to review how to handle the investment banker. They also had to review all this in the context of having to get loans. If it was going to buy the company being offered Whiteman would need a loan and the investment banker was talking about arranging the financing. Whiteman also was in the process of renewing its credit line from a bank which it used to finance its business operations when needed. They also wanted to discuss if Whiteman should try to get the financing to buy the business from its bank or some other source. All this involved review of the financial statements and other material for both companies. Since this was a meeting to plan strategy as well as a review of the facts, neither anyone from the other side nor the investment bankers were there.

Sweeney and Featherbottom were the first to arrive. They often worked together and were an odd couple. Sweeney had been in every gorgeous young woman on the planet, or at least he had that reputation in the firm. He actually had done a lot of them. Sean was a young blonde guy and seemed to be a gay as a squirrel on coke with two nuts in his mouth. He was. Since Featherbottom was often doing work for Sweeney's show business clients they were talking about a

THE DEAD ONE PROTRUDES

new show Sweeney was negotiating as they came into Lohman's outer office, where Lohman's secretary, Tina Goblat, presided. She was rather big and looked like a pro linebacker. She talked like a punch drunk boxer turned Mafia hit man. People in the firm did what she said. Period. Her nickname was Tete. When she heard what they were talking about she said, "What show? Since last fall the only show in town is the Hump Show." Then she pointed at the door to the conference room and they went in.

As they passed her Sweeney said, "No Doll, he just does the ads. He's not the show. He's just an ad - like for abortion."

Tete did not look up from her desk where she was looking at papers. She just said, "Unfortunately yours failed," as they went on in. She liked them. She didn't joke with people she didn't like.

No one else was in the conference room. There was a refrigerator holding drinks and other things and coffee making facilities. The coffee and fixings were already out on the conference table, but Sweeney wanted a Coke Zero so he got one out of the refrigerator and went and sat down next to Sean. Coke Zero has words like "Stunning", "The Star" and whatever they think up to put on the cans. Sean picked up the can to see what it said. Just as Lohman was coming in Sweeney was saying, "Stop fondling my can, Dude!"

Lohman was used to Sweeney so he just had a chuckle, since he got the joke. Sean just wiggled a bit in his chair and gave a glance to the side.

Soon all the others had arrived and got settled in. Everyone had received the financial material and other documents in advance and had read them in preparation for the meeting. Besides the usual

THE DEAD ONE PROTRUDES

discussion of certain items in the audited financial statements of the West Coast company that they wanted explanations for and determining what else they wanted to examine they also discussed the price that Whiteman might want to offer and what Trulia and Eddie Whiteman were saying about it. This involved a discussion of what amount of loan Whiteman could pay from the money the West Coast company could produce.

There was also a discussion of Whiteman's financial status and what its financial statements showed and what terms it would ask the bank for in its loan renewal negotiations.

McClurg then started to fill those present in on the particulars of the company such as where its plants were and how it got its concrete and the connections to Hump and Flinton. He also explained that Whiteman had some other companies located at its South Side location. One made pre-cast or panel concrete. Most concrete is delivered to the construction sites in fairly liquid form and poured into forms at the site where it then cures into its hard form. Pre-cast concrete is poured and hardened into panels off site and the panels are delivered to the construction site. Whiteman did this through the Whiteman Panel Co. It also had not too long ago started selling art panels which had art on its display side. It did not make the panels, but it got the orders and sold them. The panels were produced by a company named the Chicago Art Panel Company. Whiteman Panel was located next to the concrete company in a connected building and the art panel company was located in part of that building and used the panel company facilities for the panels it created. Whiteman did not own the art panel company.

THE DEAD ONE PROTRUDES

The concrete company itself had a lot of facilities besides its main building, such as those used to store cement and other materials like aggregate and steel bars to reinforce the concrete. The aggregate was mixed with cement and water added. Aggregate was largely sand and crushed stone or gravel. The steel bars were placed in the concrete at the pours. The contractors on a project usually did this, but Whiteman often sold them the steel bars as well as the concrete. The mixed cement and aggregate would be concrete in its liquid form and would usually be delivered to sites in trucks which kept the concrete liquid. These trucks had to be loaded from the mixing machines and there had to be a place to store them when they were not being used so the plant had a lot of open land around it. Within the plant building there were offices and storage and tool areas and areas where there were bags of cement which Whiteman sold to small contractors and for small jobs. There were two brands of this bagged cement. Both were shipped in from Humpy Cement in Mexico, but one brand was ordinary cement and one was billed as a very superior cement for finish, strength and durability. The ordinary bags had the Humpy Cement label on them. The others were labeled as "Excelente Cemento" and were kept in a separate area within the plant. This area had a wire fence around it and was usually kept locked. This cement was very much higher priced.

One thing Lohman brought up was that the profits of the concrete company appeared to be declining since Whiteman disappeared. He also noted that the money going to the wife's company had been going up a lot since that time as well as the money going to something called the Whiteman Consulting Group, LLC. When he asked who owned that McClurg told him that he was not sure. He said he had been told by Whiteman to set it up with a Cayman Island's trust company as the

THE DEAD ONE PROTRUDES

owner. Lohman asked him to find out who the real owner was if he could. He then remarked that the Hispanic minority contractor owned by the chef and maid was not bringing in more money since Whiteman disappeared. Then McClurg added that the son also had a minority contractor, for the odd case where the black owned company needed a black minority contractor, but that it usually wasn't needed. It did not seem to be getting more money after Avon disappeared.

Then he said that they had noticed that a company called Blackman Consulting was getting paid a lot from the Whiteman company. He asked McClurg about that and asked who owned it. McClurg said, "I don't know. I asked Avon about it, but he told me he didn't know. I asked if it was his butler's company and he said he didn't know. He told me he didn't want to get into it."

Lohman also noted that so far as he could tell Whiteman was not the lowest bidder on many of the projects it supplied, especially the public jobs. McClurg explained that on a lot of big projects only Whiteman had the equipment and capacity to do the jobs and the lower bidders were usually bidding only on part of the job. He explained how political connections help too and how Avon Whiteman's father built the company on a combination of salesmanship, political connections, and buying out the previous biggest supplier.

At this stage there was more discussion of what effect the lower profits of the company would have on its ability to do the deal and get the loans and whether any of the money going to the wife's company and the consulting company could be reduced. McClurg said he would bring this up with Trulia.

THE DEAD ONE PROTRUDES

Sean had been following all this closely. He was a CPA as well as being a lawyer. There was another thing about him that would be useful to the deal. He had worked at Whiteman Materials when he was going to college. His job had been at the main plant and he was familiar with its operations. He had been a common laborer and he was assigned to whatever needed doing at the moment. He could count and he had some questions. He had reviewed records of the company's equipment and sales and purchases of supplies and they did not seem to make sense. He broke in to the conversation with, "Excuse me, Mr. Lohman. I have some questions. I don't know if you know it, but I worked there when I was in college. At the main plant. I did whatever needed doing - not the business work - just the yard and plant work. My job title was 'laborer'. A lot of what I did was to move the bagged cement around."

Sean then paused, gave a wiggle in his chair, and looked from side to side. He smoothed his blond hair back and continued. "Everyone there was awfully butch and - well - I was fired for being gay. And, you know, well, I wasn't out then. So I sent a note to Mr. Whiteman, Avon Whiteman, saying I was fired for being gay and I didn't do anything wrong. His son was my supervisor and he refused to talk to me about it. I had been working on the cement bags. They had started selling the high priced bags soon after I started there. They had them only at the Calumet plant. I had asked Mr. Ed Whiteman why they had to be locked up and why they were so high priced. It was a nuisance to get them out to deliver to buyers. He told me it was none of my business and that they didn't want fags around and he fired me."

He continued. "Mostly the people staffing the drug bag and panel company areas were from Streets & San, that City department that deals with what it says. Streets and Sanitation. They had a yard next

THE DEAD ONE PROTRUDES

door and some of their people worked at Whiteman too. Whiteman didn't have the art panels then, but they had the regular panels. All those Streets and San guys were butch. They didn't like me. Anyway, I have been looking at the financials and the sales figures listed for the company would be for way more concrete than they can be selling. I know what concrete sells for and I know what their capacity was and the sales stated would exceed their capacity. I went to the other plants occasionally for various things like deliveries and I heard and saw things about those plants so I know what they had there. The capacity would have to have gone up more than ten times since I was there and that was about ten years ago. It would also exceed the capacity of their trucks and any conceivable amount of trucks they could rent even if they could rent any. I never saw them use rented trucks and they always had unused trucks sitting idle on the lot for times of high demand."

Sean then said, "And another thing. Those Streets and San guys were always coming in and talking to Mr. Whiteman. The father. There were more of them around when the high priced cement came in because they staffed the locked up area. I just went in there to pick up bags customers had bought to take them out to their cars. They were also talking to a guy named Blackman a lot. I found out he worked for Whiteman personally, but I was never told at what."

Lohman asked McClurg, "What about all that? Do you know anything about it?"

"No," said McClurg. "I'll ask Trulia and Eddie. I need problems like this like a hole in the head.""

Sweeney couldn't help it. "Right Dude! You already got plenty."

THE DEAD ONE PROTRUDES

Since those present were used to Sweeney they just paused a bit.

Lohman asked the accountant if he could look into the questions raised and get back to McClurg as soon as possible and then they talked about when they could meet with Trulia and Eddie and then the investment bankers. Lohman finished with, "You all know the drill. Rome wasn't built in a day but the largest company in the world can be bought in a day so let's keep on this."

5 THE DEAD ONE PROTRUDES

As usual Lohman and everyone else in the firm who was in town was in the office on Saturday. Lawyers bill by the hour and the more hours put in, the more money billed. Unless he was in the middle of closing some rush job he usually left the office earlier than usual on Saturday and this Saturday was no exception. Lohman lived about two miles north of the office in a section of Chicago called the Gold Coast and he often walked home, both for the exercise and to see what he could see. His house was on the same street as the Swifton Tower where the firm was located, but he often took other streets home because they were busier or had more interesting things to see. This Saturday he had decided to go one block east to State Street, which had once been home to many large department stores concentrated on the seven block length of the street between the elevated tracks that surrounded the downtown area. The elevated railroad was called the "el" and the downtown area it surrounded was called the "Loop". At the north end of this strip the street went under the el tracks and extended one block further until it crossed the Chicago River and entered an area called River North where there was a mix of high end apartment buildings and commercial buildings housing stores, offices and a lot of expensive restaurants and bars. On the north side of the River he was going to go one block further east over to Wabash Avenue and go north on that street which contained more interesting stores and restaurants. He could go east to Wabash along the plaza of an office building between State and Wabash.

One of the high end apartment buildings in this area, Hump Tower, was located on the north side of the River at Wabash. The office building's

THE DEAD ONE PROTRUDES

plaza was along the River between State and Wabash and Hump Tower was across Wabash on the street's east side. It was almost one hundred floors tall. As Lohman was approaching it he became aware of a lot of activity in the street in front of it. There were several police cars there blocking off the street and a crowd was starting to form. He could also hear sirens of other emergency vehicles that were apparently coming to the scene. Lohman was across the street from the Tower and the building plaza he was on extended to the north on up Wabash and it was not blocked off so he could go on north. As he did so he stopped for a while. What he saw was a big panel to the side of the entrance to Hump Tower that had evidently fallen apart. There were concrete parts all over the building's entrance steps and what was left of the concrete panel next to the entrance seemed to have something sticking out of it.

This was not just any panel. The building of the whole Hump Tower had received reams of publicity as it progressed and one of the most publicized events was the placement of the panels on the sides of the entrance, with the most publicity being given to this panel which had a figure molded in the concrete. It was Ares, the War God, and it had been specifically selected by Hump.

Lohman remembered what was not reported at the time. This was that Hump had sold the right to buy apartments in the building to many people as construction was proceeding. They had to put up big deposits. Eventually, when the building was completed, he refused to sell to them at the price originally quoted and sold the units to other people for more money. He gave the deposit money back to the original proposed buyers, but in the meantime he had received a huge amount of interest free loans. Lohman wondered for a moment if

THE DEAD ONE PROTRUDES

Hump had just gone cheapo on the construction and maybe the whole place was going to start falling apart.

Lohman was not as interested in public catastrophes as some other people and he rightly thought that the police would want to clear the area so he went on north up Wabash. He eventually got home without further incident. He and his wife, Gloria, had planned to spend a quiet evening at home and they did just that since they did not make much noise when doing you know what. They watched TV for a while and by that time all the local stations were reporting what they knew about the incident at Hump Tower. What they had found out was not much more that what Lohman saw. There was a head and other body parts sticking out of the panel and the concrete showing Ares had been poured over that and had fallen off with other parts of the covering concrete. They had also found out that the panel had come from the Chicago Art Panel Company through Whiteman's panel company, Whiteman Panel Co.

Monday morning Lohman came in early as usual. He greeted Tete and they talked about the incident at Hump Tower for a while and then Lohman went on into his office to review his scheduling for the day and the week. When he had a better idea of what was going to need doing and when it needed to be done he rang up McClurg, Whiteman's lawyer, and asked him what he knew about the panel coming apart at Hump Tower. McClurg told him that he had already talked to Whiteman's wife, Trulia, and Eddie, Whiteman's son. He hadn't heard anything about the incident until then. They told him what happened and wanted to know what they should do about it, if anything. They confirmed that Whiteman had sold the panels and installed them, but beyond that they didn't know anything. They said they got the panels

THE DEAD ONE PROTRUDES

from the art panel company which had an office attached to the Whiteman Panel Co. McClurg said that they did not know anything about how the body got in the concrete because the art panel people come in to use the panel company facilities at night when they have a project. He said they told him it is an art venture and they don't do that much business, although anything they do is sold through Whiteman Panel Co. They hire the artists on a per job basis and don't have any full time employees except for the manager.

Lohman did not spend too much time on this because he had other things to attend to. However, he got a call from Cohenstein who had heard that Whiteman may have been involved in the Hump Tower project through the internal firm discussions concerning the possible conflicts of interest between Hump and Whiteman Concrete and others. Cohenstein always got interested in things involving publicity that the firm could latch on to. While he was interested mostly in public relations, both he and Lohman agreed that they needed to know more about what was going on and Lohman agreed to try to find out more. After he and Cohenstein hung up he rang Joe DiBello and the head firm investigator, Wiggy Rodriguez, and asked them to get together and find out all they could about what was going on involving Whiteman, the panel incident and Hump and Flinton. Since DiBello had been involved in the discussions about these matters so far, Lohman told him to meet with Wiggy and fill him in on the details.

Wiggy was not Wiggy's real name. Everyone called him Wiggy because he wore a big and obvious wig. He was proud of the wig and proud of the nickname. He was short, fat, and almost round. He was born in Mexico and had a heavy Mexican-Spanish accent, although he talked English very well. Naturally he thought the other people in the firm had

THE DEAD ONE PROTRUDES

the "accent". Many large law firms had their own investigators because they often had to find out all they could about incidents and the people involved in them.

When Lohman had finished telling Wiggy what he wanted Wiggy remarked that he was aware that Hump was always tweeting things early in the morning and had still been going on about building a wall between the U.S. and Mexico until recently. He said, "Mr. Lohman, Hump is - I think - I think he is talking to himself. Who is looking for tweets at three in the morning? So he talks to himself. I don't know why. It doesn't seem like there's anyone there."

Lohman and Wiggy rang off and Lohman then got to work on the affairs of his own clients.

THE DEAD ONE PROTRUDES

6 IT WAS WHITEMAN

On Wednesday morning Lohman was sitting down at home with Gloria having some coffee before going to work. They were watching the news and were informed that the body in the panel at Hump Tower had been identified by the police as that of Avon Whiteman. It was also reported that the cause of death had not yet been determined. The body had been identified from some dental implants from a dentist who put his trademark on the inside of the implants. They had used tooth x-rays from the body to compare with the dentist's and there was a match. In the meantime they had taken DNA samples from the body to confirm the identity, but the testing was not complete

Lohman got in to the office. When he got there Tete was at her desk. She said, "The cops want to come in and find out what we know about that Hump Tower pop-out or whatever you call it. It's the same crew who came here before, Detective Bongwad and Sergeant Gilbert. Or is it Wilbert. You know, that guy who stands up all the time like he's at attention at some Army ceremonial review. Wilbert Gilbert or Gilbert Wilbert. Whatever. It's him. I looked at your schedule and fitted them in at noon. You want me to get McClurg in too?"

Tete and a lot of other people in the firm were familiar with these police officers because of a few unfortunate incidents in the past involving dead bodies and the firm and suspicions that people in the firm had some connection with the incidents. Needless to say, with the guidance of Cohenstein these incidents wound up greatly bolstering the firm's reputation, regardless of who was killed by whom.

THE DEAD ONE PROTRUDES

Since McClurg was more of a sales and maintenance lawyer he usually got other lawyers in the firm involved in anything major concerning his clients. Lohman was often involved because of his connection with Whiteman and because of his abilities. Because of this and because he was in charge of the day to day management of the firm he was going to meet the police with McClurg. At noon the police showed up and McClurg and Lohman told them what they knew about the matter, to the extent the attorney-client privilege did not require it to be kept confidential. The only new thing Lohman learned in the meeting was that McClurg had told Eddie to check the company records and they showed that the panel, along with another panel for the other side of the entry way, was delivered early on the Monday after Avon Whiteman had disappeared on the previous Friday. The records also showed that the panels were never paid for, which was par for the course in Hump matters.

When the police left, Lohman asked McClurg who was going to run the company now that Avon Whiteman was gone. McClurg did not handle estate planning matters, which is a way of referring to process of planning how to handle the assets of people who have died. However, he said he thought the son would now be in control. He explained that while Whiteman was missing his wife had been appointed as administrator by the court to handle his financial matters, but that the documents covering his estate plan provided that on his death everything was to be handled through a trust and his son, Eddie, was to be the trustee. McClurg explained that the firm's head of Trusts and Estates, Jerry Nuftdone, had done all the work on the matter and he would contact Nuftdone about the details.

THE DEAD ONE PROTRUDES

Lohman asked McClurg, "Now what about this deal we're working on? Trulia, Avon's wife, was in charge, but now she isn't. Is the son, who, what is his name - oh yes, Eddie - does he want to do it? Does he want to do it the same way? And what about the financing? We better find out quick."

McClurg said he was scheduled to meet with both Eddie and Trulia later that day and he would let Lohman know. In the meantime he said he would get ahold of Nuftdone if he could. "So, I'll let you know whatever I find out, Bumper. But I think they'll both want to continue with what we have been doing so far. They have both been in on all the discussions and planning." With this he left and Lohman was able to turn his attention to his own clients' matters. For the next week and a half Lohman was doing just that.

One other thing Lohman had to do was cancel his Independence Day plans because the Independence Day weekend was going to start with a memorial service for Avon on Friday, June 30th. His body, still mostly encased in concrete, was being held by the coroner pending further testing so there was to be no viewing and no burial. However the family had arranged for the memorial service. Because of the publicity the matter was receiving day to day on the news and because of the involvement of the Hump name and because of all the prominent people who were suddenly eager to be mourners, the service was going to be a big deal.

The family had arranged the service to be held at D'Gregor Temple which had been started by Wilfred D'Gregor, the great evangelist. He had been the Grand Deacon of the Temple. He had also been a U.S. congressman. He had evidently passed on several years ago and the current Grand Deacon was Gregory Hevencent. The Temple ran a large

THE DEAD ONE PROTRUDES

D'Gregor Institute of Theology in a group of mid-rise buildings in the River North area just north of the Chicago downtown area and it had a huge Temple building about a mile further north at the northwest corner of the Gold Coast. The large Temple was perfect for the ceremony and all the notables and press who wanted to attend.

Avon Whiteman had been a Deacon of the Temple. His wife, Trulia and, oddly enough their butler, Snively Blackman, were Deacons too and that is one reason why the service was held at the Temple, in addition to its size.

One of those in attendance was Toby Rich, the Mayor, who D'Gregor once ran against for the mayoralty. There was a large group of people from the firm too. Ronald Hump even flew in for the service. Not to be out-done by the sinners taking advantage of God's publicity, The Four Saints were there. This was a heathen nickname for the most prominent characters in the Chicago spiritual community, namely, Cardinal Brandon Samuel, leader of the Chicago area Roman Catholics, The Prophet Andy, Angelic Leader of the Evangelical Congregation of the Angel Gabriel, a world-wide and growing religion, the Rabbi Nathan Bierblatt, leader of Chicago's most prominent Jewish temple, and the Imam Akmud Muhamood. Due to the possible clashing of religious faiths Hump had demanded that the Secret Service be present to protect him, but when they declined, and after much tweeting on his part and because of the presence of the Mayor, a large contingent of police were present too. In addition, the Governor, who was more receptive to Hump than others, had called out the National Guard to protect the service.

The service was spectacular. It, including the eulogy which Hump insisted on making, was televised and it even made the national news

THE DEAD ONE PROTRUDES

and many video feeds on the internet. In his eulogy Hump said little of substance, but did manage to plant the idea that the Russians had somehow caused the death and encasement in concrete by means of "hacking".

THE DEAD ONE PROTRUDES

7 MORE STIFFS

July Fourth was set to be a glorious day in Chicago. All summer days in Chicago are glorious. The space between the bullets is sunny and clear and in case it gets too hot the breeze created by the politicians shuffling their cash about cools things down. This July Fourth was no exception. It was sunny and clear and just the right temperature. The Mayor was going to start the festivities off with the dedication of the Riverwalk, a walkway along the Chicago River that had just been completed. Then there was to be a grand Independence Day parade down State Street in the heart of the Loop. Numerous celebrities were going to participate and the whole celebration was set to take place before the Cubs were scheduled to play so there would be no conflict with televising it. To be included in the parade was the Supreme Commander of the North Korean military and a small brigade of 2500 of his troops. They had been invited by the Mayor to participate for a show of solidarity and good relations between the two countries. Flinton, upon hearing of this, had sent G. W. Sush, Chairman of the Joint Chiefs of Staff, and a battalion of 1000 troops who were also to participate in the parade. The Supreme Commander and the Chairman were going to appear with the Mayor in all his appearances and when it got to the parade, the Koreans would march in front of him and the U.S. troops behind him. There was to be Glory and Peace Divine. South Korea had not been invited to participate because Flinton had just announced the prior week that she was going to get the trade deal between the U.S. and South Korea revoked because they were taking advantage of us.

THE DEAD ONE PROTRUDES

The Riverwalk had been under construction for several years. The ceremony to dedicate it was located in one of the sections built several years ago. It was going be along the River a little west of State Street where the parade was going to start. The speaking platform was set up on the concrete walkway in front of concrete panels that had been installed to block off an adjacent roadway that ran along the River. They had moldings on them depicting the early settlement of Chicago and the River it was on. The roadway, called Wacker Drive, was a two level street. The two street levels were referred to as Lower Wacker and Upper Wacker. They ran along the south side of the main east-west stem of the River and then, further west, turned south as the River did. They enclosed the north and west sides of the downtown area and were a little outside of the el's (elevated rail) circular tracks around the area called the Loop. The platform was set up at a right angle to the wall. The Mayor would be facing east and the wall would be to his right. Various dignitaries, including the Supreme Commander and the Chairman, would be seated behind him and an audience would be in front of him along with the TV cameras.

The Mayor was in fine form. He praised this person and that person and everyone except God. Then he described the enormous effort put into the construction by the contractors, resulting in the walkway which had no equal anywhere. Then he went on to explain how he, and only he, was responsible for creating all the jobs and investment that went into the walkway. His blabber put other politicians to shame. At the moment of dedication and giving of the walkway to the citizens of Chicago, the Mayor walked over to the wall from the podium and hit the wall with a bottle of champagne. There was thunderous applause, supplemented by the sound of concrete falling from the wall and exposing what appeared to be some of the bones of a body. Had the

THE DEAD ONE PROTRUDES

television stations known this would happen they would have charged much more for their ads.

As this was happening sirens could be heard coming from the street overhead and going by to the east. Sirens could also be heard going to a point just east of the Mayor's ceremony and coming from other directions. On upper Wacker Drive, just east of where State Street crossed it and where the parade was to be held, a FedEx truck had pulled up in front of a building to make deliveries. Naturally it did not pull up to the curb where a police vehicle was parked in a no parking zone, although there was other free space in the no parking zone. It double parked in the middle of one of the two traffic lanes headed east. While it was sitting there a UPS truck pulled up next to it and parked. This being July 4th, their deliveries were very important and no time could be spared in making them. Effectively the whole east bound lanes of upper Wacker Drive were blocked off. One of our modern car drivers then came along at about fifty miles per hour because it was extremely important that he get to the next stop light immediately. It was also extremely important that he be looking for parking with the parking app on his cell phone. At the last moment he looked up, saw the trucks blocking the street and swerved towards the curb to avoid them. In the process he ran up on the sidewalk and into many of the good citizens who were waiting to see the parade. Since this was near the start of the parade route there were TV cameras there which recorded this too.

By now the media were attracting more and more viewers and listeners as the news spread that something was happening in the Loop. The show was not over though. Lower Wacker Drive was home to a substantial homeless population, which included some bad guys.

THE DEAD ONE PROTRUDES

Just at this moment warfare broke out among them. Over what, no one knew. They were using whatever weapons they could find, and quite a few of them had guns which turned Lower Wacker into a war zone. More and more sirens could be heard as more police cars and other emergency vehicles headed into the Loop.

All this occurred just south of the River on the north side of the downtown area, but soon there was a growing commotion on the east side. There was a walkway under the Loop called the Pedway. It allowed pedestrians to move about free of vehicle traffic. It had various areas with art and art objects and one of them contained concrete panels with moldings on them depicting various historical figures. Naturally one of the panels decided to fall apart at this time. Two bodies were in it.

Fairly soon the downtown area was closed off and a state of emergency was declared by the Federal, state and city governments. The Governor called out the National Guard, which was not hard to do since almost all the available personnel were set to march in the parade. Almost all available police were called in to the area. Crime in the outlying areas soared. Fairly soon air force planes and helicopters were patrolling the skies over the Windy City. All civilian flights were grounded or diverted to other areas. The expressways were closed and the CTA, which ran the buses and el trains, was shut down. The civilians present for the parade began to riot. Many had guns and shooting broke out. So did fights between individuals using anything they could find as weapons as well as their fists and other body parts. People were running for cover everywhere. Others started breaking into stores and looting them. A lot of buildings were set on fire.

THE DEAD ONE PROTRUDES

Soon the media reported that the Mayor had been taken to a secure bunker. Until then, no one knew Chicago had such a place. There was pandemonium all over town. No one knew what would happen next and it was widely reported that The Terrorists had gone on the offense.

Because of this dangerous state of affairs the Cubs game was cancelled. The whole area around the stadium and the stadium itself was one of the biggest bars in the world and by the time the game was cancelled about 60,000 people were in or around the stadium and the surrounding bars. Half were lit to the gills, both on booze and the miscellaneous drugs that were well supplied during the games. The news of the cancellation did not go down well with them. They rioted and the whole area around the ball park descended into pandemonium.

In no way were there sufficient police and National Guard troops available to quell the disorder all over town, and it was spreading. News of the problem got to the White House when the Mayor requested martial law be instituted. It was Tuesday so the President was usually available, but because of the holiday, she couldn't be found. Will, the Vice President, was filling in for her and was at a ceremony on the Capitol Mall. When he got the news he did declare martial law in Chicago.

Unfortunately this did not get any more troops there right away. The U.S. contingent of soldiers already there was relatively small and unarmed. To get more troops immediately Will Flinton got in touch with the North Korean Supreme Commander, whose troops just happened to be armed, and made a deal to use the North Korean troops under the joint command of the Supreme Commander and the Chairman. By the time more U.S. troops arrived the North Koreans had

THE DEAD ONE PROTRUDES

subdued most of the rioters, mainly by killing a lot of them and beating a lot of others to a pulp.

The next day Sillary Flinton showed up and took to the air to thank North Korea for their peace keeping efforts and to take credit for restoring peace and sanity to Chicago. She also announced that she was renouncing her affiliation with the Democrats and was now a Republican. The head of the Democratic National Committee was interviewed about this and stated that most of his party was greatly relieved.

After this nothing new happened and things eventually quieted down and the media began reporting on casualties and property damage. It took some time, but the Loop was quieted down and cleaned up within a week, with the exception of some missing concrete panels and a lot of property damage making parts of it look like it had been bombed. This did not include Swifton Plaza so life could go on as usual at good old F, P & C.

Naturally Lohman and McClurg were aware of all this, as was everyone else in the country and so was Cohenstein. They conferred and the obvious question was whether the concrete panels came from the Chicago Art Panel Company and also, who was in them. Cohenstein told them to find out while he was going to figure out some good PR for the firm.

And one more thing: there was no parade on July Fourth. Boo Hoo.

THE DEAD ONE PROTRUDES

8 MORE NEWS FROM GOOFYTOWN

By Thursday, July 6th, Sillary Flinton was back at the White House. She realized there was no further attack coming in Chicago and rescinded the declaration of martial law. Then some interesting news came out. Hump and Flinton announced that they were soon going to have a conference at the White House to foster better relations. More interesting news came out on Friday. A Congressional committee released a report on campaign contributions. Congress had been trying to investigate everyone, except themselves, since the election. One thing they had been looking into was the subject of campaign contributions - to other peoples' campaigns. The report stated that the Flinton Foundation gave substantial amounts of money to the Hump campaign and that, after the election, Hump gave large amounts of money to the Flinton Foundation.

These topics disappeared from the news on Saturday, however, when Nappy Leaks leaked materials that caught the media's attention. In early June Flinton had publicly demanded that Russia allow us to invade Syria and the Ukraine "or else", as she put it. She declared that if they did not allow this a state of war would exist and she would have to order an attack. They ignored her. The material leaked showed that on July Fourth she had ordered the attack. However, due to the fact that Congress had not raised the debt ceiling and the fact that the government had reached it, no money had been available to buy fuel for the military for some time and they had run out, leaving our armed forces with planes and rockets that could not be launched. This did not deter our President, for she convinced most of the large oil companies to deliver emergency supplies without charge and soon our military

THE DEAD ONE PROTRUDES

was set to go. However, it was then discovered that all our planes and rockets had a crucial part in their electronic systems which could be turned off by electric impulses from a satellite to disable them. These parts had been supplied by a major donor to the Flinton campaign and had been bought from a supplier in India which in turn had bought them from a supplier in North Korea where they were actually manufactured. This did not stop our President, who was a magnificent warrior, and she soon got the problem sorted out. At this stage she had hit the button to wipe out Russia and all the nearby faithless ones (which would probably include the Ukraine). The button did not work. As Nappy Leaks further leaked, the Russians had hacked our systems so no attack was possible without picking up phones and making numerous individual phone calls to individual bases and installations and somehow proving that it was really the President giving the orders. No one had ever thought of this so we were not set up to do it and there was no attack. The leaked documents further showed that Russia had learned of our intended attack through their spy systems and tried to counterattack, but could not do so because we had hacked their systems too.

While most of the rulers of the world were busy at their weekend lawn parties, the media went nuts. There were constant claims that what Nappy Leaks had put out was "fake news" and there were other claims that "fake news" was Russia's new way of attacking us. Speculation ran rampant and there were constant public demands from politicians and other prominent people for marital law and declaration of a state of emergency. No one knew where our President was. All during her campaign and since then she had been unavailable from Thursday night to Tuesday morning. No one had ever been able to have any contact with her. The press was all over the White House and secret

THE DEAD ONE PROTRUDES

Service, but all they would say was that her whereabouts was a confidential national security issue.

Much of the media attention focused on the fact that the Chairman of The Joint Chiefs of Staff, G. W. Sush, had been parading around Chicago soon after all this was supposed to be going on. He claimed he did not know anything about all these matters. Other opinion givers in the media thought his presence in Chicago was just a cover since his appearance was after all this was supposed to have happened and the administration would probably want to keep the whole thing under cover.

Lohman and everyone else, was tremendously entertained by the spectacular weekend show, but by Tuesday morning he had work to do. The crew working on the Whiteman acquisition and loan was due to meet. However, because Whiteman was known to be dead there would be a change in the arrangements for who would in control of his assets, even if it was still going to be his wife. She had been appointed by the court to serve for a missing person, not a dead one. Neither Lohman, nor other parties involved in the prospective deal knew who would be in charge. Also a few of the people involved had told Lohman they still had more work to do on finding what out what was going on with the companies so the meeting was postponed. LaRue, however, was available and in Chicago so he and Lohman went to lunch at the College Club which was a little east of Swifton Plaza fronting on an area called Grant Park which was on the east side of the downtown area between the downtown and the Lake.

Naturally Lohman wanted to know what was going on in Washington. LaRue's life and practice revolved around politicians, which is why his area of practice was called Governmental Affairs. He explained to

THE DEAD ONE PROTRUDES

Lohman that no one in D.C. knew what was going on. "Everything is up for grabs," he said. "However, in a way, that's good. It's like someone came in one of your deal rooms and threw all the papers up in the air. If you're fast you can run around and grab them and put them down where you want 'em. Let's say new opportunities and areas of influence are opening up all over."

"I can see that," said Lohman, "but doesn't anybody know what is happening with this idea of war with Russia?"

"Not that I can tell," said LaRue. "This would have been a catastrophe in the past, but all this year Washington has been up for grabs. Each day - new crazy news. Just look at the election. There were all these people running and who gets nominated? Flinton I can see, but Hump? He was never in politics. What were his connections? What influence did he have on the Republican National Committee? Who did he give money to? He didn't have any big money to give. As a matter of fact with all this investigation of campaign contributions we find out that the Flinton Foundation gave his campaign big money through intermediaries to hide a not-for-profit being involved in politics. And you know that for years he and the Flintons have been big friends. The rumors are that he just ran so he could lose and Sillary could get elected and that what he really wanted was a better bargaining position with his creditors. He raised a lot of money, I think it was about five hundred million, and his Foundation used it to buy debt from his companies. You already heard that, I think. Now, after the election and after he got the money, he is giving money to the Flinton Foundation. It's like the Flintons financed his campaign so they would have a real loser to run against."

THE DEAD ONE PROTRUDES

LaRue went on. "And look what they just did. Well, I suppose you haven't heard about this yet, but it will come out soon. Hump and Will Flinton are back in bed together. You may not have heard this, but the pols know. Will, now that he is Vice President, he would ordinarily stay at the Vice President's place. But he is married to Sillary so he lives in the White House. Where do you think his office is? He has taken over the Oval Office. At least for what he claims is dictation to his staff of administrative assistants. And they're all gorgeous. Let me tell you, everyone in D.C. is making jokes about the 'dick' part of that. So Hump is in on this too. He and Will are supposedly working forming The Grope Society. The idea is that they will grope around - search, you know - for solutions to world problems. Articles of incorporation have already been filed. Wait till this hits the news. There is going to be a staff of course and they are going to solicit rich guys and prominent world leaders for members. Now who do you think the staff will be? A lot of pretty young things. As for the members, the jokes are already floating around about the fact that there will be a lot of male members involved."

"Are they crazy?" asked Lohman. "How do they think they will get away with that?"

"Have you seen anything sane since the election?" asked LaRue. "The more you are exposed to nuts, the nuttier you get. I think the public will eat it up."

"What's all this about Flinton being gone all weekend? And Friday and Monday?" asked Lohman.

"Well the Secret Service says they know where she is. They probably do. But it's all supposed to be secret. I don't know. I don't deal with

THE DEAD ONE PROTRUDES

those secret guys. All I can say is that they are the SS and Hitler had an SS too."

"What about her changing parties?" asked Lohman. "I can't believe that. Can she do that?"

"They're looking into it," said LaRue. "But who says she will be a Republican? They haven't said they will take her. They don't want her either."

Lohman said, "Every time I talk you about what is going on in politics I am just amazed. How do they get away with it?"

LaRue said simply, "Because the media just reports what they are told in press conferences and press releases. Only the people who are involved know what is really going on and each one who knows something doesn't know all of it. You know, the President probably does not know what is going on in the government. There is even a rumor going around - well it has been going around for a long time - that the CIA won't tell anyone anything, including the President, because they claim no one meets their new security clearance rules. Then there is another rumor that the CIA does this because they don't know what is going on either and they don't want anyone to find that out. Then I was at a party at Hump's place recently and Flinton showed up with Will and Hump greeted them and everyone heard him tell Sillary that she should tell Will, 'You're fired'. She made out it was a joke."

"I thought he and Will Flinton were - you said 'in bed together'. What happened?" asked Lohman.

THE DEAD ONE PROTRUDES

LaRue said, "Did you ever hear of Hump being consistent? Besides, I think he even told his own mother 'you're fired'."

Lohman went on. "We hear about all these computers and software and hacking. Look at what we are hearing. It's like an insane asylum. Just look at the miraculous devices! And when it comes time for it to work, it doesn't. So our so-called national defense is based on complex systems that don't work. Or is that fake news? And the computers seem to be taking over our daily lives too. It gets more and more complicated. Crap! We need a password for everything." He paused and then added, "But that may be good. Pretty soon we'll need a password to die. Who can remember a one-time password? We'll have life everlasting."

LaRue said, "That wouldn't make any difference in D.C. Right now when one of them dies, another one pops right up. What D.C. needs is death everlasting. Of course if that happened I and a whole lot of people feeding off the pols would be bankrupt so everyone wants to keep the whole mess going."

"Maybe you shouldn't tell me anything more about this," said Lohman. "It makes me want to run and hide under a rock. That probably won't be safe though. Maybe I should just enjoy myself until we all blow up."

LaRue just looked at him.

Lohman added, "You guys feed the flames. You don't put them out."

"It pays well," said LaRue. "And everyone wants to hire me for more flames, not more water."

THE DEAD ONE PROTRUDES

"Yeah," said Lohman. He paused. "Tell me, do you know anything about Whiteman or his company lending money to Hump and Whiteman's wife not doing anything to collect it?"

"No," said LaRue, "but things like that are common in politics to hide bribes and payments for other reasons. You aren't giving people money or bribing them if they supposedly have to pay you back."

"There's something else I have heard," said Lohman. "Sean - you know Sean Featherbottom who works for us - he told me recently that Hump hasn't paid a lot of people who worked on his campaign. He says one is a consulting company that we represent. Do you know anything about that?"

"Not that specifically," said LaRue. "But I hear he's a deadbeat."

After that their conversation turned to more enjoyable topics as they finished lunch and got back to the office.

Tuesday morning was also a Flinton day. She was back at work. But where? In the Vatican. Almost all television, radio and streaming services throughout the world interrupted their normal programming at five o'clock Rome time which was eight in the morning on the U.S. west coast, ten o'clock in Chicago and six in the evening in Moscow. The view in the Vatican showed the Pope standing between Flinton and the President of Russia, Vlad, The Putin. The Pope read a short statement through interpreters that basically said that the U.S. and Russia had declared Peace Everlasting, the end of all sanctions and trade restrictions, and creation of a permanent committee to be staffed by representatives of both countries to effectuate these principles. The Pope then ended the presentation and said there would

THE DEAD ONE PROTRUDES

be no questions and further news would have to come through the White House and the Kremlin. All three then turned and walked out of the room with the Pope first and Sillary and Vlad next, side by side, holding each other's hands. On the way Vlad disengaged his hand and put his arm around Sillary's waist and as they approached the door slid it down to her butt which he patted for all the world to see.

THE DEAD ONE PROTRUDES

9 THE COPS AGAIN

By Wednesday, July 12th, Lohman had made some semblance of order out of all his clients' matters so he knew something messy would come along soon. The deal the Whitemans were considering involving buying the West Coast concrete company and the status of their company's loans had been put off pending finding out who was authorized to act for Whiteman's company, now that it had been determined that he was dead. Lohman had scheduled a conference with Shannon McClurg about the status of the deal. He had asked Mrs. Whiteman and Eddie, Avon's son, to come in too. McClurg came into Lohman's office and they greeted each other. As McClurg was sitting down Lohman said, "What's the status of this Whiteman deal?"

McClurg said, "That's what everyone wants to know. I told everyone that we are just trying to sort out the details and will contact them when we have someone officially in charge."

"No one is?" asked Lohman.

"I think there is, but I want to check for sure with Jerry." He was referring to Jerry Nuftdone, head of Trusts and Estates. "He did the work on Avon's estate plan. I just want to be sure of the details. Everything winds up in a trust and Avon's son Eddie is the trustee. I think the whole family knows that, but I want to make sure of the details before getting back to the deal parties." McClurg paused and then added, "I also want to clear up what the police are doing. They have been interviewing everyone at the concrete company and the panel company."

THE DEAD ONE PROTRUDES

"Yes," said Lohman, "that's something the lenders won't like if they find out about it. We have to assume they will."

At this time Mrs. Whiteman and Eddie Whiteman were led in by Tete. After everyone greeted everyone else and got seated Lohman wanted to get down to business. He asked them if they knew who was in charge now and they both indicated that they knew all along that if Avon died Eddie would be in charge of almost all Avon's assets, including the company, as trustee of a trust holding the assets. McClurg added that they were going to see Nuftdone later to go over the details.

McClurg said, "It isn't a conventional estate plan for this size of estate, but the end result will be that the assets will be in trust with Eddie as trustee. A lot of transfers have to be checked out and Jerry is having that done so we are not meeting with him right away. It will probably be later this week or next week. We have to wait for word from him"

Besides knowing who was in charge, Lohman also wanted to know if Eddie still wanted to go through with the deal. Both he and Mrs. Whiteman did. Those present then discussed some further questions about the deal, but everything was waiting on the results of the due diligence investigations being made of the subject company and Whiteman's company. After some small talk, the meeting ended and McClurg and the Whitemans left.

As they left Sean Featherbottom was in the outer office talking to Tete. Lohman had called and asked him to come in to discuss a contract matter. Sean came in and they began to go over the contract questions when Tete rang and told Lohman the police had come to see him and were waiting downstairs with the receptionist. She said she told them

THE DEAD ONE PROTRUDES

Lohman was busy and had mentioned that it was with Sean and she said the cops told her that they wanted to talk to him too. They had also told her that they wanted to talk to McClurg. Lohman told her to tell the receptionist to send them up and he asked her to try to get McClurg back in his office and that they would all use the conference room.

Soon Detective Smokey Bongwad and Sergeant Wilbert Gilbert arrived. Lohman and Sean had already moved into the conference room and Tete showed them in there. They greeted Lohman and just looked at Sean. They knew him from other unfortunate incidents involving the firm which they had been convinced he was responsible for. Bongwad sat down and Gilbert stood at attention. He was very militarily inclined. Nobody except Bongwad would dare call him Willy. Bongwad said, "At ease Willy," and Gilbert relaxed. Bongwad sat down, and hauled out his notebook and pen. McClurg joined them soon thereafter. Gilbert remained standing.

When all the others, except Gilbert, were seated Bongwad said, "Well, I'm sure you've all heard that it was Avon Whiteman who popped out of Hump Tower. A guy owns a concrete company and he's poured into his own concrete. We have been asking everyone at the plant about it, but no one knows anything. The records show the panel he was in was delivered to Hump Tower on Monday, September 15, 2014. He disappeared late on that Friday, September 12, 2014. No one saw him after that and they tell us down at the plant that concrete takes about 24 to 48 hours to dry. It takes a lot longer to what they call cure, but these panels weren't load bearing so they could be shipped when dry. It's not like the concrete that is poured on site. That goes into place when it's wet. Anyway, he must have died and been put in the concrete

THE DEAD ONE PROTRUDES

sometime late Friday or at the latest early Saturday. We heard the art panel company was doing a pour that Friday night, but we still have to confirm that."

He went on to say, "We have been examining the premises. It isn't actually a one company site. The concrete company has a plant down there on Lake Calumet and then next to it is a panel concrete company. Separate company, same owner. Something they call panel concrete is made there. Concrete slabs which are hauled to a construction site and placed there instead of liquid concrete being poured into forms at the site to harden. Then there is an art panel company which has an office attached to the regular panel company. We are told the art panel company is not owned by the Whitemans and that it just supplies the art work and makes the panels with art on them. It uses the panel company facilities at off hours when the panel company is not working."

Bongwad then said, "The concrete company has a big yard with various things in it and a lot of parking for trucks and cars. All the buildings are interconnected. There are doors between the concrete company and the panel company. More than a few. Some are huge so the panels can go through. We were told that they are never locked. Same for the passage from the panel company to the art panel company. It is usually open, but we were told on occasion it is locked. Then on the other side is a Streets and San warehouse and lot. So basically you have a big yard in front of the concrete plant and it has facilities for putting wet concrete into the trucks on one side of it. If you are entering the yard, the plant is in front of you and the tower for loading the trucks in on the right. Behind the plant, along the lake are storage facilities for materials and a railroad spur that comes in from the right. To the left of

THE DEAD ONE PROTRUDES

the plant is the attached panel company building and to the left of that is the art panel company, but it doesn't go all the way back along the panel company plant. It's only an office. The panel company building and the art panel office both have doors into the Streets and San yard. And Streets and San, well that's just what it says. They do a lot of the City's work on the streets and sewers and water systems. They have a big yard where there are a lot of trucks and they have a big road salt storage area. They get deliveries by water, just like Whiteman. They both get rail deliveries too."

This was not news to McClurg, but Lohman found it interesting since he had never been to the plant.

Bongwad asked, "Do we have it right so far?"

"Yes, that sounds right," said McClurg.

Lohman asked, "How do you know it was Whiteman?"

Bongwad said, "The ME, the Medical Examiner, says he had the trademarks of a dentist in the inside of some dental implants. So we got ahold of the dentist and he had records from which the body could be identified once we gave him the ME's x-rays of the teeth."

McClurg said, "They do that? Dentists put marks on the implants?"

Bongwad said, "Yeah. For fifty thousand you get marks on the inside of your implants." Then he went on. "So what we want to know is who owns that art panel company and who will own the concrete and panel companies now. We were told the Whitemans don't own the art panel company as I told you, but no one down there says they know who the owner is. Apparently there is just one full time employee, the manager.

THE DEAD ONE PROTRUDES

David Delez is his name. He used to work at the panel company. They hire artists on a job basis and the pours of the art panels are apparently done by Streets and San people working part time, usually at night. We talked to Delez, but he says he doesn't know who owns the company. He only knows who hired him and that was a lawyer named Sam Meacham. Delez says Meacham told him that he set up the company and is the agent for the owner, but who the owner is is confidential. We can see by the Secretary of State records that the lawyer is the registered agent, whatever that is, and we talked to him. He says everything is confidential and covered by the attorney-client privilege and he won't tell us squat. And then Delez tells us he doesn't keep records of who was working there in 2014 because they came from a temp agency. We haven't been able to follow up on that yet. Delez says he gets orders from the owner through Meacham."

At the mention of Meacham McClurg and Lohman exchanged a worried glance. Meacham and his firm, Finebaum & Akhbahr, had a reputation best reserved for something exuded by a snail or a mold product. In fact the firm was often referred to as Slimebaum & Akhbahr.

"So," said Bongwad, "who owns the art panel company? Who is running the concrete and panel companies now?"

McClurg's eyes passed the buck to Lohman who said, "Avon Whiteman's son is in charge now. The company is owned by a trust of which he is the trustee, or it will be soon. We are working on the details. But in any event, we can't tell you the details because of the attorney-client privilege. We'll look into that and see if our clients will give consent to tell you. As to the art panel company - well I don't know anything about it. Do you Shannon?"

THE DEAD ONE PROTRUDES

McClurg said, "I don't know who owns it either. Whenever I have dealt with it I talk to Delez."

"So nobody knows nothin'," said Bongwad. "That's why we cops have jobs I suppose." Then he looked at Sean. "And you, Featherbottom. You worked there. We hear you were fired."

Lohman started to wonder if they were after Sean for murder again.

Sean had been following all this intently, even though he knew all about the physical aspects of the plant. He even knew that the art panel company office was once occupied by the panel company as a storage area. He gave a little butt wiggle in his chair and responded, "Yes, I was."

"So why?" asked Bongwad.

"I'm not sure," said Sean. "They started selling a new brand of bagged cement. It was supposed to be way better than regular cement and it was very high priced. They kept it locked up. I had mentioned that the way they started locking up some of the bagged cement they were selling for smaller jobs made it difficult to deal with the bags. The next thing I knew Mr. Eddie Whiteman, who ran the day to day business, told me I was fired because they didn't want homosexuals there."

Bongwad looked at Gilbert who looked at Sean with a raised eyebrow. Then he asked, "Were you - whatever you do - chasing after the guys there?"

Sean said, "No. I wasn't even out then."

"Out where? In the yard?" asked Bongwad.

THE DEAD ONE PROTRUDES

Lohman broke in. "He didn't even realize he was gay."

Bongwad said, "Yeah, I'll bet. Listen to your dick kid." Then he asked Sean, "So why did he say that?"

Gilbert spoke up. "Sir - look at him."

Sean gave Gilbert the open eyed look of a deer caught in the headlights. Then he said, "I don't know why. Just the week before he had told me that I was doing a good job and that they were lucky to have me there. He had told me I was doing a good job at other times too."

"So did you think that came from his father?" asked Bongwad.

Sean said, "I don't know. All I know is that is what he told me. I had seen his father around a lot and we had spoken at times and he never seemed upset with me."

Lohman interjected, "He said 'fags' didn't he? They didn't want fags?"

"Yes," said Sean.

"So we'll be following up on that," threatened Bongwad. "We know your type. Anyhow, we want to find out more about that art panel company. What do you know about it?"

Sean replied, "I don't know anything about it except what I have heard recently. It wasn't there when I worked there and they didn't get art panels from any other source to sell so far as I knew."

At this stage the cops had covered what they came for and Bongwad said they were leaving. Lohman said, "Wait a moment. What about

THE DEAD ONE PROTRUDES

those other three bodies that came out of concrete panels on July fourth? Were those panels delivered by Whiteman?"

McClurg interjected. "Yes. Whiteman did those jobs too with panels from Chicago Art Panel. We looked it up."

"So who were they - the bodies?" asked Lohman.

Bongwad said, "We don't know. The ME is doing tests. They think they can tell us something, but so far - nothing. The tests take time. We got lucky with Whiteman. He had markings on his teeth we could trace."

Lohman then asked, "How did he die?"

Bongwad answered, "Don't know. The ME is working on that too." Then as they rose he said, "Let us know as soon as you can if you can get consent to tell us more." They went on out and McClurg got up and left too.

Sean stayed to continue reviewing the contract matter with Lohman. After everyone was gone he did some more butt wiggles and patted his blond hair as he said to Lohman, "I think I was there the night he disappeared."

"Oh Christ!" said Lohman. "Not again!" He was referring to the recurring effort by the police to pin murders on Sean just because he may have had the opportunity and motive.

"I didn't kill him," Sean added. "But I think I was there at his house. I remember in 2014 I went there one Friday night. I think it was in September. I can check my time records. Mr. McClurg wanted me to deliver some papers to Mr. Whiteman. Mr. McClurg didn't want to use a delivery service and he had to get the papers there right away so he

THE DEAD ONE PROTRUDES

sent me. He also wanted me there to explain the papers if needed. When I was at the door it opened and Mr. Eddie Whiteman came out. He didn't seem to remember me. I hadn't told Mr. McClurg about getting fired. I was new here. I didn't want job trouble here. I was scared. I didn't know what to do except go deliver the papers. He asked who I was and what I was doing there. I hadn't expected to see him. I told him what I was there for and he let me in. Then he recognized me and asked if I had worked for him. I said yes and he seemed really glad to see me and told me he was glad I had a good job. Then he left. I saw a white Mercedes in the driveway, but he drove off in another car. The Mercedes was still there when I came out. When I got in I said 'Hello' several times, but no one answered. I got into what looked like an office and then Mr. Whiteman showed up. He said, 'Did Blackman let you in?' I said, 'Who?' and he said, 'The butler'. Then he said, 'Oh that's right - he said he was leaving.' Then I gave him the papers and told him what they were. He didn't have any questions so I left. I was still a little nervous about going there so I didn't mention to him that I had worked for him. He didn't recognize me so I wanted to leave well enough alone."

Lohman looked at him for a while. Then he said, "Well, I'll bet we're off and running again. Try to go over everything you can in your memory and refresh it. I'm sure they'll be after you again, especially when they find this out. Anyway, let's get back to this contract." They did just that and soon finished up their session and Sean left.

THE DEAD ONE PROTRUDES

10 MORE OF THE CONFLICTS COMMITTEE

The next Saturday a Conflicts Committee meeting had been scheduled again to follow up on what to do about the potential problems caused by Hump and concrete and debt. They all gathered in Lohman's conference room. As usual Ruhlman had his rottweiler with him and as usual the dog was a sweety, wandering around and getting his cuddles from all those present. The name of the rottweiler by the way was Rottweiler. Cohenstein had been in Lohman's office to discuss a matter concerning one of his clients and when he learned the Conflicts Committee was going to meet he decided to stay.

The members of the Committee started coming in and they were all greeting each other. The last one in was Sweeney. Cohenstein was glad to see him because he always liked the salesmen, but he was surprised to hear that Sweeney was on the Committee, instead of being just another associate or young partner handling a specific task for the committee. Lohman had asked LaRue to attend too because of the political aspects of the matter and he was there too.

Lohman started the meeting by reviewing the problems that could arise with Hump wanting to get concrete from Whiteman's company and at the same time being the major supplier of cement to Whiteman. He reviewed how The Bank, the firm's largest client, was a major creditor of Hump and that the loan was past due and how Hump wanted to borrow more money from The Bank to do the project. He also reminded everyone of the fact that The Bank wouldn't do the loan unless they could sell it off to investors which would bring a hefty fee into the firm's coffers. On top of this he added the fact that Avon Whiteman had lent money to Hump or his foundation and the loan was

THE DEAD ONE PROTRUDES

still outstanding. He also reminded everyone that the concrete business involved a lot of relationship building with government officials and that an additional problem might be that Hump and Flinton were possibly in bed together. He shouldn't have used that term.

Sweeney said, "What? They're gonna' do a horror show now?" Knowing that St. Charles and his ilk were not there, everyone had a laugh.

Then Ruhlman started saying that he couldn't understand how Hump was such a big deal. He said, "He's such a big debtor from all I can tell. If he's so rich, why can't he pay The Bank what he owes them. He could just go elsewhere and get a loan to pay off The Bank. I hear from Graybee that The Bank is always complaining about problems with him." Graybee was the nickname for St. Charles, although sometimes his partners called him Grabby. Ruhlman went on. "He proposed getting rid of all debt in his campaign. It was real popular. Government debt. Private debt. How? Did he say? No. But everyone bought it. He said if we get rid of the debt we will still have our assets. Try telling that to The Bank. All their assets are debt - what the borrowers owe them. Debt is an asset. And I'm not even going to go into all those securities they are investing their dough in these days. So you remember he said we should just abrogate all the debt and reallocate all the assets. Trouble is that one man's debt is another man's asset. He was a threat to the rich guys. Me too actually. My practice is state and local debt. Screw the bastard!"

"Oh come on," said Cohenstein, "you know that Hump guy didn't believe all that. He was just probably saying he'd like to get rid of his own debt. He was just bedging his hets."

THE DEAD ONE PROTRUDES

"Hedging his bets," said Ruhlman.

"That too," said Cohenstein. "You know Hump is a problem where ever he appears. I don't think anyone was ever happy to have done business with him - or even to have been anywhere near him. Of course, I don't know. I never had anything to do with him. Anyway I do think he's good at getting publicity. But he screws it up when he gets it. What he is is an advertisement for retroactive abortion. Anyway, what are we going to do here?"

DiBello chimed in. "Talking about debt and Hump - you know how he had gambling casinos and went bankrupt with them? I read something on the internet recently saying what he did was bleed about three billion out of the casinos and put it in other things before he put the casino business into bankruptcy and he got the money out in a way that it couldn't be recovered by the bankruptcy trustee. And talking about bank loans - who would lend him anything? Anybody can make a loan, but the banking business used to involve making good loans which is not easy. Now who cares if the loans are any good. The banks just want to make loans and sell them to the suckers. They can make shitty loans and get paid a big fee for putting the deal together. And they don't even want to be in the loan business anymore, they just want to get fees for putting together mergers and acquisitions and besides that they only want to get cheap money from deposits and the Fed and engage in trading financial assets with it." He paused. "Well, anyway I suppose that's irrelevant here where we're supposed to figure out what to do about our possible involvement in conflicts."

"Right," said Lohman, "On both points." Then he turned to the group and said, "Did anyone find out anything new?"

THE DEAD ONE PROTRUDES

"I did," said McDade, the firm Business Manager. "We represent a consulting firm that Hump's campaign owes money to."

"Who?" asked Lohman.

"It's Rich Consulting, Inc.," said McDade. It's owned by one of those Delaware corporations which it turns is owned by a Cayman Islands trust company and the trustee - the trust company down there - gives the orders. We don't know who really owns it. That is, we don't know who is the beneficiary of the trust. You may be surprised to know that the Mayor, Toby Rich, does a lot of the consulting, but he claims he just is an independent contractor and doesn't own the company. "

"So," said Lohman, "we've got this mess and with all the things these parties are involved in we could find more potential conflicts as we go along. One thing is that we should think of who we can keep as a client if worse comes to worst. I think the answer is The Bank. But let's look at what we actually have showing up as conflicts. There is a present conflict between The Bank and Hump. So we have to avoid representing Hump. Hump and the concrete company are on opposite sides of the fence so once again we can't represent Hump. Then we have this consulting company that is adverse to Hump. Then we have this walled city idea and that is where we could get into trouble. The concrete company has to be involved because they are the only one that can do it. But Hump wants to be involved too. Will they be partners? Adverse supplier and buyer? Hump wants to borrow more money from The Bank for this. Will the concrete company have an interest in the terms of that loan since they will benefit from it - it ultimately will be the source of their payment? I think that's where we could get into trouble. And if we in any way cooperate with Hump are we helping a party adverse to several of our clients? Then what about

THE DEAD ONE PROTRUDES

what is going on with Hump and Flinton and the fact that they may be co-owners of the company shipping most of the concrete to Whiteman? I think it all depends on how the facts develop. That means we have to keep these things in mind when representing Whiteman and The Bank and that consulting company. And we have to keep an eye on politics too because of all of these politicians involved. What do you think Zenon?"

Cohenstein said, "You think I can think? Thanks. I'm thinking of how we can get some publicity out of all this. We got bodies, we got clients involved, we got publicity already. At least we could get our name involved too. I'm working on that. Can't we get some TV station to do a news report on Whiteman where we explain there is nothing to indicate Whiteman did anything wrong - like a sub did all the work and like that. I know a lot of these news guys. I'll get to work on that."

"What about you?" Lohman asked McClurg.

"All I can do is watch out for the possible conflicts," he said.

Cohenstein added, "You'll do the news conference too. Start rehearsing. The key points are that our guys didn't do it and we represent every big guy there is and we know about these things. I'll get the PR firm to contact you - be available."

"And we should all look for other potential conflicts too," said Lohman. "Does anyone have anything else at this time?"

Ruhlman's rottweiler got up and came over to Lohman and put his front legs on the table and rose up and tried to lick him. Lohman ducked and pushed Rottweiler down. "Well Rotty, at least being

THE DEAD ONE PROTRUDES

friendly is a good idea in general," Lohman said. Lohman called him Rotty.

"What about that thing we did that other time or talked about?" said Cohenstein. "You remember that we talked about the lawyers representing the conflicting interests being put in another firm and getting our share of the profits by subleasing space to them and getting it out in rent?"

"I'd hate to rely on that," said Lohman. "How would that firm be truly independent from us. I know we have hundreds of lawyers running around here and that means we are constantly exposed to rampant idiocy from people who consider themselves geniuses, but when push comes to shove on that one I think a court might not buy it."

"So," mused Cohenstein. "By the way, what is going on with the situation at the concrete company and with all that stuff about the Whiteman body? Have you heard anything?"

Lohman filled those present in on what he had heard so far, except for some of what he had learned from Sean. He did tell them the cops were interested in Sean because he had worked at the company and been fired, but he did not tell them about Sean's visit to Avon Whiteman.

"You think we got a problem there?" asked Cohenstein.

"Well, yes," said Lohman. "The officers are the same ones that have been assigned to the murders that involved our firm before. They always seem to be after Sean. I don't think he's a murderer though."

THE DEAD ONE PROTRUDES

"Yeah, that Fluffbottom kid," said Cohenstein. "We should rent him out to do hit jobs maybe. But the truth is I don't think he did it either. He's a good kid. Good lawyer too. I still have to find a way to break it to Grabby that we got some fruits here."

Lohman then said, "I think you all have heard that the Hump Tower body was Avon Whiteman and the panel came from his company that sub-contacted it from an art panel company that shares their premises. He disappeared on a Friday night in September 2014 and the panel was sent to Hump Tower the next Monday. The cause of death isn't known. So another one of our clients was murdered. That is, I think so. He probably didn't pour himself into the concrete."

Lohman added, "One more thing. We all have to remember the political aspects of this. We have to avoid getting involved with one side or the other."

"Yeah," said Cohenstein. "Just remember - don't get specific about anything in politics. If you do you lose. Try to stay away from it period. That is until I figure out what's gonna' get us traction here."

"What about you Bungus?" asked Lohman as he turned to LaRue. "Do you have anything to add that's new?"

"Not much," Bungus said. "There are just some new rumors in D.C. Talk about conflicts, you should hear what they're talking about. I hear Flinton's psychiatrist, who is a guy, quit and won't say why. The rumor is that the real reason is that his psychiatrist is a gorgeous woman who just happens to be Hump's psychiatrist - or she was. She quit on Hump about month before and supposedly just sent him a handwritten note saying 'I give up'. I'm not making this up. Someone else may be, but not me. Anyway this is going around and it's not going around as a joke. Actually this is all good. No one wants to hire me when everything is predictable and going according to Hoyle."

What the meeting then descended to was a discussion about who to bill for all the time the cops would be taking if they started talking to a lot of people in the firm like they had done in prior instances. Lohman finally reminded them that false billing of clients for work not done on their matters was a breach of ethics and may be civil fraud and even a crime. They did have to be reminded.

THE DEAD ONE PROTRUDES

11 TO BUY OR NOT TO BUY, THAT IS THE QUESTION

The next Monday, July 17th, Lohman had the Whitemans coming in to go over where they stood in respect to the West Coast concrete company and the loans they had been considering. Before the Whitemans came in he was meeting with the lawyers who had been working on the matter, namely DiBello, Sweeney, Featherbotton and Cook. He and McClurg met with them first thing in the morning in Lohman's conference room. One of the accountants from the outside accounting firm was there too. They all reviewed what they had discovered about the West Coast company and the Whiteman companies. Naturally the investment bankers wanted to get the West Coast company sold to someone, but the Lohman crew was asking some questions about its financial statements. Basically their examination of the financial statements showed a wide divergence between the income of the West Coast company measured by one standard and its income shown in its financial statements which was measured by another standard.

The accounting firm had gone there and gone through its financial and other records from which the financial statements were supposedly compiled. For instance if a company sells a product to a buyer it has records of the order and records of the sale and it has records of buying goods to make the product with and paying for labor to make the product and other things relating to the order, production, shipment and sale. It also has records showing payment and deposit of the funds. It would seem rather simple to simply categorize all these things and add them up and report the results. Not so fast. What if you got the order, made the product, and shipped it out one year, but got

THE DEAD ONE PROTRUDES

paid the next year? What if you paid for the supplies you purchased to make the product the next year? What figures go into your financial statements for the year you made, sold and shipped the product? There are countless adjustments that have to be made to come up with the type of financial statements that are used in most businesses. Needless to say, the more complicated the matter, the more opportunities there are for "adjusting" the numbers. In this case the accountants had decided that the West Coast firm was improperly adjusting its numbers to show higher income in the financial statements than it actually had.

This made the price the investment bankers wanted for the company more expensive. It meant that for the price they were asking the buyer would get less actual income than was claimed. In other words the buyer would have to pay more for the actual income. The price was higher for each dollar of income. The accountant went through the details of this and DiBello, who had gone out to examine the West Coast company with him, added that the bank that Whiteman Material's credit line came from was concerned about this too. Then he explained that that bank had also been asking him about the decline in earnings for Whiteman Materials since Avon Whiteman disappeared. The bank was concerned that the combination of paying too much for the West Coast company and the decline in earnings might influence them not to renew the credit line or to limit its amount.

McClurg added that the investment bankers and the potential lenders for buying it also wanted to know what was going on at the Whiteman company since it was found out that Avon Whiteman had died, and under circumstances that would make anyone wonder if something was wrong at the company. He added that they also wanted to be filled

THE DEAD ONE PROTRUDES

on in exactly who was in charge, beyond his general statements to them that Eddie Whiteman was going to be in charge.

Lohman said, "It seems pretty clear that we have to talk to the Whitemans about this. Do they still want to pursue the deal? At any rate they will probably want to consider a lower price, and it would take a while to figure out what they want to offer. I know the investment bankers are shopping the West Coast company around at a price that nobody is going to pay. Everybody will come back with their own offers after examining the company, but the Whitemans will probably revise whatever offer they were considering now." He turned to the account and asked, "Do you know if they had an offer in mind?"

"No," he said. "They're waiting to hear from us."

"OK," said Lohman. They're coming in soon. Anybody else have anything to say?"

Sweeney spoke up. "Yeah Dude, I got something. Maybe. Maybe not. You know you sent me down there to the Calumet plant and some of the other plants too to just check things out. I was down there and they were showing me all around. Eddie Whiteman was taking me around. He showed me the cement bags and some were locked up. He told me how it was - he called it luxury cement. Real high priced compared to the other bagged cement. Excelente Cemento was the brand name. The other bags came from Humpy Cement in Mexico he said. That Hump guy owns it. He told me the Excelente bags are sold by Humpy too and shipped in by Humpy with the other cement. He tells me that the bags are mostly bought by small contractors or by someone doing small jobs."

THE DEAD ONE PROTRUDES

Sweeney continued. "Then I see this guy in the place. He has one of those hand trucks, or maybe it's called a dolly. He is in the fenced off area with one of the Whiteman employees and Eddie Whiteman points him out to me as one of the customers. I've seen this guy before and someone told me something about him." He looked at Lohman and added, "You want to hear about that?"

Lohman knew that asking Sweeney to say something was always risky, the risk being that the denizens of the proper world might faint, but he decided to risk it since those present were accustomed to him. However, he decided to ease into it. ""Where did you hear it?"

"At one of those show business parties for agents and performers," said Sweeney. Sweeney represented a lot of people involved in show business.

"And who told you what - what happened?" asked Lohman.

Sweeney said, "Well, I was there with Trisha. Her agent wanted her there. It was a big event in the ballroom of that hotel over on Michigan Avenue. The one that got renamed. I forget the name. Now you know that drugs are part of show business. Frankly, one of the big reasons some of the show crowd wants to be around me is that I can see that they get their drugs. I know who the dealers are and who sells what and how the users can get it. I don't sell the stuff. Don't use it either. Or I should say I don't use it beyond my knowledge of it. So Trisha and I are talking to this dealer when we notice some guy getting loud and arguing with someone. Trisha says, 'Someone should tell him to can it.' The dealer says, 'Stay away from him. He's dangerous. He cuts it down to nothing. And he'll kill anyone who bitches about it.' Now that's the guy I saw at the plant buying the cement."

THE DEAD ONE PROTRUDES

"So?" commented Lohman.

"So I don't know," said Sweeney. But it's odd that someone at one of those show gatherings would be anywhere around a joint where they work with their hands."

"So," said Lohman, "you're just telling us you noticed something unusual?"

"Yeah, Dude," said Sweeney. "And another thing - that Hump guy with the Humpy Cement - I hear he's coming back on TV in a show where he's a vampire who gropes and sucks blood out of Muslim women who will then become promiscuous and suck blood out of Muslim men. The show is gonna' be called Humpula. I also hear Hump's trying to sell a new show called "The Truth" which he will explain each week. And that's not all. The newspapers are going to add a new cartoon strip called Sillarytoons. These are the biggest deals being discussed on the circuit these days and everyone is trying to get in on them. Actually I think some of it might be con man scam to get investor money."

Everyone just looked at Sweeney for a while. Finally Lohman said, "For real?"

"Yeah Dude. It's show business," Sweeney said. "You know that Hump guy is bad. Everybody on the circuit's talking about him. Everything about him is possible script matter. I even hear his mother called him a son of a bitch once."

McClurg said, "Oh come now. She must have been joking."

Sweeney replied, "Shit no Dude! She was braggin'."

THE DEAD ONE PROTRUDES

Lohman said, "Look, the Whitemans will be here soon, so lay off all the show business stuff will you."

And just then Tete opened the conference room door and announced the Whitemans. They came in and, after everyone greeted each other, got settled. All but Lohman, the accountant, and McClurg excused themselves Then McClurg and Lohman went over what they had learned with the Whitemans. It was ultimately decided to put the matter of buying the West Coast company on hold and to merely tell the investment bankers what their concerns were and ask them to look into the matter. They would stay negotiations with the proposed lender for the deal too. In the meantime they would proceed with renewing the credit line with their regular lender which wouldn't be a problem without the issue of buying the other company being involved.

The topic then turned to what had happened to Avon Whiteman. Lohman said, "You know we are going to see Jerry Nuftdone about what is exactly going on with the implementation of Avon's estate plan tomorrow, but everyone wants to know what happened to Avon. Do you know?"

Trulia Whiteman, who was a rather tall white blonde beauty, said, "No. We don't know. We want to find out too. The day he disappeared I had gone to the Calumet plant to pick up something I left there. I got there a little before 4 in the afternoon. When I left home Avon was still there. I was at the plant for a while and then I went to see a movie that I had been thinking of seeing. Avon was occupied with business matters and he didn't want to see it anyway. He was going to come down to the plant later after I had left and then we would meet up at home later. The movie was in a mall out there. I walked around for a while, but I

THE DEAD ONE PROTRUDES

didn't buy anything. I just saw the show. When I got home he wasn't there. And he never was again - or anywhere. We couldn't find out anything. We reported it to the police and came in here to talk to you guys about what to do. Avon's car was still there when I got home, but he wasn't. He's got - he had - a white Mercedes. I had a black BMW. He told me to get a white one because we were the Whitemans. He thought it was good public relations. But I liked black better. I was driving around in that. To the plant. To the show. Home. I got home about 10 at night, just about when our chef and maid got home. They had gone to some sort of family gathering they said."

Eddie added, "I was there that day too. After she left I came in to see dad. We talked about several things involving the business and then I left. When I was leaving this guy from your firm came in with some papers. I think his name was Sean. I let him in. Blackman - he's the butler - he was out. The chef and maid were out too. Just me and dad were there. So I let your guy in an left. I recognized him. He used to work for us. As I remember it he was a good worker."

Lohman said, "He says you fired him. Did you? What was that all about?"

Eddie looked into the distance for a minute. Then he said, "Oh yes. Now I remember. Maybe that's why he was looking funny. I did. I remember he was telling me how locking up the new bags we started selling made it difficult to serve the customers. They had to get clearance, someone with authority had to go in and unlock the place and lock it up again and supervise the whole thing, things like that. So I told dad and he just told me to fire Sean."

Lohman asked, "Did he say why?"

THE DEAD ONE PROTRUDES

Eddie said, "No, other than saying he should mind his own business. He told me to tell him he was being fired because he was a fag."

"Was that a problem?" asked Lohman.

"Well," Eddie said, "some of the guys were making jokes about him, but I never noticed any problems. I got a complaint from one guy, but when I asked him what Featherbottom had done I found out he was just complaining that he was a fag. So I told him to sit on it. But, how come you assigned him to work with us? "

McClurg said, "He didn't tell me anything about being fired. I think he was afraid to."

Trulia added, "You remember Eddie that you said Featherbottom said he was there to deliver papers. I found an envelope from this firm there on his desk the next day. It wasn't opened."

"Yes, I remember you telling me that," said Eddie.

Lohman asked, "Was that the last time you saw your dad?"

"Yes," said Eddie. "After I left, my wife and I went to an event at a hotel downtown. Some big contractors were going to be there and we wanted to be with them - prospective customers. One more thing. You know the cops asked us all about these things. One thing I remembered was that one of my dad's friends asked me a few days after he disappeared where he was. The guy's name is Cassidy Tyreservski - I think that's it. Cass is what we call him. He was a friend of dad's. He's in finance and he and dad were always playing golf or something. Basically they were hitting each other up for deals I think. He said he had stopped in to see dad that night. It was after I left. He said they just

THE DEAD ONE PROTRUDES

talked and then he left because dad said he was going to the plant. He said no one else was there, or at least he said dad told him that."

"So how did your dad seem? Did he seem OK when you talked to him?" asked Lohman.

"Yes," said Eddie. "I didn't notice anything unusual. He was there at his desk in the usual way fiddling with his ring. Always his ring. Not his wedding ring. It was on his right hand. He would twist it around and take it off and play with it and put it back on. Any problems and he would stop that. That's how I could tell what mood he was in."

Eventually the meeting wrapped up and Lohman and McClurg bid the Whitemans goodbye until the next day when they were all scheduled to meet with Nuftdone.

THE DEAD ONE PROTRUDES

12 THE ESTATE PLAN

The next day, Tuesday, July 18th, his eminence Jerry Nuftdone was finally free to meet with the Whitemans. For some reason lawyers who handle estate plans for the rich are usually big snobs. They want rich and by God they are rich (supposedly) and the rich hang only with the rich, some of whom actually are wealthy. And "Wealth" is the name of the game. "Wealth Management", "Wealth Planning" and so forth. "Money", "Loot" - words such as this are unmentionable. "Assets" is an OK term, but it shows you are just one of the staff.

Earlier that day it had been reported in the news that the bodies in the Riverwalk panel and the Pedway panel had been identified. Both panels had been delivered in late 2014. The body in the Riverwalk panel was that of a prominent politician and evangelist, Wilfred D'Gregor. He had been a congressman and had earlier run against Toby Rich for Mayor and lost. He was the Grand Deacon of D'Gregor Temple on the North Side where it had a huge physical temple and a seminary. The news stories said D'Gregor was identified from a ring which he prominently displayed in public appearances and which had the Temple symbol on it.

The bodies in the Pedway were identified as a Mexican drug lord and a Streets and San employee who was also a driver for the Whiteman panel company. The drug lord was Mezamo Guzalemonez who had been arrested in Mexico and then escaped and who then disappeared from Mexico in early September 2014, before the panels were delivered and also before the panel containing Avon Whiteman was delivered. It was reported that after that the drug wars in Mexico vastly increased. The panel he flopped out of had a bust of him on it and it is

THE DEAD ONE PROTRUDES

that that fell off and exposed his body. The scene on the panel around his bust was supposedly a depiction of his drug activities in Mexico. Guzalemonez was identified from some DNA which matched up with DNA taken from him in Mexico and the driver had been identified from a distinctive ring also. The police had heard about that in descriptions of him and then were able to get a positive id from medical records. Both had been shot in the forehead and the driver and D'Gregor both had broken thumbs on each hand. It was further reported that the Guzalemonez's drug supplies to the U.S. came mostly through Chicago where he was the main supplier. It was also reported that the police did not know who the major supplier was now.

It was also reported in the news that the panels came from the Chicago Art Panel Company by way of the Whiteman Panel Co.

Before the Whitemans came in McClurg and Lohman met with Nuftdone and six of his junior lawyers to brush up on the details of the Whiteman estate plan. They were meeting in one of the conference rooms on the 43rd floor. McClurg and Lohman had also got Sweeney, DiBello, Featherbottom and Cook there because of their work on the possible deal for the West Coast company. There was some discussion about the morning's news, but no one knew anything more than what had been reported, except McClurg who had already been informed by the client that they had supplied the panels. With regard to the estate paln, McClurg explained that Avon had not too long ago told him and Jerry that he wanted to give more to his wife, but then right after that and shortly before his disappearance he had changed his mind and told them to hold off on giving his wife more.

Nuftdone was going to have one of the associates quickly explain the details of the plan to the other lawyers, but the Whitemans arrived

THE DEAD ONE PROTRUDES

which cut short the lawyer's meeting. Since the audience had arrived the show was on. Therefore Nuftdone himself, his eminence, led everyone through it. Whiteman had set up a trust with himself as trustee while he was alive and Eddie as trustee after his death. Ordinarily people who set up such trusts transfer all their assets to the trust. The trust then owns the assets, not the person who set it up. Therefore when that person dies he or she has no assets and there are no assets to go through a court probate proceeding. The trust usually contains various features designed to reduce estate and other taxes and says who will get what. Avon's trust did all this except he did not transfer his assets to the trust.

Nuftdone explained that Avon did not want to transfer his assets to the trust while he was alive. (Clients can be so tiresome - which, of course, is an opportunity for higher billings). To avoid probate all his assets were put in joint tenancies or had pay on death designations. The trust was the joint tenant or pay on death designee. This also avoided probate because no court proceeding was necessary to transfer the assets or to determine who got them. He then explained that all the assets were now in the trust and that Eddie was the trustee.

They then went over the major assets which included the concrete company, Whiteman Materials, Inc. They reviewed its plants. It had the plant on Lake Calumet where most of the supplies of cement and aggregate were delivered and it had plants on the near Northwest and near Southwest sides and more plants in the suburbs and in several Northern Illinois cities and St. Louis. They mostly got their supplies from the Lake Calumet plant by rail or truck. The land for most of these plants had been owned separately by Avon as a way to get pre-tax money out of the company in rent and that land had been held in joint

THE DEAD ONE PROTRUDES

tenancy between Avon and another trust of his. Eddie was now trustee of that trust too. A separate trust was used so getting pre-tax rent money out of the company could continue.

Nuftdone then explained that there was a marital trust that would qualify for the marital deduction under the estate tax, but the trust was not big enough to eliminate all estate taxes. He told everyone that he was still working on methods to reduce the tax and they had not yet come to a conclusion.

Then he told everyone that, apart from a few minor gifts to specific people and charities, the trust said Trulia was to get the income from the marital trust for her life and that anything that was left would go to Eddie or, if he was not alive, to his descendants, and if there were none, to Avon's heirs as determined by the law.

The Whiteman Panel Co. was reviewed and there was discussion of the dead bodies in the panels, at which time everyone was reminded that the bodies were in panels supplied and made by the Chicago Art Panel Company, although it had used the Whiteman Panel Co's. facilities. Trulia Whiteman explained that they had just started selling the pre-cast or panel concrete not too long ago and that the art panel company started up after that - in 2014. She repeated that they did not own the art panel company and she said she had thought David Delez, the manager, did. When questioned she said she just assumed this. She added that he used to work for their panel company.

There was more discussion of other assets like bank accounts and brokerage accounts, The Nudie Mansion, and other real estate and some art and collectibles and that wrapped up most of the assets and it

THE DEAD ONE PROTRUDES

was explained by Nuftdone that nothing more needed to be done with respect to re-titling or transfer of assets.

At this stage Sean Featherbottom asked, "What about Whiteman Consulting Group, LLC? I have seen a lot of money going to that in the financial records. What is that?"

Trulia said, "That's not ours." She said nothing further.

"No Whiteman owns it?" Sean asked.

There was no answer. No one spoke. Sean looked around and twisted the ring on his finger back and forth.

Lohman was curious. "What is that? What is going on there?"

Eddie started to speak, but Trulia spoke over him. "It's a consulting company."

"And --?" asked Lohman.

"And what?" said Trulia.

"Who owns it?" said Lohman.

"We don't know," said Eddie.

"So who runs it?" Lohman went on.

Eddie looked at Trulia. She paused and said, "It's one of those minority companies that we have to use sometimes to get government contracts."

"So don't you have to show that it is minority owned?" asked Lohman.

THE DEAD ONE PROTRUDES

Trulia looked around and then said, "I think our butler does, Snively Blackman. He owns it."

"Isn't he white?" asked Lohman. "What is the minority status?"

"Oh," she said, "with us white is a minority. Anyhow, I think he told me it is owned by a Cayman Islands trust company so it can be transferred around to whatever minority we need."

Lohman decided to let well enough alone for the time being. So did everyone else.

At this stage Eddie asked, "What about organ donation? Didn't Dad sign up for that?"

Nuftdone looked at one of his associates who had the file. "We did that didn't we?"

The associate said yes and Nuftdone said, "We did that, but after almost three years I don't think any viable organs existed.

Eddie was looking at Sean Featherbottom as he was considering this and all of a sudden he said loudly, "Wait! Where did you get that?" He pointed at Sean.

Sean said, "What?"

"His ring," said Eddie.

Trulia looked and added, "Yes. Where did you get his ring? Avon's ring?"

THE DEAD ONE PROTRUDES

"Avon's ring?" said Sean. He looked at his ring finger where the ring was. It was a gold ring with a purple glass star and it had a small white plus sign in the middle of the star. "This is Avon's ring?"

"Yes," said Trulia.

Eddie said, "Right! He always had it. He had it the night he disappeared. I saw it. He had it off and was moving it around with his fingers like he always did. Just before you came to the house. How did you get it?"

Lohman interceded. "How do you know it was his ring?"

Eddie said, "He had it specially made. He told me it was his lucky ring. He had it made a few years before he disappeared and the first day he wore it he got a huge contract. The contract to supply concrete for that Hump Tower building. 96 stories. A lot of concrete. He got it from a jeweler in the Loop and he told me he had them promise to never make another. He said he had it in writing."

"Have you seen the writing?" asked Lohman.

McClurg said, "I have. He wrote it off on his tax return. He said it was a business expense. He thought it was responsible for him getting a lot of business that year. I couldn't talk him out of it. He got it trademarked too. We may still have it. I'll look. Anyway, I'm sure it was a one of a kind ring."

Sean had been following all this with wide open eyes. Now he looked from one of the speakers to the other and back and forth. He said nothing.

Lohman asked him, "Did you see it on Whiteman that evening when you were there?"

THE DEAD ONE PROTRUDES

Sean said, "I don't remember seeing it. I wasn't there long."

"So where did you get the ring Dude?" asked Sweeney. "This gets interesting."

Sean looked sideways at Sweeney and then back at the others. He said, "I bought it at a resale shop at a Church."

Lohman knew that Sean was a collector of little art type things, like jewelry, china and little ceramic figures and other things, called objects d'art by some. He even had a display case in his office. "What church?" he asked.

Sean said, "It was at that D'Gregor Temple. Up on LaSalle Street. It was at that theological seminary they have up there - the school."

"When?" asked Lohman.

Sean said, "I can't remember. It was after I saw him at his house. I can try and see if I have anything on it."

"Do that," said Lohman.

McClurg then asked Sean, "How come you didn't have it earlier? I think I would have noticed it when we were meeting before."

Sean answered, "I don't wear it all the time. Just when it matches my outfit."

"Outfit?" asked Nuftdone in a derogatory tone. "What is that?"

Sean just looked at him. Sweeney broke in with, "His clothes, Dude. He likes to have all the things on him at one time match up. Like the dolls, Dude."

THE DEAD ONE PROTRUDES

Everyone there just went on pause for a moment except Sean who wiggled his butt and glanced up and across the ceiling.

There was some more talk about the details of the transfer of control from Trulia to Eddie and then they all got into some talk about the details of the business again and the possible purchase of the West Coast company and the loans.

At this stage Sweeney started talking about his visit to the Lake Calumet plant. "One more thing," he said. "Remember what I was talking about in our meeting yesterday? Maybe the Whitemans know something about it." He turned towards Eddie. "They sent me down to the plant to look over things - you know - that due diligence stuff about the West Coast company deal and the loan." Due diligence involved people who were not the parties to a deal, such as the lawyers and accountants and investment bankers, investigating the companies they were representing to see that what they were claiming was true and to see if there was anything special that needed to be disclosed. These people could be held liable for their clients' fraud if they did not investigate adequately and passed on the fraud.

Sweeney continued. "So you may not know this. I have a lot of show business clients and in show business there are drugs. I don't do the stuff, but I know who does and I often know who to get the stuff from if someone asks. I don't sell. I just know who does." There was total silence and lack of movement around the room. Nuftdone was appalled at such a discussion in his presence. Lohman and McClurg were hoping Sweeney wouldn't get further into the Hell pit of improper discussion. The Whiteman's were interested. "So I am down there and you are showing me around and I see this guy who I know deals. What do you think he's doing? I ask who he is and they tell me his is a

THE DEAD ONE PROTRUDES

contractor. He's buying cement in bags. He was in that locked up area so it must have been the high class stuff. You remember Eddie? You were taking me through the place. I said, 'Stay away from him Dude! He deals.' Then you told me he's a regular customer. You said he's a contractor on small jobs and he couldn't be a dealer. He wouldn't have time."

"Yes," said Eddie. "He's still a customer."

"What kind of jobs?" asked McClurg.

"Small ones, he says. I don't know the particulars."

"What if he is a dealer?" asked Sweeney. "People tell me he sells the stuff. Then we have this drug guy from Mexico popping out of your concrete. Is there a connection?"

"Of course not!" said Trulia. "What do you think? Do you think - are you suggesting we have anything to do with drugs?"

"Well, somebody does," said Sweeney. "Look at that drug guy from Mexico. He was supposed to be the main source of drugs in Chicago and now he's gone. But the stuff is still coming in here. He probably wasn't the big shot anyway. It's just like Prohibition I hear. Remember that President Johnston's father - that Old Joe he was called - he was one of the main sources of booze brought into the U.S. during Prohibition. I hear rumors that there's a big guy in control. Just like Old Joe."

"Who?" asked Nuftdone.

"Johnston's father. President Johnston. Remember him."

THE DEAD ONE PROTRUDES

Nuftdone exhaled in an insulted fashion. The offense was not so much denigrating the family of an exalted President, but the degeneration of the meeting into the discussion of drugs.

Sweeney went on with, "And I hear a big guy is in control of the drugs here in Chicago like before. We hear that the Outfit, the Syndicate - you know - the same as the Mafia in other cities, never went into the drug trade. Instead after Prohibition they morphed into gambling and now that's all gone. So we are told independent street gangs are in control. But I hear a big guy here is over it all. Who, no one says. Maybe it's poo poo. But that's the word in show town."

Lohman said, "Yeah. You think we would have learned something from Prohibition. Those who want drugs get them and making them illegal just creates a group of crooks supplying them. On the other hand our mayor and all the past mayors and the police chiefs say there is nothing like the Outfit or any big guy running the drug business here."

"So," said Sweeney, "did they ever say anything about Old Joe in the twenties and thirties?"

"Well," asked Eddie, "what would it have to do with cement? And us? You think we sell drugs? You looked over our business. The accountants came in. Where are the drugs? We sell concrete and cement and allied products. That's it. And we get most of it from Humpy. That's Ronald Hump. You think he sells drugs?"

At least this changed the subject. Sweeney said, "Hump! He's bad! No wonder he lost. I think he's just here to show us God ain't perfect. If God is all good and all powerful, how did Hump get here? Or Flinton?"

THE DEAD ONE PROTRUDES

He paused and then said, "But maybe not. Maybe God has just sent us something to test our faith. Never can tell with that God guy."

Nuftdone had had enough. "That's it. The meeting is over. We all have other things to do."

With this everyone started to leave. Lohman left with Sweeney and Sean who were going to go to his office with him to discuss some matters involving Lohman's clients. On the way down the hall Sweeney said, "How about that organ donation stuff? I hear a lot of people do it. I remember several years ago St. Charles had me working on the estate plan for an old guy client of his. Real rich guy. So what else? When does he deal with anyone who isn't rich? I had to meet with the guy several times."

Lohman asked, "Who?"

Sweeney said, "I don't remember. I just wanted to forget him. But he was a basshole."

"What's that?" asked Lohman.

"A bickering asshole," said Sweeney.

"Oh," said Lohman.

"So I am meeting with St. Charles and some other associates and we get to discussion of organ donation," said Sweeney. "Zenon was there too to talk about something else with St. Charles. He did some work for the client too so he stayed when we were talking about the organ donation. The client wanted us to look into not just organ donation, but preserving his body in frozen form until science could figure out how to bring him back to life. Zenon says, 'He's in such bad shape that I

THE DEAD ONE PROTRUDES

wouldn't think anyone would want his organs.' I said, 'He's such a big asshole I'd think someone could use that.' After that St. Charles didn't have me working on any of his stuff."

"I wonder why," said Lohman.

THE DEAD ONE PROTRUDES

13 CHICAGO ART PANEL COMPANY

Lohman had earlier assigned DiBello and the firm's head investigator to find out who owned the Chicago Art Panel Company. Many large law firms had in-house investigators because they often had to take the initiative in finding out the actual facts of any particular matter, at least when they were not the ones making up the facts. F, P & C's head investigator was Wiggy Rodriguez. He was short, fat and almost round. Wiggy was not his real name. It was what everyone called him because of his monstrous wig, which he was very proud of. He was born in Mexico and was proud of that too. Both he and DiBello were good at their jobs which is why Lohman used them whenever he could. Both of them had been nosing around the concrete company's plant on Lake Calumet in connection with evaluating the company for the loans. By Thursday Lohman had them in his office to report what they found out.

Lohman asked, "What did you guys find?"

DiBello said, "Nothing. That is if you want to know who actually owns that outfit. We looked at all the available information and talked to David Delez, the Manager of the company. He says he takes orders from a trust company in the Cayman Islands. The records show that the company is a Delaware corporation. It's registered to do business in Illinois. The Illinois filings show that they were made by the Finebaum & Akhbar firm, the same firm that did the Humpy Materials, Inc. filings. The registered agent in both places is one of those corporation service companies that act as registered agents for a lot of companies. There is no public record of the Cayman ownership. And even if there was, it would only show that trust company and there is no way of finding out who is the real beneficiary of one of the trusts there. That's why

THE DEAD ONE PROTRUDES

they're set up there. Anyway, Delez says he doesn't know who the real owner is. He seems cooperative, at least after Whiteman's son asked him to tell us what he knew."

Lohman asked, "Did you check anything else? Are there any other public filings?"

"Yes," said DiBello. "A lot of the filings in Illinois, like the papers to qualify the corporations to do business here and the annual reports to the Secretary of State, show Sam Meacham or his firm, Finebaum and Akhbahr, were involved. They probably represent the company."

"That guy everyone was badmouthing in our conference the other day?" asked Lohman.

"Right," said DiBello. "I never dealt with him myself, but I've heard other people say he's - well - let's not say too - oh - ethical maybe. I can't remember the details."

"At least we don't represent the art panel company," said Lohman.

Wiggy said, "Maybe we don't know who owns that company, but we found out some other things about it. We got dates. Dates the panels were delivered." He pointed to a notebook in his hand. "I have them here. We got the date the panel with Whiteman was delivered. That was September 15th. The panels with the Pedway bodies and the Riverwalk body were delivered later that year. The Pedway panel was delivered on September 22nd. The Riverwalk panel was on October 31."

DiBello broke in. "Those panels were thicker than the usual panels. The usual concrete panel or precast panel might be four to eight inches

THE DEAD ONE PROTRUDES

thick. They can be made a lot thicker and the panels with the bodies were thicker. They'd have to be to conceal the bodies."

Lohman asked, "What are they doing there? What are art panels?"

DiBello said, "Panels with art on them. The art panel company hires artists on a per job basis to design whatever art needs to be on the panel. The artists supply a cover panel of their own material or a molding into which the art panel workers can pour concrete. It's like an inverse sculpture. In effect it is like a flat surface with a hole in it. The concrete goes into the hole which is sculpted so that the cured concrete has something sticking out of it that is whatever the artist wants to depict. In the case of these panels with the bodies in them human faces and body parts were depicted. Evidently the concrete covering the bodies was not thick enough. Anyway, it didn't last. Maybe because it was too thin. The son, Eddie Whiteman, had told me that, 'Concrete is forever'. Apparently not these panels. And I hear Avon Whiteman was a real big guy. It might have been hard to cover him up without making the panel too thick."

Wiggy added, "Finito. No more bodies popping out. Either whoever did this stopped it because it didn't last or they learned how to do it better. I hear that Whiteman guy was big, maybe 300 pounds. That's what they say down there. Maybe that had something to do with it. Maybe he was too big for the panel."

"What else do you know about that company?" asked Lohman.

"Not too much," said DiBello. "At least not much more than you know already. The artists don't work there. They do their work elsewhere and they are only hired for specific jobs. The company is located right

THE DEAD ONE PROTRUDES

next to the Streets and Sanitation yard down there. It's the biggest Streets & San yard in the city. The art panel employees are all part time too. They all work at the Streets & San yard."

"Yes," said Wiggy, "Streets and San work and workers are interesting. A lot of them don't show up for work unless someone is coming around to check on them. They hear about that in advance. Patronage workers they were. You know, people hired to get out the vote for the big wheels and not to actually work at the jobs where they got paid. Streets & San used to have another problem too. It's where the mob - the Syndicate - used to put their people on the payroll. They were in other departments too, but Streets & San used to be the big one. What they were was Syndicate street crew members. Those were the guys who went around and did the mob's dirty work. Collecting the juice, putting out the hits and beatings. Things are better now, but I think there's still some of the funny stuff going on there."

DiBello said, "We asked Delez about all his workers and he told us that he gets people from Streets & San because it is right next door and the art pours are usually at night and a lot of them want extra income and are free at night. There is a door between the panel company and the Streets & San lot. It is kept locked Delez says and they have to ring to get in. He also says he hires from a temp agency and most of the people he gets from there are Streets & San people from next door. He doesn't keep much in the way of records though. He says there aren't any records of who was working there when the panels with the bodies were made. Another thing - he says he pays mostly cash."

Wiggy chimed in. "Streets & San. They have a bad rep. You know I have sources in the police department and I asked about these art panel guys. We got some of their names from Delez. The cops are working on

THE DEAD ONE PROTRUDES

this too - or some of them are. I think some of the cops are still part of the old system and don't want to get into anything involving Streets & San. My source tells me the guys at the art panel company, or the names we got, - most of them don't show up for work at Streets & San. He tells me some of them have a lot of arrests on their records, but no convictions. All seems like a little bit of the old system. But the Syndicate is gone. What gives? And another thing. The panel company area has a door leading out to the Streets and San lot next door. I'm told it is usually locked and you have to ring to get in."

"Right," said DiBello. "Bad records. Secret owner. It says there is something more than we know that is going on there. There's another thing too. Delez told us that the panel company van driver who was found in the Pedway panel left his car in the Whiteman lot the night Avon Whiteman disappeared. He says he saw it there when he left about five. It gets stranger and stranger."

"With me too," added Wiggy. "I came in to see Delez one day and was told he was out at a restaurant so I went over there and he was there with some Streets & San guys. I had talked to them all before except one. They introduced me. Said he was - a weird name - Snively Blackman. So I thought he might be Streets & San. But I found out later he was Whiteman's butler. What he was doing down there I haven't found out yet. Mr. Lohman this is trouble."

THE DEAD ONE PROTRUDES

14 MORE NEWS

Friday, July 21st, was the last day of big news before all the politicians, emperors and those media persons who dutifully reported what the politicians and emperors wanted reported left for their weekend estates. It was raining, gloomy and the start of the weekend off for many of those who would spend the weekend complaining about the long and arduous hours they had to work.

The big news of the day was that Mexico and Canada had really bought into the wall idea - the idea that a wall should be built around the United States to keep us in. Their prime ministers announced in a joint press conference that they were forming a coalition of countries across the world to pay for it. Soon thereafter it was reported as "breaking" news that Hump had been tweeting that he was going to pledge ten million dollars to the effort, but he would have to be the cement supplier and concrete contractor and then only on the condition that no Mexicans who were not U.S. citizens could work on the project. In a hastily called press conference later in the day Hump announced that he had formed a company to do the work and he was planning to sell interests in the company to finance it. He announced that he had also formed a company to operate screening of the traffic through the wall by checking credentials and authorizations as they went through the wall and to operate the air traffic control system and security to do the same. He explained that the revenue to pay for all this and the revenue to pay off money borrowed to build the wall would come from charges imposed on people who wanted access and egress.

THE DEAD ONE PROTRUDES

Apparently none of this was news in D.C. because it was also reported that just that day a bill had been introduced in Congress to implement all this.

What our President would have to say about all this would have to wait because, it being Friday, no one could find her. This had become so routine that there was no comment about this. On the other hand it was reported that the annual dinner for the ambassadors from all the countries with relations with the U.S. was to be held at the White House that evening and Vice President Bill would be hosting it in the absence of the President. A few of the ambassadors were interviewed about this and they indicated that they could care less about which Flinton was there - or if any Flinton was there.

Lohman had heard some of this on the radio before he left the house and Tete had filled him on new tidbits during the morning so he had some idea of what was going on. One thing that she also informed him of was that it had been reported in the local news that the probable cause of death of Avon Whiteman had been determined to be fentanyl, the drug with opioid like effects, but many times stronger than heroin. This had been based on finding traces of it in his remains. She told him that the news had also contained a description of fentanyl. Apparently just a little bit could kill. She mentioned that they added it could be taken the same way as opium and also in liquids since it dissolved in water.

At noon St. Charles, Cohenstein and Lohman were due at the Pullman Club. When they were not required to be elsewhere they usually met there on Friday, supposedly to discuss firm business. However, they usually ran into the Three Stooges there and ate with them. One of the Three Stooges was St. Charles. The other two were Arthur Swifton and

THE DEAD ONE PROTRUDES

Biffster McCain. They were not referred to as The Three Stooges in their presence. Arthur Swifton, known as Swifty or Arty, was the head of The Bank and the Swifton Corporation, a large family organization involving many of the businesses their forefathers had engaged in such as farm machinery, meat packing, truck manufacturing, packaged foods, household products and real estate, in addition to The Bank. Biffster McCain was known as the Biffster, which was his actual first name. He was an old line, Social Register, CEO and part owner of a large conglomerate. Swifty and the Biffster also happened to be clients and when they were there the F, P & C people ate with them.

Today all the Three Stooges were present so Lohman and Cohenstein were doomed to lunch with them. They all had got seated at one of the larger tables when one of the older members of the Club came by on the way to his table. Older, as in way older than the Three Stooges group. He and St. Charles were friends because of his eminent standing as a rich guy. Because of his age and his standing, he continued to wear old clothes. He wore suits with wider than fashionable lapels, pleated pants, and wider than fashionable ties. All the details were wrong. All were out of date. Out of fashion. He would not be accepted anywhere in today's world - except he had loot. On his way past the table he paused to greet St. Charles and shake hands with him. All St. Charles had to say, besides "Hello," was, "You should see my tailor. Hans Gregor. Try them. Magnificent attire."

The old guy sniffed and then moved on. As he went out of earshot St. Charles said, "He is an embarrassment to our class. But what can you expect. I understand his father was a common laborer."

Cohenstein said, "That's not so bad. My wife Zelda is too."

THE DEAD ONE PROTRUDES

"What!" exclaimed St. Charles.

"Three kids," said Cohenstein. "She's been a common laborer three times."

Lohman tried to control his facial feature controls which were about to twist the edges of his mouth up. The other two Stooges just looked blank.

Then St. Charles said, "He reminds me of Gerry Ruckus in our Lake County office." He looked at the other Stooges and said in the confidential tone used between the intelligentsia. "Our litigation partner up there, don't you know. The leading lawyer up there. But he dresses in old clothes. Disgraceful. And our Management Committee lets him get away with it. You know Arty, you too Biffster, we who lead large firms have to put up with really outrageous behavior sometimes. I tried to take him into Cook & Brothers for a fitting one day when he was down here for lunch. It is right on the way back to the office from here. I just casually said we should go in and look. And you know they clothe the majority or our class who do not have their own tailors. But he just refused to go in. Said something about having to prepare for trial."

Cohenstein spoke up. "Gerry doesn't dress that way all the time. Remember we discussed this before when you brought it up at the Management Committee? He's a trial lawyer. He wants to dress down for the jurors. He doesn't want to make them think he's from another world. They aren't usually the people who can afford expensive and up to date clothing. But when the clients who like to see that meet with him he dresses the way you like. He keeps a change of clothes in the office. You just don't see it because he's up there in Lake County and

THE DEAD ONE PROTRUDES

you're down here. And that day you wanted him to go into Cook & Brothers - remember I was with you two guys? He had the old suit and things on because he was in court that day. Clothes schmooze. Actually most of the clients don't care if he's naked if he wins."

This was a jaw dropper for the Stooges.

The Biffster asked, "In court?"

After a period of stunned silence St. Charles, who apparently did not hear Cohenstein, said, "He gets clothes at resale stores. As you know I am a director of numerous charities and one day I and some other directors of various charities were being shown through a resale store that wanted help from us. And there he was, buying clothing. I was so shocked I couldn't even speak to him, nor did I want anyone to see that I knew him. I just turned and walked out."

St. Charles then turned the conversation to the menu which everyone had started looking at as a way to avoid entering into the clothing conversation. Soon they were served and proceeding through the luncheon. The conversation had turned to the news of the day. The subject of Avon Whiteman's cause of death came up.

Cohenstein looked at Lohman and asked, "You knew him, Bumper. Was he a drug addict? Did he take too much?"

"He wasn't an addict that I know of," answered Lohman. "At any rate, he didn't pour concrete all over himself."

Cohenstein said, "Could someone have done that to save face? They found him dead from an overdose and then put him in the concrete as

THE DEAD ONE PROTRUDES

if he was killed? They didn't want everyone to know the head of the company was an addict."

"Good Heavens!" said St. Charles. "People don't do things like that!"

The Biffster, being a person who said what he thought, when he had a thought, which was not often, said, "Oh come on Graybee. What if your partners find out you're an addict and died from an overdose? Don't you think they'd cover it up?"

Swifty added, "Yes. Like Marshall Field's son - you know the son of that guy who built up the big wholesale and retail department store business? He died in one of the whore houses in the vice district way back then and after that they took his body home and said that's where he died."

"Certainly not!" exclaimed St. Charles. "How could you possibly think I would do such things?"

"They're just making an illustration," said Cohenstein.

St. Charles said petulantly, "Well such an illustration is impossible. My doing such things is unimaginable."

"So did you hear about building that wall around us?" asked Lohman as a way of changing the subject.

Cohenstein said, "Won't happen. We shouldn't waste time trying to get involved. We should tell everybody in the firm to stay away from it. Bad PR."

Swifty and the Biffster looked at each other. "Good advice," said Swifty.

THE DEAD ONE PROTRUDES

Then Swifty remembered Hump and his involvement in walls. "What about us? We lent a lot of money to Hump and we're negotiating renewal." Then he added in a confidential tone, "I can say this because it's been in the news. We're negotiating renewal. God forbid if he can't pay. Then it shows up as a loss on the income statement and a hit on the balance sheet. If we roll it over that doesn't happen. We can still claim it's a good loan. Anyway, thank God he lost. When it looked like he might win he was asking for terms we wouldn't give anyone and for a lot more money to boot. We're talking about more normal terms now. Actually we'd like to get paid, but he can't. At least it doesn't look like it. No one else will lend him the money to pay us."

Cohenstein said, "Maybe you should have had him win. Then he could use the leverage of being President to get some money to pay you with. Anyway, even if he is a rich guy, I think he got the money by not paying anyone. But I hear you Christ guys got a hymn that says, 'Everybody talkin' 'bout Heaven ain't goin' there.' As lawyers we know that everyone who's claiming to be rich ain't."

"Well I certainly am," said Swifty.

"Me too," said the Biffster.

Soon the rich guys got up and went back to their offices.

THE DEAD ONE PROTRUDES

15 ESTATE ADMINISTRATION

Lohman spent most of Saturday and part of Sunday in the office. Monday morning he was scheduled to meet first thing with a potential client that Sweeney had dug up. Lohman had met him at a party where Sweeney and the prospect were and Sweeney had indicated that Lohman was an expert in business matters. Sweeney had later told Lohman the guy wanted to come in to discuss starting a new business. He told Lohman that the guy was an agent for show business clients, some of who were well known. None of them were Sweeney's clients. He told Lohman that the guy had said he wanted to do a "startup" and had access to "equity funding" from show business people. He also told Lohman that he had reservations about the guy and he wanted Lohman' s opinion about taking the guy on as a client as well as help in the legal matters involving the business venture.

Sweeney and the prospect came into Lohman's office. After the greetings and getting settled they got down to business. The guy wanted to start up a credit card business where the card would have super privileges. It was going to be called "The Hump Card" and it would be endorsed by his show business clients and, he hoped, by Hump himself. The endorsers would all get fees of course. The business plan would be to sign up rich people who would get special deals from participating providers of goods and services, one of which would be resorts owned by Hump. He wanted to patent the idea. He explained that he had met Hump, but he wanted to prevent him from using the idea.

Lohman explained that they couldn't get a patent, but maybe they could get a trademark. He cautioned however, that if they were going

THE DEAD ONE PROTRUDES

to use Hump's name they would have to get his cooperation. Especially if he was publicly endorsing the card. Lohman asked if the prospect had discussed this with Hump and they guy explained that he had not and he wanted to protect the name before he did. Lohman remarked that Hump did not own the name "Hump" because other people used it and Hump certainly did not own it as a word identifying a particular credit card. He then explained that if it was all set up to involve his identity, getting his consent would probably be required. Lohman told him that it would probably be a good idea to get Hump's cooperation before proceeding. However, he also indicated that they could have their trademark lawyers look into that.

The prospect then proposed setting the business up as if Hump was not involved. He asked if they could use the "Hump" name then and get a trademark and then later go to Hump for his endorsement with more leverage. Lohman once again said they could have their trademark lawyers look into that. Lohman also told the prospect that when someone else is using a name, even for something else, it is good idea just to come up with another name and avoid the cost and delay of litigation over the matter. In other works, stay away from name conflicts. Just don't even come close. Clients usually didn't like this advice and the prospect didn't seem to hear it.

Funding was discussed. The prospect did not have any idea of the amount of money needed. Lohman indicated that the thing that might get Hump to cooperate was showing him that the prospect could raise the money for the project. For this, Lohman told him, he should be talking to people involved in funding new businesses such as "private equity" people and investment bankers. To get them involved he

THE DEAD ONE PROTRUDES

should have some source of funds interested already, such as his wealthy show business contacts.

Lohman also told the prospect that he should be working with an accountant to develop financial projections for the project.

The trouble was that the guy seemed like a sleaze. Lohman did not want to refer him to any of the accounting firms that F, P & C did business with. The guy did have his own accountants at a fairly sizeable firm so Lohman indicated that he should talk to them. They scheduled another meeting, just in case something would come out of it and the meeting broke up.

After this Lohman was scheduled to meet with Eddie Whiteman, McClurg and Nuftdone about matters concerning the administration of the trust assets, the financial status of the company, tax matters and the status of the West Coast company deal and the loan negotiations. Sean Featherbottom was included because, being a CPA as well as a lawyer and having worked at the company, he had been assigned to review the financial materials and tax matters involving the company and trust assets.

The meeting got started and one of the problems discussed was the need to raise money to pay the estate taxes that had to be paid. A lot of this depended on the value of the company. The outside accounting firm was working on an appraisal, but it wasn't completed. In this regard there was a potential problem with appraisals. To get a loan to buy another company the lender would want an appraisal. Also to renew its credit line the company needed an appraisal. To get loans borrowers want the highest value possible for assets to be used as security for the loan. In this case the security would be the ownership

THE DEAD ONE PROTRUDES

interests in the Whiteman Materials, Inc. company and some of the company's assets. On the other hand, when it comes to estate taxes which are based on the value of the assets in the taxable estate, the taxpayer wants a low appraisal. As a result of this it was decided to stop pursuing acquisition of the West Coast company.

"But what about the credit line?" asked Eddie. "Don't we have to show a high appraisal there?"

McClurg said, "The accountants are still working on that. I spoke to them and they are aware of the different uses of the appraisals and they think the estate tax appraisal will satisfy the bank. They don't think the appraisal for the West Coast company loan can be used without having to up the appraisal for tax purposes. Anyway Eddie, we are scheduled to meet with them later this week. Right now they are holding everything pending what is decided. I talked to the bank and gave them a predicted value and they think it is OK."

Nuftdone reminded everyone what the probable amount that would have to be raised for estate taxes was and explained that, "This is a problem too. So far as we can determine you will have to borrow a lot of this. This will probably have to come from your credit line or loans to individuals in the family and we haven't worked out the exact amounts yet. Anyway, once again, the lower the appraisal for estate tax purposes, the lower the value of the assets the lenders will see. You can't use an appraisal for estate tax purposes that is lower than other appraisals you know about without explaining the difference. Sometimes the different appraisals are conducted according to different standards, but we would have trouble doing that here. Did you talk to the accountants about that Shannon?"

THE DEAD ONE PROTRUDES

"Yes," he said. "They don't think they can work out separate appraisals that would work. They think they can use the rules to shave a little off the estate tax appraisal and add a little to an appraisal for lenders, but nothing much. Anyway, they think there are enough assets around to get enough to pay the estate tax. This is going to require not just you, Eddie, but Trulia to personally guaranty the loans and put up your separate assets as security."

Eddie said, "Yes. You told me. I spoke to Trulia about it and she understands this too. She told me you already talked to her."

"Yes," said McClurg, "but with her just like you, the details still have to be filled in as we go along with the accountants. So where we are is this. We drop the West Coast deal and start talking to the bank about increasing the credit line or getting other loans to pay the estate tax and about what sort of appraisals and security they need and, as we are doing that, keep the accountants involved."

Nuftdone then went on to discuss another problem. When a missing person is declared dead pursuant to a statute saying that after a person has been missing for a defined period of time they are to be presumed dead the Internal Revenue Code takes that as the time of death. The period during which an estate tax return must be filed runs from that date. However, when the missing person is found dead within the statutory period before the person is presumed dead the law is not so clear as to determining the date of death for tax purposes. Is the date of death when the person is found? Is it sometime earlier? He discussed the fine points of the law on this and finally recommended that they were going to use the date on which it was discovered that Avon was dead. Otherwise they would have a very late estate tax return with penalties and interest due.

THE DEAD ONE PROTRUDES

Lohman then said, "There could be another problem with all this. Shannon, remember Sean said the company appears to be selling more concrete and cement than it has?"

Eddie had not heard this before. It was a difficult subject and McClurg probably had not wanted to discuss it with him, especially since when it was brought up Eddie was not in control of the company and it was not known that Avon was dead so no estate tax questions had arisen. Eddie said, "What? How can that happen?"

At this stage Sean gave some visible butt wiggles in his chair and some vigorous ceiling looking. Lohman said, "He worked there and he had reviewed the company financial statements. Based on his knowledge of the physical quantity of concrete and cement that passed out of there when he was there and his knowledge of the prices charged and estimates about activity at other plants he came to the conclusion that the sales reported in the financial statements far exceeded the amount actually being sold. In fact he thought the present sales might exceed the capacity of the plants."

Eddie said, "Well, he didn't work at all the plants. How could he tell? Where did you get this idea Featherbottom?"

Sean wiggled again. "From the things Mr. Lohman indicated. I didn't do an audit or anything. But look at the financials yourself. Then take your physical sales volume. That is, the actual physical quantity of materials sold and not the dollar amount stated in the financial statements. Multiply the physical amount by the prices you charge and see what you get. In other words, do not conclude from the sales stated in the financial statement divided by the price that the resulting figure is the

THE DEAD ONE PROTRUDES

physical amount being sold. Just figure out the actual volume from truck loads, physical amounts in inventory and other sources like that."

"Well I never noticed anything like that," said Eddie.

Sean added, "There is something else too. The sales stated in the financial statements rose a lot after Mr. Whiteman disappeared, but the profits declined, mostly because of much higher payments to the consulting companies."

"Did you handle the financial matters, Eddie?" asked Lohman.

"Dad did all that," said Eddie. "You know, I'm not an accountant. I think we should get the accountants on this."

"Not now," said Lohman. "It's best that you look into it first. Proceed as Sean has indicated. If it comes out that the financial statements show more sales than the amount actually being sold then something may have to be explained. One thing though, since the accountants prepared the financial statements and audited them it is highly likely that the money indicated for sales actually came in. That is where you should start. Check the bank records. Did you actually get that much money? We'll have Sean help you. He's a CPA and he knows something about the business so he can handle your questions. But don't talk to anyone else about this right now. No one. We don't know what we will find. Can you work with him? You fired him?"

Eddie said, "Yeah. I didn't have anything against him. It was Dad who told me to fire him. Actually he was working twice as hard as anyone else. He didn't even take breaks. That's one thing dad mentioned. He said you can't have someone around who is upsetting the other employees that way."

THE DEAD ONE PROTRUDES

"Well what about being gay - is that a problem?" asked Sean.

"I don't care," said Eddie. "I don't care if you screw toads."

"Well, I don't," said Sean. "Either sex."

"Saying you were fired because you were gay was Dad's idea," said Eddie. "I think he just didn't want anyone except the people he designated fiddling with the Excelente cement. He had special people he wanted to handle it. He said we were going to make a lot of money on it.

Another thing they had discussed at an earlier meeting was the terms of who gets what. Basically Avon had given Trulia the income from a part of the trust qualifying for the marital deduction and given everything else to Eddie, subject to an obligation of the trust to pay the marital trust income to Trulia. This had been discussed before and both Eddie and Trulia had said they had been aware of this before Avon died. Nuftdone now brought this up again and noted that the amount going to Trulia was not all that large and thus the marital deduction for the estate was not too large.

McClurg said, "He was going to change that and give her more. Then he took it back and said he didn't want to. I don't know why. I told him he could get a lot bigger marital deduction. I had discussed it with you, remember Jerry?"

McClurg asked Eddie, "Did you know anything about it?"

"Well, I don't know anything about estate taxes. I don't think Dad did either. But he told me what he was doing there. He didn't say why. But I have an idea. Not long before he disappeared he told me he thought

THE DEAD ONE PROTRUDES

Trulia was cheating on him. He even told me he wondered if it was with Snively - Snively Blackman, the butler. That's something I wanted to stay out of, you know. Anyhow, he was always thinking she was up to something with some guy"

The others just looked at each other and no one pursued the subject any further.

Lohman decided to follow up on what he had been asked about Avon. "Eddie, you've heard about the cause of death, haven't you?"

"Yes," said Eddie.

"I got asked if he was an addict Friday. I never got any idea about that. Did you?" Lohman asked.

"No," said Eddie. "He wasn't. I never saw anything like that. He didn't even drink much, just his evening drink at his desk and a drink or two at parties. I never saw him - what - plastered - drugged - or whatever."

Lohman then told Sean and Eddie what to do about getting together and McClurg summed up about dealing with the accountant about the company value and the meeting adjourned.

THE DEAD ONE PROTRUDES

16 THE GOLD COAST ASSOCIATION

The following Saturday, July 29th, a gala society event was to be held. This was the annual officer installation meeting of the Gold Coast Association. The Gold Coast was an area of Chicago starting about a mile and a quarter from the center of town and extending to about 2 miles north. It was along the Lake Front and was about one quarter of a mile from there to its western boundary. It had originally been swamp and sand dune land with a cemetery thrown in, but one of Chicago's old time rich guys developed it into an area of large houses. After that, in the early part of the Twentieth Century, came the large apartments. After World War II came the smaller, but expensive, apartments. The Gold Coast Association was the neighborhood organization and was quite popular with the snob set.

The meeting's purpose was to install the new officers for the coming year. The President was going to be Arthur Swifton, our dear Swifty. His main residence, a large palace on the Lake, was in the tony North Shore suburb of Lake Forest, but he had a town house in the Gold Coast. It was not a town house as the word is used by developers these days to indicate a house attached to a row of other houses built by the developers. It was a mansion that happened to be "in town". The meeting was to be held at the Ambassador West Hotel which was just one block from Swifty's place. There was also an Ambassador East Hotel which was across the street and on the same block as Swifty's house. There was going to be drinking (called a cocktail hour), then dinner, then the installation ceremony and then more drinking and mingling and then leaving. It was to be a festive occasion where all present did not have to endure mixing with their inferiors.

THE DEAD ONE PROTRUDES

Naturally those present wanted to have their friends who did not live in the Gold Coast attend and they wanted everyone to know what glorious people they were so there were guests from out of the neighborhood and members of the press present. Lohman lived in the Gold Coast and he attended. F, P & C had several tables reserved for some of their partners and their guests as well. McClurg also attended, as did St. Charles and Cohenstein. Everyone had their spouses in attendance.

During the cocktail hour Lohman saw Cassidy Tyreservski, nicknamed Cass, Avon Whiteman's friend, who Lohman also knew. They got together and started talking and as they were so engaged Swifty came by and greeted Lohman who introduced him to Tyreservski. Lohman turned the conversation to Avon Whiteman because he was curious about what happened and because Cass had been there. He asked Cass what happened. Cass told him the things Lohman had heard before. One thing Cass told him that Lohman hadn't heard before was that on the evening Avon disappeared Cass came in to see him because of a phone call he received from someone to do so and pick up something. He couldn't remember who called him, just someone calling for Avon. At any rate Cass explained that it couldn't have been important because they didn't even talk about it. He said he came over, parked in the driveway next to Avon's car, and they just talked.

Lohman asked, "What can you remember about the person who called you?"

Cass said, "Not much. It was a woman."

"So what happened then," asked Lohman.

THE DEAD ONE PROTRUDES

Cass explained that, "I came in and we talked. He was there alone. He had told me the butler and chef and maid were gone. Blackman he said. He always referred to the butler by name."

Swifty chimed in. "Blackman. Oh yes. I have seen him at Avon's place. Parties, gatherings, don't you know. I have seen him elsewhere too. I thought maybe he was with a catering company. I have seen him at parties up on the North Shore at that fellow's place, what's his name? I think he represents that Humpy Cement here in the U.S. or something. Jared Bannon. That's his name. I've seen him there. You mean he only worked for Avon?"

"So far as I know," said Cass. "Anyway, I was about to leave and Avon poured himself his evening drink. He always had one. He had the fixings there in his office. There was a glass and a small crystal pitcher with booze in it on a silver tray. It was scotch he usually drank. It wasn't in the bottle. It had been put in the pitcher. Then there was the one glass. He asked if I wanted a drink. I have had a drink with him before in the evening and he had to get Blackman to get another glass. Anyway he had told me no one else was there and I didn't want to have a drink and I had to get on to somewhere else so I declined. I had just enough time to get to dinner with my wife at home. I was there from about five thirty to six. I remember looking at my watch when he asked me if I wanted a drink and seeing that I had to go."

"Did you notice anything else? Was anybody else there?" asked Lohman.

"No," said Cass. "At least he told me no one else was there."

"So who called you?" asked Lohman.

THE DEAD ONE PROTRUDES

"I don't know," Cass responded. "It was a woman. I couldn't tell who it was. It wasn't Trulia, unless she was trying to disguise her voice. Now that I think about it, the voice sounded funny."

"So what did you talk about?" asked Lohman.

"Nothing important. I think he told me he was going to go to the Calumet plant, but he didn't say anything about why or when. We talked about the usual stuff. He just wanted to shoot the shit and I didn't have anything on my mind." At this stage Lohman was grateful that Sweeney wasn't there.

Cass continued, "We talked about maybe golf, cards, how to play, etcetera. We talk about that a lot. Broads. We talked about getting some ass. I can't remember the particulars. Bullshit it was. Just the same stuff we talk about when I'm in the neighborhood and drop in. So I left. Oh - one thing. I saw one of his trucks when I left. It was a van. Not a big truck. He owns or he owned, a panel concrete company and it had trucks and vans and they are very distinctive. As I was coming out I saw one of the trucks going north on State Street. That's the street the house is on. The street out in front of this hotel. He's just a few houses north up the street. You know that. The van looked like it was going to turn into the driveway, but then it went on north."

What was it doing? Do you know? Did Avon mention it?" asked Lohman.

"No idea," said Cass. "As I was coming out it was going north in the street. I assumed it was some of the workmen going home. Or maybe to a plant on the North Side. Don't know."

"Oh, before I forget," said Lohman, "did you see Avon's ring?"

THE DEAD ONE PROTRUDES

"His ring?" asked Cass. "Why would I see that?"

Lohman replied, "Well, I hear he was always taking it off and putting it on and playing with it."

"Yeah, I think he did," said Cass.

"So you saw it that night?" asked Lohman.

"No," said Cass. "Not that I can remember. I don't pay much attention to that kind of thing."

Lohman wanted to make sure. "So you did not see it that night?

"Cass said, "I can't remember. Why are you asking about it?"

Lohman said, "Someone was seen wearing it after he died."

"That's strange, "said Cass. Who?"

"Actually one of our young lawyers who was there that night before you were there. The strange thing is that he bought it at the D"Gregor Temple resale shop after Avon disappeared. Just, once again, let me get it clear. You did not notice whether Avon had the ring or did not. He could have had it or he could have been without it. You didn't notice."

"That's it. I didn't notice one way or the other," said Cass.

The conversation then turned to other subjects and shortly after that they all broke up and moved on to conversations with other people.

Later, at dinner, the Lohmans sat next to Bungus LaRue and his wife. Bumper was next to Bungus and to the left of Bungus sat the two

THE DEAD ONE PROTRUDES

wives. The wives talked to each other and Bungus and Bumper were talking to each other. They got to talking about the Avon Whiteman affair and all the crazy things that had been in the news lately

Bungus said, "The politicians like all the wacko publicity because it takes attention away from what they are actually doing or not doing. In the meantime it gives them publicity to latch on to when they want to. Anyhow, what are they really doing lately? Let's just say that with all this craziness going on they are talking to me more often these days."

Lohman wasn't going to ask about what. He turned the conversation to the bodies. Along the way he asked, "What about the other victims? Is Whiteman going to be linked up with them? And since he is our client - or was - are we going to get bad publicity out of it? Avon was a Deacon in the church or temple run by D'Gregor. Blackman too. His butler."

LaRue said, "D'Gregor Temple. That's something. Do you know how many politicians are on its payroll? The Temple supposedly gets large religious donations from people who might ordinarily give the money to politicians. Political contributions are not usually deductible for tax purposes. Charitable or religious contributions are. Put two and two together there. Now you remember the concrete company gets a lot of contracts to supply the concrete for public projects like road building. They give a lot of campaign contributions to politicians too. So Whiteman was a Deacon of the Temple. I think we should prepare something to gloss over all that if it comes up."

Cohenstein was next to them and heard what they were talking about. "Let's set up a meeting for this. I think it will come out in public.

THE DEAD ONE PROTRUDES

Anyhow, we have to be prepared. I don't know why I wasn't on this already. I think my train of thought got stuck in the station."

"I'll set it up," said Lohman.

LaRue added, "Trulia Whiteman. She was a Deacon. Still is. Whiteman's butler. He is. Blackman gets a lot of money from the Temple. Me, I'm a Deacon too. That's how I'm in on all this. Come to think of it, being a Deacon of that place is dangerous. Avon gets it. D'Gregor gets it. And he disappeared abound when the Mexican Deacon was brought back for burial."

Lohman asked, "Who was that?"

LaRue said, He was a guy who was like a reclusive monk. He started up a D'Gregor monastery in Mexico. He died down there, but they brought him back here for burial because he came from here. We were all at the funeral. Me, Trulia, Blackman, D'Gregor. Hevencent presided at the funeral though. After that D'Gregor went out of town to visit some of his locations. No one ever heard from him again. He didn't show up at any of the places he was going to visit. The Deacons set up a committee to try to find out where he was - Trulia, Blackman, a few others - but I never heard what they found out, at least about the details."

"Nobody knows anything about it?" asked Lohman.

LaRue said, "I don't know. I'm not in on that. I guess things are going on OK as usual so no one pays much attention to the matter."

THE DEAD ONE PROTRUDES

Lohman wanted to ask LaRue what he did as a Deacon and if he got any money out of the Temple or put any money in to it. The "Don't Ask" rule came to him just in time.

LaRue went on. "A lot of the Temple money comes in as cash and I think it is off the books. I don't know where it really comes from. Churches don't have to file tax returns you know. Then the Temple runs a string of substance abuse treatment centers. It actually makes big money off of them, but I was never told the details of how. They have a separate advisory board and a separate corporation because, for one thing, they have to file a return. Avon was active on the board there."

Then LaRue violated the "Don't tell" rule. "The cash is something else. I'm not sure where it goes, but I can guess. The money on the books shows a very big volume of donations too. Then there are the politicians. It has lots of politicians on the payroll. Other government employees too. New ones are added all the time. Normally if you want to influence a politician the legal way is through campaign contributions. But a lot of politicians are restricted in how those funds can be used and they often have to report what is going on with them. This way they get the money free and clear. It's salary. Much easier."

"So who is running all this now?" asked Lohman.

"I think Trulia does," said LaRue. "But at Deacon meetings Blackman seems to do a lot of the talking. He gets paid a lot there through a consulting company he owns. As a matter of fact, D'Gregor used to have meetings, dinner meetings, at the Whitemans' house. I assume Blackman was there as a butler. None of the other Deacons were invited. But since Avon disappeared I don't know the details or who is

THE DEAD ONE PROTRUDES

running the show except Trulia tells me whatever D'Gregor would have told me and I deal with her about anything that comes up. On the other hand I don't start asking questions about things like this."

Lohman thought that he couldn't ask too much about it now either without risking hearing something he didn't want to hear.

LaRue added, "And another thing that is interesting. That substance abuse program has drugs. Drugs for what they call withdrawal and then they have drugs for what they call 'maintenance'. That's like methadone. You've heard about that. Who knows all the drugs. They buy the drugs from drug companies of course. But Avon told me that he and D'Gregor were going to start their own drug company to supply the clinics. There are a lot of clinics all over the country so it would have a lot of business right off the bat. I don't know if they did it or not."

At this stage Cohenstein spoke up. "Talking about drugs, you remember the news a little while ago? It was in the news. It didn't get too much play. The source was supposed to be that Nappy Leaks outfit and everyone was saying it was fake news. Hump and Flinton have foundations, for charitable giving you know. But foundations have money. They just give away the income from their investments. So it was reported that both of their foundations have big investments in a drug company that makes opiates, amphetamines and methadone and that fentanyl we keep hearing about. And it said the foundations both also own part of a shipping company together. With all the crazy things they are doing these days I think maybe they use the stuff. I hear, maybe from that Sweeney kid, Hump is going to do a new TV show called The Truth. What truth? I think they're all wacked out. Fake news, real news - what's the difference these days?"

THE DEAD ONE PROTRUDES

"Yes, I know," said Lohman. "Who knows what is going on. And even if someone is telling us about something real all we hear is bull poo. No one can state facts today or get specific. At best they pass off opinions as facts. There's so much bullshit flying around. It has legs and runs around all over the place."

"Well, we're lawyers," said Cohenstein. "We gotta have wiggle room."

LaRue chimed in. "When it comes to politics you can't get specific. Every time you do you lose votes. The voters hear one thing they disagree with and they think you are horrible. They won't vote for you. That's why they won't talk politics with each other, even with their best friends. If my friend says something I disagree with he's no longer my friend. He's horrible. Take it from me. Every time I got specific about something I lost a lot of votes. That's why politicians are usually different. Not always, but usually. Their talent is getting elected and re-elected. This means they don't get specific about anything so the job attracts people who can't. They are incompetent at dealing with anything. That involves getting into the specifics. Instead they have a talent most of us don't. They can talk on forever and please everyone that hears them with their promises of eternal everlasting glory and benefits."

Cohenstein said, "Isn't it that fentanyl that killed Whiteman?"

"Right," said Lohman.

"So where'd it come from?" asked Cohenstein.

"Good question," said Lohman. "They didn't say."

THE DEAD ONE PROTRUDES

At this point Lohman noticed Eddie Whiteman walking by holding a couple of drinks. They all greeted each other.

"Eddie," said Lohman, "we were just talking about the D'Gregor Temple. Bungus here was telling me about it. Do you know who has been running it since D'Gregor disappeared? Who will run it now that we know he is dead? Avon was involved wasn't he?"

Eddie said, "Well, I know dad was active there, but I didn't know the details. I think Trulia and Snively are active there too. I don't know. Dad said there were charitable and tax matters involved, but I never got into that. I never handled the taxes or legal details. I just handled the plants and production and delivery. I didn't even do too much with sales. Hell it was just recently that you guys showed me how much Trulia's company was getting. I knew Trulia's consulting company was getting paid, but dad told me a lawyer recommended that. I don't mean her minority company. I mean the consulting company. When I heard about it I asked Shannon why he recommended it and he told me he didn't recommend it. So who did? I don't know. I asked Trulia and she told me her company was acting as a collection agent to shield our main company from liability. I heard about Blackman's company too and she told me that was just used to funnel money to him and he would get it back to us. Something about taxes and liability she said. As for the Temple, I don't know. I just thought they were all friends. Sometimes I used to see them all down at the Calumet plant. That's here we had our main offices."

"Who did you see there?" asked Lohman.

"Dad, Trulia, Snively, D'Gregor - them. They all seemed to be talking business. And I know dad talked about huge contributions to the

THE DEAD ONE PROTRUDES

Temple and then about getting big salaries from there and the treatment centers. It all sounded complicated," said Eddie. He continued. "And I didn't understand all this. And while this was going on one thing dad had told me was that he thought Snively was stealing from him and at the same time he said he wasn't going to tell the cops. I asked why and he told me he couldn't. He wouldn't say why he couldn't. Then I told Trulia about all this and asked her what was going on and she just told me she didn't believe it all."

Eddie then indicated he had to get on and get the extra drink to his wife and they bid goodbye.

Soon it was announced that the installation ceremony was starting and everyone standing returned to their seats and quieted down. Swifty and the other officers were installed and glory returned to the Gold Coast.

After the dinner and installation ceremony the Lohmans and McClurgs headed to the exit together in an attempt to avoid the rush of others who wanted to leave. They got to talking about what Cass had said. As they were starting to walk down the outside steps at the entrance to the hotel McClurg said, "What about the panel company truck that Cass said he saw driving north that night up there the night Avon disappeared? Did you hear anything else about that?"

They had just come out of the doors, one of which was still being held open for them by the doorman when they were discussing the van. The doorman knew Lohman because, being a nearby resident, he attended events there a lot and passed by a lot. Often they talked. The doorman said, "I saw that. When I heard on the news about when Mr. Whiteman disappeared I remembered all the neighborhood gossip I heard about

THE DEAD ONE PROTRUDES

him being missing. The date was on the news and I put two and two together and remembered that night I saw a van labeled Whiteman Panel right here. It was going that way." He pointed to the south. "It was going south and then it pulled up here in the driveway. I went toward it to see if anyone was coming out, but it just paused here until the street was clear and then it made a U-turn and headed north. I didn't think much about it until all the recent news. What gives Mr. Lohman?"

"That is just what we would like to know," said Lohman. "I take it they weren't working or delivering or picking up anything here were they?"

"Not that I know of," said the doorman.

Lohman and McClurg and their wives then parted and then went on to their respective homes to pass out as well behaved old people do early on Saturday night.

THE DEAD ONE PROTRUDES

17 WIGGY REPORTS

The next Monday Lohman went to Wiggy's office to find out what Wiggy had discovered. Lohman went to other people's offices when he could. He did not give a damn how this affected his reputation as the magnificent Managing Partner. It got him out and around and he found out a lot about what was going on in the firm this way that he wouldn't have found out if he had insisted that everyone come to his office. Wiggy had been down to the Calumet plant of Whiteman Materials and had rung up Lohman and told him he was back in the office.

When Lohman got there he and Wiggy greeted each other and then Wiggy began telling Lohman about his visit to the plant. He described the plant and what was going on there. Then he got into another aspect of the plant that Lohman had not heard much about. Wiggy said, "I think something is going on down there. I don't know, but at least in the past if you heard about Streets & San you thought of the Syndicate. The Outfit. The organization Al Capone was running here. So I didn't find any illegal stuff there and the Outfit is mostly gone because they were getting money from illegal gambling and most gambling is legal now. And they never got into drugs. But I still don't think Streets & San, where they put their guys on the public payroll in the past, could have completely cleaned up yet. And that place is full of Streets & San guys who work there."

"Well what do you think is going on?" asked Lohman.

"Don't know, Mr. Lohman," said Wiggy. "One thing I saw was a guy who I know is in one of the drug gangs buying some cement. It was that bagged stuff they have locked up. I saw a lot of people coming in for

THE DEAD ONE PROTRUDES

the cement. It's supposed to be for the small jobs. A lot of them came in with cars, not trucks or vans. Do small contractors use their cars to haul things around? And a lot of the vehicles, cars or trucks, have out of state plates. They don't have dealers on their states? They make trips all the way into Chicago for a bag of cement? So, I don't know."

"Don't know what?" asked Lohman.

"What is going on," said Wiggy. "I asked about the drug guy and I was told that he is a contractor. They gave me his company name. Salerno Contractors. I looked it up and found out its address. It's a small place on the West Side. Right out there in slum land with all the vacant lots. It used to be an Italian neighborhood way back when. It's a small store that has the company name on it. There's a small lot out back with a truck with the company name. An old, beat up thing. There's also a building with a Salerno Funeral Home sign on it next door. There wasn't anyone there at either place, but I talked to several neighbors and they said they didn't know anything about the company. One told me he wasn't going to talk to me. I looked more and I couldn't find a city license for the company. Then I checked my source again and I am told the guy is still in the gang. My source doesn't know just what he does though."

Lohman thought about this. Then he said, "See if you can find out anything else about this. I am starting to hear more about drugs in connection with Whiteman and other people connected with Whiteman."

"Will do," said Wiggy. "Another thing. I heard this guy, the contractor guy, talking to one of the guys in the bagged cement area. They were

THE DEAD ONE PROTRUDES

talking about a Fat Tuna, Dat Tuna, something like that. I couldn't hear it too well. It isn't a quiet place and I wasn't too close to them."

"So, see what you can find out," said Lohman. "There's something else too. What about the guy who was found in the Pedway panel? He was a driver for Whiteman Panel. Did you find out anything about him?"

Wiggy looked at his notes and said, "I found out when the panel was delivered to the Pedway. It was delivered on a Monday, September 22nd. And that Riverwalk panel. I got that date too. It was delivered on a Friday, October 31st, 2014."

Lohman said, "We heard something about a Whiteman van this weekend, Friday it was. The night Avon Whiteman disappeared several people saw one of his panel company's vans on the street where he lived. One of the people was a friend who was leaving his house about 6 in the evening when he saw it. He said it was going north. Then the doorman at a hotel down the street, the Ambassador West, said he saw a Whiteman panel van come from the north and turn around in front of the hotel and go back north. The doorman didn't give a time. He knows me so if you talk to him, use my name. He's on in the evening. He's usually there on weekends, but I don't know exactly what days he's on."

"What's his name?" asked Wiggy.

"George. That's all I know. Don't know his last name," said Lohman. "He's at The Ambassador West."

"I'll see what I can find out," said Wiggy. "I did find out that all vehicles are checked in and out of the lot down there after work hours. The work day ends at four there. The check in includes the license number

THE DEAD ONE PROTRUDES

of the vehicle and the id of the driver. There isn't any check in during work hours, except for the workers arriving for the next shift. There is a separate gate for them to enter. They swipe their id cards and if they are registered to work on the upcoming shift the gate opens. But this is only up to one hour before the shift starts. If they aren't registered or they get there too early they have to go in through the regular check in gate. So now that we know who that guy in the Pedway was, maybe we can find out if he had anything to do with the van. The panel company manager already told me they don't have good employee records though. And since we know when the panels were delivered maybe I can find out more about what they do know about who was there around then. First I'll try to find out when these people disappeared."

"Good," said Lohman. "What we want to do is avoid any bad publicity out of this. There are too many big names attached to what Whiteman was doing. The publicity might get to us." Then he added "What about the Streets & San lot next door? Are those guys checked in? There is a door between the panel company and the Streets & San lot."

Wiggy said, "I asked about that. No, they aren't checked in. I think that's because the door is locked and someone has to let them in. Then the art panel company doesn't keep records of who was working around then. Streets & San doesn't check people in and out of their lot either."

Wiggy paused and then said, "Bad news brings more bad news. There's something else. I hate to tell you this because maybe you'll think I'm in with the crooks, but one of the guys in the Pedway had a mark of a Syndicate kill. The guy in the Riverwalk too. The one in the Pedway with the broken thumbs was the Streets & San guy who also worked as a van driver at Whiteman Materials or the panel company. They were all

THE DEAD ONE PROTRUDES

shot, but they can tell the two guys in the Pedway were shot with different guns. The cops have concluded that. They told me. I know the Outfit is supposed to be gone, but at least at one time they often gave a signal to anyone interested that they were the ones who had done a killing. Sort of a watch it message. The mark of their kill was broken thumbs in each hand. Now I don't know that first hand, but I heard that from several sources. But now all my sources tell me that the Syndicate is gone. The drug gangs have their own territories and get their stuff from the big drug cartels, usually from out of the country. Like I'm told that all the drugs from South America as well as Mexico and Central America mostly come through Mexican drug outfits and then the drug gangs here take over from there. They're all independent."

Lohman said, "Maybe one of the drug gangs adopted the broken thumb signal as their own. These gang guys are always fighting and killing each other aren't they? God, I hope we stay out of it!"

Wiggy said, "I don't know. I'll ask around. I'll let you know what I find out."

They talked a little more and then Lohman excused himself and went back to his office to actually practice law.

THE DEAD ONE PROTRUDES

18 PANSY'S PARTY

The next Saturday, August 5th, one of the snob empire's favorite events was to be held. It was time for Pansy's party. Tonight the excuse for the party was to honor Swifty's elevation to the leadership of the Gold Coast Association. Pansy was Lady Fitch-Bennington. Her first name was Elizabeth, but everyone called her Pansy, except her dyslectic butler James who called her m'Lady or Lady Bitch. Pansy was a member of the English aristocracy and had her home in London. She had extensive American agricultural interests so she had a residence in Chicago too to look after them. Actually The Bank's Wealth Management department looked after them and if any legal problems arose, F, P & C took care of them. Pansy was not a snob, but due to her station in life and the people she mingled with, she did not know any other life style. Actually she was one of the nicest people in town, but that isn't why so many people flocked to her parties. The snobs went because that was where all the superior people were found. Then there were a lot of people who went because people with money would be there and they were after money. Then there were a lot of neighborhood residents who just liked to go to parties in the neighborhood and mingle with each other. Due to the nature of the neighborhood, they tended to have a lot of loot too.

Pansy's husband usually stayed in London. Just as well because Pansy usually had some sort of boy toy around.

Pansy had a penthouse on the top two floors of a 70 story building on Michigan Avenue. Michigan was the street on the east side of the downtown area and it extended north from there across the River up to the south end of the Gold Coast, which started two blocks

THE DEAD ONE PROTRUDES

north of Pansy's building. The wealth of the Gold Coast extended beyond its boundaries so, while Pansy did not live in the Gold Coast proper, her address was included in its elite aura.

F, P & C people naturally were invited to most of Pansy's parties and this one was no exception. St. Charles of course was always there. He belonged with the aristocracy. This evening the Cohensteins, Joseph Pavlik, the partner who handled agricultural matters for Pansy and his wife, the McClurgs, the Lohmans and some assorted other firm personnel were going to be there.

Bumper and Gloria were walkers. It gave them exercise and an excuse to get out and around and see people. Whenever Pansy had a party they walked there. They lived on a street called Dearborn towards the north end of the Gold Coast. Dearborn was three short blocks west of Michigan Avenue where it ended at Oak Street so tonight they were just going to walk straight south on Dearborn and then over to Michigan on Oak Street and then two blocks south to Pansy's place.

Lohman was anxious to get out and walk and he was waiting for Gloria at the front door of their house. She came down the stairs and he held the door for her and they went out and down the outside steps. Across the street was the most exclusive private school in town, The Roman School of Chicago. Their children had gone there and they were still involved in various ways with it. They noticed that people were entering the building. "Must be having some sort of event tonight," said Gloria. "Did you hear what it was?"

Bumper said, "I think it was some kind of show with the grade school kids in it."

THE DEAD ONE PROTRUDES

Gloria said, "Sounds like Pansy's party."

"Yeah," said Lohman, "but usually some of the people at Pansy's graduated from sixth grade."

They went a little further down the street and they noticed one of their neighbors sitting on his porch. He was a client of Lohman's, or that is he had been for years. Now it was his guardian who was the client. He was sitting with a young and beautiful woman, enjoying the nice evening. He wasn't completely gone in the head and he came and went, but he wasn't all there. The guy started waiving to the Lohmans and saying, "Hello! Hello!"

The young thing was his girlfriend. The guy had told Lohman, when he was still competent and they were discussing his estate plan, that she was mainly interested in his money and that was just fine with him because she actually liked him. He wanted to give everything to her if she was still with him when he died. It seemed like a good deal to him.

The Lohmans waived back and the guy motioned for them to come on up to the porch which they did. The guy looked at Bumper and said, "It's nice to see you. Who are you? You look familiar."

This didn't seem odd to the Lohmans. The guy had always been pretty plain and direct. He was merely saying what he thought. He thought he recognized them and he thought he liked them, but he couldn't remember who they were. Bumper told him and they chatted for a while and then they left and walked on down the street.

They soon came to St. Tom's of Christ Church, an Episcopal church which was the only church in the Gold Coast. The pastor, the Reverend Pratton Cuthbert, was very active in neighborhood affairs and meetings

THE DEAD ONE PROTRUDES

and he and the Lohmans were good friends, although the Lohmans were members of Seventh Presbyterian Church, on Michigan Avenue, just across the street from Pansy's building. St. Tom's may have been in the Gold Coast, but Seventh Presbyterian was where all the most important people (and God) were members. Anyway, neither Cuthbert nor the Lohmans gave a damn where God hung out. As they were waking by Cuthbert came out of the parish building in full uniform. They greeted each other.

Cuthbert asked, "You going to the Squash Club?"

The Squash Club was on the other side of the street a bit south of the church.

It was the only club in the Gold Coast. The Lohmans were members, although neither one played squash, which could be said about most of its members. "No," said Bumper, "we're going to one of Pansy's parties. You going?"

"No," said Cuthbert. "There's a wedding over at the Club. I'm doing it. They didn't want to do it there."

They walked with Cuthbert to the crosswalk and they all went to the other side of the street and he went into the Club and they went on down the street towards Pansy's. When they got to Oak Street they turned east towards Michigan Avenue. Oak Street was a commercial street and it was home to many of the high end stores in town. Gloria liked to walk down it and window shop so that's the way they went. They got to the intersection of Oak and Michigan and turned south and walked the two short blocks to Pansy's building. There they went

THE DEAD ONE PROTRUDES

through the security system and took the elevator up to the penthouse.

As usual, Pansy's butler, James, greeted them. He knew most of the guests. "Welcome, welcome," he said. "Lady Bitch welcomes you Mr. and Mrs. Lohman. It is wonderful to see you again." He then extended his arm in the direction of the grand hall where most of the people were.

The Lohman's went on in and began to mingle. Soon they came across DiBello and his wife. They were talking to Pansy. They all greeted each other and began to talk. At this stage James came over with a drink for Pansy. He recognized DiBello. He said, "Why hello Mr. DiBello." Everyone who knew him knew he was dyslectic so they didn't comment about things like this. James continued with, "Thank you. I want to thank you again for all the work you did for the Association." He then gave Pansy the drink and started back to the entry area, but Pansy motioned for him to wait.

"What association, what's that?" asked Lohman as he preempted Pansy's question.

DiBello said, "Mr. St. Charles asked me to do it. He said Avon Whiteman asked him to do it as a favor for his butler. That Blackman fellow. Naturally Mr. St. Charles wasn't going to do it himself. He delegated the work to me. He said he had heard about it at some publicity event he attended at the - that place where Whiteman lived. He said McClurg wasn't there for some reason so Whiteman talked to him."

"But what was the association?" asked Lohman.

THE DEAD ONE PROTRUDES

"Oh, yes," said DiBello. "It was the American Manservant Association. It is an organization of men 'in service' as they put it. James is a member." He motioned towards James who nodded. "Mr. St. Charles told me he didn't deal with details and to talk to James here and Mrs. Whiteman about it. Mrs. Whiteman told me some of the details. She said her butler wanted it, but that I could talk to James here about most of the details. So I did and we got it organized."

"Wrong Sir," said James. "It was a pleasure. Mr. Blackman doesn't actually deal with details. He is very highly placed. Actually he doesn't much buttle. He just supervises the underlings. So he had me handle it. So I didn't." Thankfully those present knew enough to interpret what James had just said.

Gloria asked, "Do they allow women?"

Pansy said, "Don't be silly dear."

Lohman had enough confidence in DiBello to trust that he had complied with laws against sexual discrimination in setting up the organization. And he had enough sense to remember the English upper class traditions of what sex butlers were. So he nudged Gloria and that was the end of that subject.

Pansy then said, "Oh look - there's that fish fellow." She pointed to someone across the room."

DiBello asked, "Mr. Bannon? Jared Bannon? I've met him. He's Hump's agent here in the U.S. Bannon's his name, not Fish."

James interjected, "Dat Tuna m'Lady. It's a namenick."

"Ah, yes," she said. "I think I shall get over to see him later.

THE DEAD ONE PROTRUDES

Soon the group broke up and the Lohmans moved on about the room. They were looking for people they knew when they spotted the Firm Fruit, Winter Goren, one of the partners, standing with Sean and some other people the Lohmans recognized as clients of his. Winter was an effeminate and flamboyant old guy. He was dressed in a double breasted cream color suit with a lavender shirt and a cream colored tie. He had cream colored patent leather shoes on and was wearing white rimmed tinted glasses with glitter on them. Who could miss him? He was called the Firm Fruit because, while not the only one, he was the most prominent in his fruitiness. He had actually coined the name himself. He had a lot of wealthy clients and so he was very acceptable to the other partners. St. Charles did not approve of homosexuals. However, Winter had the rich clients so to St. Charles he was merely "artistic".

The clients Winter was with were a young man and his boyfriend. Both were clients of his and both had a lot of inherited money and controlled several successful businesses. Sean Featherbottom was with them because Winter had him working on matters involving the clients. One of the clients was very outgoing and the other was shy and inhibited. They actually ran the businesses themselves and their talents complimented each other's. Winter had suggested they come to Pansy's party to start getting the inhibited one accustomed to social events and dealing with people. He also wanted to introduce both to the group of wealthy people he had access to.

Bumper and Gloria were great fans of Winter who was actually a great guy. They had also met his clients before and found that they were usually great guys too and also that they were hardly inhibited about being gay. Winter had told Bumper what he was trying to do for them.

THE DEAD ONE PROTRUDES

As they approached Lohman greeted them with, "Hello! What's this, a pansy fest?"

They all laughed and Winter said, "Sort of, but I was just going to tell Herb here (he put his hand on the shy one's shoulder) about Little Jack Horner." Then he turned to Herb and said, "Little Jack Horner sat in a corner - and missed war, famine, pestilence, and the assorted evils mankind inflicts on itself. He attracted no notice, especially from the Devil. So he is the one who got to Heaven - where he attracted a lot of notice because he was cute."

Herb said, "I thought you said I should get used to be more outgoing. You're just telling me I'm going to Heaven the way I am."

"It's a fairy tale Herb," said Winter. "And that doesn't mean a tale for fairies. It's just for your self confidence. To illustrate that there's nothing wrong with you. Lack of self esteem is one reason people are inhibited around others. Outgoing socializers and networkers get to Heaven too."

After a little more of this the Lohmans moved on and ran into John Sweeney and his client Trisha DeLang. They were all moving on towards the next room and they ran into St. Charles and Cohenstein and their wives and a couple they didn't know. They were the Horatio Bingbutts. Bumper and Gloria had seen them at other parties, but had never met them. St. Charles was trying to get business out of them. They were prominent in society circles and supposedly had immense wealth and this alone qualified them to be F, P & C clients. Cohenstein realized that these people were buying the St. Charles act so he was just playing along as a subordinate of St. Charles'.

THE DEAD ONE PROTRUDES

The Lohmans' group greeted the St. Charles' group and stopped to talk to them a while. St. Charles had just been talking about a prominent local figure who he claimed intimate contact with and the advice the prominent one had given which resulted in some magical solution to someone's problems of life. St. Charles called the advice "sound", "very substantial" and "very solid". He claimed to be very close to the figure and others of similar suitable standing. The prominent figure turned out to be Toby Rich, the Mayor.

Mrs. Bingbutt said, "He is so impressive. We know him well. We joined with him in endowing a scholarship fund at the University of Chicago."

St. Charles took the hint and added, "Very impressive. I too take an interest in promoting education and other matters benefitting mankind, perhaps because I am constantly involved with people such as yourselves with similar interests. I am thinking of creating an endowed chair there at the Law School. It will be the St. Charles endowed chair. Our firm had been thinking of it, but I thought it would be more suitable if I myself was the benefactor."

Lohman, Cohenstein, and Sweeney just looked at each other.

Mrs. Bingbutt's attention then turned to Trisha. Trisha was not dressed properly. All young people these days seemed to be unaware of polite society's standards of dress, but Trisha, being the hot little star she was, pushed the envelope. She had a fairly short skirt on for one thing and her dress was bright red with orange highlights in it and it had sequins and, to top that, a few reflective strips of the kind found on sports clothing or road workers' jackets to reflect vehicle lights. Mrs. Bingbutt looked her up and down and said, "And you young lady - what did you say your name is?"

THE DEAD ONE PROTRUDES

Trisha said, "Trisha DeLang."

"And what are you doing here." said Mrs. Bingbutt. She didn't ask that. She said that.

Sweeney interjected something at this moment which he often had to remind people such as the St. Charleses and the Bingbutts of when Trisha was around. "Her grandfather was The Lion."

Mrs. Bingbutt gave her snootiest raised face and said, "Who?"

Lohman decided to help out. "Edgar Ivan O'Brien. I'm sure someone of your standing knew him - you know, the wealthiest person in Chicago?'

Mrs. Bingbutt, seemed to calm down a little. And so did St. Charles, now that he had been reminded of this. He added, "Our client, don't you know."

The Lion had been found dead in a disabled stall in one of the firms' men's rooms not too long ago.

Sweeney said, "Trisha is one of the best selling pop artists. Actually, the top grosser."

Mrs. Bingbutt could care less. She turned to her husband with a look of disapproval, indicating that he should deal with a problem of this nature. He turned towards Trisha and said, "Young lady, do you know who I am?"

He shouldn't have asked. She said, "No, but I'm sure you're at least a sultan."

"What's a sultan?" he asked.

THE DEAD ONE PROTRUDES

"Oh, you don't know?" she said. "Then I'm sure it's someone way beneath you. You don't live on a cloud do you?"

"What?" he asked.

"Or maybe you're a ningle twit," she added.

"What?"

"Anyway," she said, "I can tell you're real important."

"Exactly," he said.

"And where do you live?" asked Mrs. Bingbutt. The location and nature of one's abode is important in evaluating one's standing.

"The Gold Coast," answered Trisha. "Not too far from here. But I travel a lot. I'm out of town a lot."

"And you grew up where?" Mrs. Bingbutt went on. "Where did you originate?"

"Around here," said Trisha. "What about you" Where are you from? Did you grow up in Chicago?"

Mrs. Bingbutt said, "My ancestors were great landowners and ranchers on the Great Plains. You ask where I grew up? Idaho."

"My, you sure are," said Trisha before anyone could grab her mouth. Fortunately the Bingbutts and the St. Charleses had no idea what she was talking about.

"So, young lady, where did you go to school?" asked Mrs. Bingbutt.

"F U," said Trisha.

THE DEAD ONE PROTRUDES

Mrs. Bingbutt asked, "What is the proper name?"

Sweeney grabbed Trisha before she could respond and he said, "I think it was Fordham."

At this stage Lohman sensed that no good would come out of this group so he said, "Well, it's so nice to have met you, but we have to get on. We are late for hooking up with someone over at the bar." He then put his hand around Gloria and they started off. Sweeney and Trisha went with them. As they were walking away Trisha said, "God! Thanks for getting us away from them."

Sweeney said, "Trisha, you know you should leave the talking to me with the snobs."

Lohman said, "You aren't much better. Christ!"

"Well, what do you expect," said Sweeney. "What creeps. Horatio Bingbutt. Horatio? Dude, what's a whore ratio? Whore's per guy? Per month? Per block? What?"

Lohman said, "It's his name. H. The letter H. H-o-r-a-t-i-o."

"Yeah, I know," said Sweeney.

Trisha said, "We were just putting them on. These bitches on stilts with their head in the clouds are hard to take. Some of these guys too. They all think they are so important. Crap! The places he takes me to just to meet people." She motioned to Sweeney. "I'm supposed to get some publicity, promotion, contracts. Stuff like that. From a lot of people who are strange. Tell him what you said to that guy over by the entrance. The guy who was talking to Zenon when we came in." She looked at Sweeney and then to Lohman. "They were talking about

THE DEAD ONE PROTRUDES

women's sports and Zenon was talking about some game he saw. He said, 'It's women's basketball. No, no, I think it was volleyball. I forget.' The guy he was talking to said, 'Good Lord! You don't even know the difference.' So John says, 'What's the difference? It's all the same. Broads running around in shorts and bouncing their boobs. Who cares what the game is called.' You think I gotta mouth!"

Lohman didn't know what to say. He was just glad he got them away from the highly placed ones.

Then Sweeney said, "And how about that endowed chair for St. Charles? Who would name a chair after him? Now the Graybourne St. Charles endowed toilet I can see. Just because you sit on it you don't have to call it a chair."

"What do you mean?" said Trisha. "Sittin' on his special toilet and crappin'? That's gross. Look what happened to my grandpa." Her grandfather had been found dead in one of the disabled stalls at the firm.

"Oh Christ!" said Lohman. "Can it!" He shouldn't have said that.

"Now you're talkin' about what I'm talkin' 'bout." said Trisha. The Lohmans looked defeated. "OK, OK. Just jokin'."

Sweeney then said, "Bumps, I remembered something about that night Whiteman disappeared. I saw Sean at a party that night. But I want to get over there and talk to an agent I see," He pointed across the room, "so I tell you later. I remembered it because I remember his telling me he had just delivered some papers to the Nudie Mansion earlier that evening. He was kind of snowed by it."

THE DEAD ONE PROTRUDES

Sweeney and Trisha moved on and the Lohmans looked around a bit. Just then they heard Zenon behind them. "Bumper. Gloria. Look who's here."

They turned and Cohenstein was standing there with The Prophet Andy, Angelic Leader of ECOTAG, The Evangelical Congregation of the Angel Gabriel, a large and growing worldwide religion. People like The Prophet and other religious leaders were often at Pansy's parties for the simple reason that they were after the loot. Churches cost money, and in the case of ECOTAG, that need was increased by its headquarters, the 2500 foot tall Aspire at the mouth of the Chicago River

Pansy was with them. Just then Mrs. Cohenstein arrived carrying a drink. She said, "Did you miss me Zenon?"

He said, "You were gone?"

"Silly," she said.

Pansy said, "Bumper - we were just talking about that Bannon fellow. You know, the tuna fish. I had mentioned him to The Prophet. He thinks very little of the fish. Right Andy?" She looked at him.

The Prophet was not accustomed to being addressed as Andy, but considering the source, he tolerated it. "Mr. Bannon has abandoned our true faith. At one time he was a contributor to ECOTAG, but for some time he has abandoned us. He has been a very large contributor, and a member of, The D'Gregor Temple. As you know, we try to work with other religions in our interfaith efforts, but there are limits. The Temple is a fraud, a mere politicians' feeding ground. They have a flawed conception of God.

THE DEAD ONE PROTRUDES

"Oh my," said Pansy. "I don't think he's that bad. You know him don't you Bumper."

Bumper said, "Not really. But I think some of our firm members do." Then he took a dive. "But I don't know anything about religion."

"I should think not," said The Prophet. "You're a Presbyterian, aren't you?"

"Yes," said Gloria.

The group then broke up and the Lohmans went on their way through the crowd for the rest of the evening and then to home where they engaged in unmentionable acts.

THE DEAD ONE PROTRUDES

19 SEAN AND THE COPS

The next Tuesday, August 8th, Lohman had a meeting scheduled with Sean Featherbottom in the morning to discuss something Lohman had Sean working on for one of Lohman's clients. They went over the matter and then the conversation turned to what went on the day Avon Whiteman disappeared because Sean told Bumper that the cops had called on him and started asking questions about it.

"What were they asking you about?" asked Lohman.

"A lot of things," said Sean. "They started by asking me about his ring. I told them where I got it and when and they took it. I had it on that day."

"Did they give you a receipt?" asked Lohman.

"No," said Sean.

"I hope it didn't cost too much," said Lohman.

Sean paused and then said, "Then they asked me about what happened that night. I told them about delivering papers to Mr. Whiteman that night and seeing his son, Eddie Whiteman. I told them what I told you and everyone else. They already knew Eddie Whiteman fired me and they asked all about that. They didn't seem to believe me when I said that he just let me in and that he wasn't mad at me. They said they would check on that. From their tone I could tell they didn't believe me. Anyway, how else could I get in? Eddie Whiteman will tell them. I hope. Then they wanted to know what else I did. I told them about meeting Mr. Whiteman and giving him the papers and about

THE DEAD ONE PROTRUDES

how I didn't notice whether or not he had the ring on. Then I told them how I had gone to Mr. McCain's house. He lives in the Gold Coast too so he wasn't far away. I was supposed to deliver papers to him too and explain them. It was a trademark memo. I think Mr. St. Charles is his lawyer, but someone in IT did the memo. Mr. St. Charles' secretary had me deliver it. I gave it to Mr. McCain. Is his first name really Biffster?"

"Yes," said Lohman. "More properly, The Biffster."

Sean looked at him for a moment. Then he continued, "I had to go over it with him. He's hard to get through to. Then I went home and changed and went to a reception at the Artists' Club Mr. Goren wanted me to attend. It was a reception to honor someone who was a set designer. I forget his name. There were a lot of art and show business people there. Mr. Goren wanted me to be there with his client who I had done some work for. He wanted to impress the client."

"Who?" asked Lohman.

"A fellow named Herb. Herb McCraken, and his boyfriend Temple McHoff. Mr. Goren calls them the two Mics. To their face. Anyhow, they're nice guys. Herb is real inhibited and Mr. Goren is trying to get him around to get used to being around people. Temp - that's what we call him - he's so outgoing you sometimes have to restrain him. Herb's real tall. Temp's real short."

"Do you know these guys? Apart from working for them?" asked Lohman.

"I see them sometimes at social events that have nothing to do with the firm. I've been to gatherings at their apartment. Yes, I know them."

THE DEAD ONE PROTRUDES

"Did you refer them to Winter? What kind of work did you do for them?"

"I didn't refer them," said Sean. "I did some work organizing and creating several corporations for them. That's how I met them in the first place."

"So what happened at the reception?" asked Lohman.

"Not much of any importance," said Sean. "I ran into John, John - John Sweeney and Trisha DeLang there. They were in the process of leaving because Trisha had to appear somewhere at eleven thirty. Herb and Temp were really impressed by her. So then the reception ended and I went home and went to bed. Got in here around nine on Saturday. I told the police all this."

"I take it you didn't go anywhere near a Whiteman plant that day or that weekend?" asked Lohman.

"No. Why would I do that?" asked Sean.

"Well," said Lohman, "someone had to pour concrete all over him. If you were not the last person to see him alive, and you weren't - his friend Cass apparently was - then if your whereabouts can be accounted for you don't look like the killer. So I imagine the key is to find evidence supporting your movements - to show that you did not have any more contact with him. For instance, you could have come back after Cass left or after you saw The Biffster or after you left the party. You could have killed him and taken the ring then."

Sean gave a butt wiggle in his seat. He looked from one side of the room to the other. Then he gave another butt wiggle and smoothed

THE DEAD ONE PROTRUDES

back his hair. He said, "I didn't come back. But I see what you mean. That Detective Bongwad and that Sergeant Gilbert, they don't like me. But they didn't give me a MIranda warning so they must not think I did it."

Lohman said, "I don't think they need to give you that warning about having a right to remain silent until they take you into custody. That can be a big reason why they don't arrest suspects. Anyway, I want to ask you about that Calumet plant. Are there a lot of small contractors buying the bagged cement? Or were there when you were there?"

Sean answered, "Yes. Most of them bought the cheaper kind. They didn't sell or stock too much of the expensive bagged cement - at least while I was there. And that went to a different kind of customer - or at least they seemed different to me."

"How?" asked Lohman.

"They just seemed different from the other customers," said Sean. "A lot of them didn't even have trucks. And more of them dressed in street clothes instead of like construction workers like the other buyers of the lower priced stuff. And the bags - when I was going through the financial material I noticed sales that seemed to exceed what they actually sold. And this wasn't just the recent years when I wasn't there. We reviewed financial material from years back, including for when I was there. I based the other years review on my knowledge of the Calumet plant and what I knew about the other plants from being there once in a while. Bags were only sold at Calumet, at least when I was there, and the accounting material for recent years does not show any bag sales from the other plants. What I noticed in particular was high sales numbers for the high priced bags that seemed to far exceed

THE DEAD ONE PROTRUDES

what they actually had and could have sold when I was there. The only other alternative is that they were charging way more than I thought they were or what they had told me the price was.

"How was all this paid for?" asked Lohman.

"I don't know," said Sean. "I was just classed as a laborer. I didn't do any accounting or bookkeeping or handle any sales. I just helped out in moving the bags. Payments made at the plant were made in the business office and there was a cashier there. I think there must have been a lot of cash sales because I saw Brinks trucks there regularly. Several times a week. I don't think Whiteman paid cash for anything or paid anyone in cash so the trucks must have been there to pick up cash. Why are you asking about all this? Didn't we discuss the sales discrepancies earlier?"

"Drugs," said Lohman. "I keep hearing about drugs every time we get into this. Avon was killed by fentanyl. Hump and Flinton supposedly have investments in a company that produces it. Or at least their foundations do. Hump is the supplier of cement to Whiteman. D'Gregor, that guy who was found in the Riverwalk, he ran the Temple. D'Gregor Temple. That's where you said you got the ring. And the Temple runs, or at least owns, a big string of substance abuse treatment clinics. And they use drugs in treatment. Wiggy and Sweeney say they have seen characters at the Calumet plant who have connections to drugs or who are at least rumored to. Then there was that Mexican drug lord found in the Pedway. Did you hear anything about drugs when you worked there?"

THE DEAD ONE PROTRUDES

"No," said Sean. "Nobody ever mentioned it when I was there. At least to me. But then I was just a laborer on odd jobs. Nobody talked business to me. They just talked about what I was supposed to do."

"When you were at Avon's house did you see anything odd? Did you see him drinking?"

"No, I didn't see him drinking," said Sean. "I remember a beautiful crystal container behind his desk. It was on a silver platter. There was an exquisite glass on the platter too, but Mr. Whiteman was not using any of that."

Lohman said, "You notice those things, don't you. We should make you the firm's art and fashion consultant." Lohman wasn't joking. Sean was flattered. "Did you see his ring? Have you thought more about that? His friend who came in later said he didn't notice if Avon had it."

Sean said, "I really don't remember. I wasn't looking at his hands. I was more interested in the crystal. And I was kind of scared anyway because of having been fired."

Lohman said, "Look for anything that can confirm when and where you got the ring. Do you have a receipt or a cancelled check or charge card records?"

"I'll look," said Sean. "This is scary. They're always after me. I didn't do anything. When they finished talking to me and asking me all these questions Detective Bongwad left the room first and Sergeant Gilbert followed. On his way he turned to me and said, 'We're going to get you this time queer.' I don't think they like me." He wiggled.

THE DEAD ONE PROTRUDES

Their meeting then broke up and Lohman accompanied Sean out to the reception area. Sean left and Lohman turned to Tete and asked her to get Seans's time records for the weekend when Avon went missing and wound up in the panel.

All lawyers in the firm have to enter what they did and how long it took which was the basis for the firm's bills to its clients. For associates the firm required entry of the start times and end times of the work as well as the total time. They also had to enter the time by the end of the day when the work was done, even if they were not in the office, and this they had to do starting in 2010 when they all were required to have the equipment to do it with. The firm's computer system was set up so they could to this with a cell phone or computer connection and they were required to have those. The firm's IT guy had also set up the system so the firm could tell when the entries were made. The object of this was to prevent the lawyers from making up the time and work descriptions. Lawyers very often wait till the end of the day to enter their time. Because they cannot remember the details accurately, this can lead to inaccurate entries. Also, lawyers, being who they are, often just make it up anyway, usually saying they did work and spent time they did not. You would think the partners would be subject to these requirements, but they were only required to report their work and hours by the end of the month. They had objected strongly to being subject to the same requirements as the associates.

At any rate Sean was subject to the requirements and his time records supported what he had told Lohman. After seeing this Lohman asked Tete to get in touch with the IT department and check on when the entries were made and to see that they preserved all the information.

THE DEAD ONE PROTRUDES

20 ASSOCIATE MATTERS

Later that afternoon the firm had scheduled a conference for new associates who had just graduated from law school and for law students who were still in law school, but had been hired to help for the summer. The firm had these conferences regularly to give them instructions and get feedback. The associates and summer workers involved mostly did research (finding out what the law applicable to specific situations was) and reviewed documents and accompanied the other lawyers to meetings and to court.

Lohman explained these things to them and informed them that part of the process was to get them involved more with clients and opposing counsel, but gradually. He explained that this was part of the process and, in effect, they had to learn how to conduct themselves with these people. He advised them to not just sit in on the meetings, but to see how the more experienced lawyers conducted themselves. His point was that clients are customers, not just people who were bothering them and they should act accordingly.

Then Lohman got into highly insulting matters. He told them all that they had to be on time. Not just about on time or soon after a meeting started, but set and ready to go by the appointed time. He reminded them that if you are not on time in court you get dismissed. Same with clients. He told them point blank that they had to meet deadlines. He added that they couldn't meet deadlines by starting the work at the time of the deadline and they had to be aware of things that were coming up in the future, not just what today's matters were, and thus they should review their calendars well into the future each day. And yes, Lohman did have to explain this to the little geniuses. He explained

THE DEAD ONE PROTRUDES

that many of their supposed deadlines were just pulled out of the air and they had no relationship to when something actually could be done. He told them in that as soon as they knew a deadline could not be met they had to tell the person who set it. Then he told them if that didn't work to contact him. Or better yet, Tete. In case of arbitrary deadlines that could not be met set by the morons or in case of people who could not do the work on time, Tete would handle it. He also told them they did not want to be handled by Tete.

He went on to explain that none of the associates had other people to do the work, like the servants a lot of them thought must be working there, so they had to do it themselves and on time. Naturally, all this was highly insulting to some of the entitled little dears who came from the top law schools, but part of what Lohman was doing was trying to get rid of the useless ones.

Then he talked about deals. The firm did many high end things called deals. This involved one company buying another or selling to another company or stock or bond offerings or large loan financings and also many just plain contracts between large companies. He explained how the timing was absolutely crucial to a lot of these deals and if the client's expectations of doing the deal yesterday is not met you lose the client and you get no more referrals from other people to participate in this kind of work. He also explained that this frequently required nothing but long hours, interrupted only by sleep, till the deals were done.

He further explained that they have to work like this because if they don't they don't get the business. Therefore anyone who needs help should ask for it right away and this is not a sign of failure. He said. "It's

THE DEAD ONE PROTRUDES

what everyone here does. If you are telling your partner you need help that can be a plus. It adds to the bill."

He then went on to describe the time entry system.

After that he talked about lying. "Don't lie. Period. Don't cheat. Don't steal. You can get disbarred. Not always of course, but that is the risk. And, while it may help with client relations in the short run, it most usually results in losing the client in the long run unless they are crooks too. Now, you may say that some of our partners are liars. But if you examine what is going on I think you will see that they may be exaggerators or, let us say, slingers of the poo. Even there they aren't real liars. When we find evidence of real lying or stealing we have to act on it. In the long run it doesn't help us keep clients, except ones that do that themselves and even they don't want their lawyers to lie to them."

Then he talked about behavior and trying to be nice to everyone, even the assholes which he did admit were in the firm and on the client list. He instructed them to report bad treatment by a superior to him. He said that was not unusual and the bad guys got more complaints so don't be afraid. He also told them they get a lot of complaints about associates who are bad guys so, as he said, "Behave. And just do your work and be nice and forget about whether we like you."

Following this he explained the need for actual contact with other people and how use of emails and text or voice messages, which was becoming universal, was just a way of avoiding narrowing things down or getting specific about anything. He said, "If I give one of you a call and ask when something is going to be done and you aren't there and I leave a message and you text me or email me that it will be done as

THE DEAD ONE PROTRUDES

soon as possible you have not answered my question. Tell me exactly when or tell me you do not know and tell me why. If you don't, I have to contact you again and you never answer your phone. Stop acting this way. Actually talk to others. If I can't get anything out of you, who needs you?" Brutal bastard!

He was starting to get offensive, at least to the message givers on their "devices". He continued, "A lot of you are privileged. You are some of the highest paid people at your age level, you went to the top schools, you had high grades and so forth. But a lot of you were coddled. You were told you are deserving. You are part of the internet and iPhone world where you never learned to deal with other people or produce. Any problems and you just hit another app. But here you have to produce so get with it. Answer calls. Talk to others in person. Yes you can be pinned down, but that is the way we get results."

Then Lohman got to the top complaint of the day from the partners. Papers towels in the washrooms all over the floors. Lohman told them about the complaints and then told them to be sure they put the towels in the containers for them. He explained that this required looking at where the towels had gone and that they were piling up on the wash room floors all over the office. He said, "Now, I realize that at our residences we have someone else to do this for us. For some of us it is the footman. For others it is Mommy. But around here Mommy and the footman are usually out back screwing so stick it in the can." Lohman then realized what he had said and decided the best thing to do was move on.

What he moved on to was the dress code which was much more liberal in law land than it had been in the past. He explained that in this area the biggest problem was everyone complaining about how others

THE DEAD ONE PROTRUDES

dressed. He told them to read the firm's policy before they complained. However, he explained that the dress standards in court had not been liberalized and to also check what the dress code said about court appearances.

He explained further about how they could get reimbursed for expenses and then went on to the subject of client relations.

He explained that just like any business a law practice has to keep the customers, who are called clients, happy. He also explained that just like any person having a job anywhere the boss has to be kept happy. Then he explained an unfortunate fact of life in the halls of the elite. "You have to understand that we deal with large companies and the average owner or officer of a large firm thinks he or she is God. So act accordingly. And remember that God wants worship and obedience, not just a job done. And God wants his or her magnificence displayed to all. So when you feel like telling such a person off, just remember what your job is. Smile and be nice. You don't have to do much else because they'll do all the talking."

"Also remember," he continued, "that many clients are difficult at best and many are bad guys. This applies to lawyers too. Difficult people are found in law offices - on both sides of the desk. Remember that we handle something called 'disputes' and people are fighting about things. Another thing to remember is that our clients think they are superior. Now I know many of you think you are very superior too, but put that on pause. Look at it this way - to be superior you need inferiors. The more inferiors you have, the more superior you are. Without inferiors, who are you superior to? And the sanctified need the sinful for the same reason. So just accept this. We have to deal with people like that."

THE DEAD ONE PROTRUDES

Lohman then paused and looked around. Then he said, "Now you may be asking yourself what this clown in front of you is talking about. What I am saying is that you will be treated poorly by a lot of people you will come across in practicing law. Just try to make them happy and stay away from confronting them. Try to smile and look interested and be cooperative and when you can't, try to keep your mouth shut. Then when it is all done, don't feel abused. Instead take satisfaction in the fact that you successfully dealt with a difficult person. When you are thinking you did OK you will feel much better that when you feel abused. And you will get better at it."

"One caveat," Lohman added. "Just because someone is nice and is smiling at you does not mean they are your friend. They can very well be your enemy. Just smile back and remember what you are there for."

Then Lohman got on to the subject of legal research. This involved looking up the law applicable to a particular situation. In the past humans prepared indexes to all the things in reports of court decisions and statutes and administrative rules. Currently these had faded into the background and, just like in any other area, word search software was being used. You had to use the exact works used in the law to find it. For an example he mentioned the original grocery chain, A&P. He explained that a search for A&Poo would not find out anything about it, even if it had once been called that. Maybe some search software would show it, but most would not. Synonyms and related subjects and other words used to express the same idea could not be found this way. Also lawyers were beginning to think in terms of key words. If other words were used to express the same idea they would not know what you were talking about. Lohman explained all this and what could be done to get around the problem. Then he went on to the constant

THE DEAD ONE PROTRUDES

use of newly coined words in speech and writing and explained that if you can't explain something in plain old fashioned simple nouns and verbs, you don't understand it. On the other hand, if you explained something so everyone could understand it many people would think you were a simpleton because everyone, they would think, knew what you were talking about. On the other hand, the people who could use the information would be appreciative of your mode of expression.

From here Lohman went to the subject of politics and other controversial areas. He told the associates to just plain avoid these subjects with clients - and may of the lawyers too.

Then Lohman threw the floor open for questions. He added that no one should be afraid to ask a stupid question or one that seemed stupid because it might not be stupid. He also mentioned that what is stupid to some is not stupid to others and anyway he was still going to answer it and that he asked stupid questions every day.

At this one associate asked, "Who are you to be telling us all these little things? You're always giving us lectures. I think I had to sit through two last year."

"I'm the Managing Partner," said Lohman. "What I say goes. I'm your boss."

The associate had a hard time believing this. "I thought you were just some kind of aide to Mr. St. Charles. You should get it out who you are. Anyway, I don't need to be told what to do, by him or you either. I know what I'm doing. I went to Harvard. Second in class."

"Just follow the rules," said Lohman.

THE DEAD ONE PROTRUDES

"I'll think about it," said the associate.

"When?" asked Lohman. "On your way to another job?"

The next question had to do with St. Charles and Cohenstein. The associate who asked it said, "What is going on? Who do I try to be like? Who do I follow?"

Lohman said, "First you have to realize there isn't any dichotomy. Mr. St. Charles just wants proper behavior. What used to be called good manners. Just behave and say 'yes' around him. Mr. Cohenstein is, let us say, less formal. You can be less formal with him. He's more interested in performance, even if you do talk or act funny."

Then another associate asked about how they could contact Lohman. He told them to do it by phone, email or just coming in to his office. The associate then asked, "Do we have to deal with your secretary? She's brutal. She treated me like some sort of underling."

Since this probably meant that Tete had not fawned all over the associate Lohman did not lend too much credit to the comment. He said, "Just tell her you want to talk to me. She'll arrange it, even if she's being brutal."

Eventually this all wrapped up and Lohman went back to his office where he had an afternoon meeting scheduled with DiBello, Sweeney, Featherbottom, Wiggy and Tambola Cook. They were going to review what they had found out about the Whiteman matters.

DiBello started describing what they had found out. He said, "One thing we reviewed was the materials from that Congressional investigation where they went in to the foundations set up by politicians. Then we

THE DEAD ONE PROTRUDES

looked into that drug company. Its name is Progressive Pharma Concepts, Inc. Who really owns it or controls it, we don't know. The Flinton and Hump foundations have investments in it and the Congressional investigation materials show that, but they don't seem to have controlling interests and it isn't a publicly held company. Ownership of most of the stock is probably held by a Cayman Islands trust company and of course we can't find out who is the real beneficiary of that."

He went on. "Then there is the shipping company that ships the Humpy cement up here. Wao Tang Nu, LLC is its name. Same thing there. It's a Delaware limited liability company owned by a Cayman Islands trust company so far as we can tell. McClurg says he was told that Hump and Flinton own it, but we can't confirm that. We asked Jared Bannon, who is the agent for Humpy, and he says he doesn't know who owns it. Of course, he probably wouldn't tell us if he did know. We found out that D'Gregor had been a manager of that shipping company. The Hump and Flinton foundations own interests in that company too and they got large contributions from it. Same thing with the drug company. It's circular. All this is described in the Congressional investigation papers."

He then said, "And we can't find out anything more about who actually owns the art panel company. Now, I think I told you this before. The art panel company corporate filings in Illinois were made by Finebaum & Akhbar. They also made the filings for Humpy Cement. We were told about that Blackman consulting company and guess what? The organizational filings were made by the same law firm."

"Now the D'Gregor Temple," he said. "That is organized as a not for profit corporation which is a church. As you know, churches don't have to make as many filings as other companies. But we got a copy of its

THE DEAD ONE PROTRUDES

organizational papers and bylaws from Mrs. Whiteman who is a Deacon. It has a self perpetuating board of Deacons. The current Deacons appoint their successors. The Temple owns substance abuse clinics which are organized as separate not for profit corporations. They take in alcoholics and addicts and detoxify them in a process that is like hospitalization. Then they provide them with continuing treatment. Mostly the alcoholics and addicts are supposed to be free of the alcohol and drugs as a result of the treatment, but some are put on what they call maintenance. That involves continuing use of drugs but in controlled and low level doses. That's mostly for opiates. The church gets big contributions from the clinics. It seems like a really profitable business. I don't see why it's not for profit."

"No tax," Lohman said. Then he asked, "If they use drugs, where do they get the drugs?"

"We asked Trulia Whiteman that," said DiBello. "We had to get McClurg to ask her. She said she didn't know, but he pushed her to find out and she said they mostly came from that Progressive Pharma."

"Great," said Lohman. "And could this Progressive have supplied the drug that killed Avon Whiteman? We are in strange waters here. Whiteman was involved with drugs and so were Hump and Flinton but what were the details? We don't know. What we do know does not say that Hump and Flinton controlled the drugs and that the drug that killed Avon came from them. Then another thing. I heard that D'Gregor who ran the Temple, and I suppose the clinics, wanted to start his own drug company. I think I was told he and Whiteman wanted to start it."

There was more discussion about these matters, but no more light was shed on the subject. Lohman wound up dismissing them and telling

THE DEAD ONE PROTRUDES

them to report anything further they found out about these matters to him, but he also told them to get back to their regular work. In effect, to get back on the bill. This is just what Lohman did too.

THE DEAD ONE PROTRUDES

21 THE FUZZ BALLS AGAIN

By Friday, August 11th Lohman had gotten back to working on his clients' matters and all was well in law land. Naturally that couldn't last so it didn't. Lohman was just about to pick up his phone to call a client when Tete rang him. "What's up, Tete?" he said.

"Your free time," she said. "That Detective Bongwad and Sergeant Gilbert, or is it Wilbert or Gilly Willy or whatever, they want to see you. Mr. McClurg too. They want to come in as soon as possible."

"What about?" asked Lohman.

"Didn't say," said Tete. "Bongwad was talking to me. He just said they want to ask you guys some questions."

"When do they want to see us?" Lohman asked.

"Soon as possible," said Tete. "It's been several years since all those guys died, so they have to see you right away."

Lawyers get used to the fact that everyone wants to see them right away, except the other side. Lohman looked at this calendar. He had a paper calendar and when some of the younger lawyers saw it they asked him what it was. Lohman said, "I can see them any time today. What about Shannon?"

Tete said, "I talked to him. He can do it this morning after ten.."

"Well, tell them to come in then," said Lohman. "I take it they want to come here."

THE DEAD ONE PROTRUDES

"Right," said Tete. "I'll arrange it. Here in our conference room, right?"

"Right," said Lohman.

Later that morning Bongwad and Gilbert did show up and they went into Lohman's conference room with him and McClurg. After everyone got settled Bongwad said, "We want to ask you some questions about things." Gilbert was still standing, seemingly at attention. He always did this so Lohman didn't offer him a seat.

"Go ahead," said Lohman.

Bongwad said, "We have been doing a lot of work on all these bodies in concrete panels your client installed. That means we have been down at the plant where they came from talking to people there and getting records. One of the things we found out is that your people are all over the company too. What is going on?"

McClurg said, "For one reason we have been investigating the financial status of the Whiteman company in regard to a proposed purchase by them of another company and possible loan it would take out to get the cash. Also the company is renewing its credit line. That's another loan they have for regular operating needs. For cash they might need from time to time in the regular operation of the company. People who might lend money to a company look into its financial status. And we would be giving financial and other information about the company to those people. Everyone involved wants to be sure that the financial information is accurate. In other words, are the financial statements accurate? Checking that out requires some investigation and that often involves going to the client and asking people question

THE DEAD ONE PROTRUDES

Lohman added, "We also have to settle the financial affairs of Avon Whiteman. This involves dealing with his assets which include a business and various legal entities. This often involves asking people at the businesses things."

"So you mean this has nothing to do with the bodies?" asked Bongwad.

Lohman said, "Mostly no."

"So what did you find out? Anything unusual?" asked Bongwad.

Lohman said, "These companies are our clients. What we find out or know about them is privileged. Even if we wanted to disclose it, we can't, at least without the client's consent."

"Yeah, I've heard that one before," remarked Bongwad. "Anyhow, we've heard that you have been asking about drugs. Or at least the people you have working on the matter have. What's all that about?"

McClurg and Lohman looked at each other. Then Lohman said, "The subject of drugs keeps coming up and in investigating all the various entities here the subject comes up again. A lot of this is public information that stems from the recent Congressional investigation into campaign contributions in the election last year. Out of that we learned that the Hump and Flinton foundations both own interests in a drug company that supplies a network of substance abuse treatment centers. That network is owned by the D'Gregor Temple. And D'Gregor's body was one of the bodies in the Pedway. I believe we heard that he was going to try to start his own drug company to supply the clinics, but we don't know that."

THE DEAD ONE PROTRUDES

Lohman then said, "And there is Avon Whiteman himself. His cause of death was a drug. Then there is the drug lord found in the Pedway, I forget his name. So we find out about drugs all over. What their connection is to the Whiteman companies or Avon Whiteman's death we don't know. So far as anyone we asked knows, Avon Whiteman was not an addict. We have someone here who used to work at the company before becoming a lawyer. Sean Featherbottom. You know him. He says he never heard anything about drugs when he was there."

Sergeant Gilbert gave Bongwad a knowing glance. Bongwad said, "We'll get to him later."

Then Bongwad said, "What about your investigator. We hear he was down there asking question about some guy buying the bagged cement. We found out who he was asking about. One day when we were down there the guy came in and bought more. We know this guy. He's a suspected drug dealer. We haven't caught him doing anything yet, but our sources tell us he's involved. He has a little contracting company on the west side. How come your investigator was asking about that guy?"

Lohman said, "Probably because of the same sources. He says he had heard about the guy from his sources and saw him down at the plant one day when he was there. Our investigator's name is Wiggy Rodriguez. He mentioned the guy to us. But he didn't tell us anything more."

"We know Wiggy," said Bongwad. "How about Featherbottom. Where is he? We can't find him."

THE DEAD ONE PROTRUDES

Lohman said, "I think he's down in Texas on a deal. They're closing on the purchase of a company down there." Lohman knew this because he had to approve sending an unusually large contingent of the firm's lawyers down there on short notice."

"When's he gonna' be back?" asked Bongwad.

"Can't tell," said Lohman. "Depends on how quick they get it done."

"Can you tell us when he gets back?' asked Bongwad. "We want to talk to him again."

"Sure," said Lohman. "I'll have my secretary call you." As he said this he was thinking of ways not to have this happen.

"We went over his story," said Bongwad. "He says he went to the Nudie Mansion with papers for Mr. Whiteman and got there about 4:30 in the afternoon. He says he saw Eddie Whiteman coming out and Eddie let him in. Then he says he left and went to another client to deliver and explain papers and then he went home and then went to a party. We have someone who says they saw Whiteman after Featherbottom left. But he isn't home free. He could have come back and killed Whiteman some time later. We can't place him down at the plant, but he could have been working with someone else down there. Whiteman fired him. He had Whiteman's ring. He says he got it from D'Gregor Temple's shop, but he can't show us any papers and the Temple doesn't have any records on it. He was seen at the other client's place. McCain, that's his name. He confirms it. And he was seen at the party later. But that doesn't cover all his time. And he had the motive. So far we can't find anyone else with a good motive. The other people who saw Whiteman that evening all have alibis. We haven't

THE DEAD ONE PROTRUDES

checked them all out yet, but if they checkout, they're good. What do you guys know about him being fired?"

"Nothing directly," said McClurg.

Lohman added, "Eddie Whiteman says he did the firing, but he says it wasn't his idea. His father just told him to fire Sean because he was saying locking up some of the cement bags made it hard to deal with them. Eddie says Avon told him to tell Sean it was because he was gay. By the way, Sean hadn't even dealt with the fact that he was gay then. Anyway, Eddie says Sean was a good worker and he had nothing against him."

"He's gay", said Gilbert.

"So you think Sean did it?" asked McClurg.

"Yeah," broke in Gilbert. "How many people is he going to kill before we get him? Someday we're gonna catch that poof with his pants down - er - you know what I mean." In the unfortunate incidents of the past where the firm was involved in killings in one way or another, the police had always thought Sean was the murderer. And Tete had often remarked that at least Sean had killed the right people.

"I take it you do not have the facts to back that up," said Lohman. "And how could he get in if he came back? Do you know if the house was unlocked so anyone could walk in?"

"Yes, we know," said Bongwad. "It was usually kept locked we are told. Eddie Whiteman says it was locked when he was there. Mrs. Whiteman says it was locked when she came back later. Blackman says it was always locked. There isn't any proof that Avon Whiteman didn't unlock

THE DEAD ONE PROTRUDES

it, but why would he? As for Featherbottom, when he came back Whiteman could have let him in. That's kind of obvious."

Bongwad added, "So we don't have the proof yet, but he can't be ruled out and we know he was there to begin with. Let me tell you what we know so far. First the drug. Fentanyl killed Whiteman. How did he get it? We don't know for sure. It was probably in his drink. There weren't any signs of an injection or any other way he got it. His butler says he usually had the drink pitcher filled every day by the maid. She can't remember if she did it the next day. She says she does remember one day in the morning she saw the empty pitcher on the kitchen sink. She says it was usually in Whiteman's office each morning and she got it from there and it usually had something in it because he didn't drink much. She thinks the day she saw it in the kitchen was the day after Whiteman disappeared, but she can't remember for sure. It was one of those fancy things with a plug in the top. Whiteman's friend, that Tyreservski or something like that, he says Whiteman was preparing to have his evening drink while he was there. So we don't know for sure how the drug got in Whiteman."

"How did it get in the drink? Do you know where it came from?" asked Lohman.

"No," said Bongwad. "There isn't any sign of it anywhere, but why would there be after all this time? Anyhow, Featherbottom was there and he probably was the one who put it in the booze. He was alone in the office before Whiteman came in there."

"Did he commit suicide?" asked McClurg. "Any possibility of that?"

THE DEAD ONE PROTRUDES

"Anything's possible," said Bongwad, "but there isn't any indication of his being in that frame of mind."

"Any indication anyone else was there?" asked Lohman."

"At that time, no," said Bongwad. "All we can find out is that Avon Whiteman was home alone. Then Eddie Whiteman came in and left. Then Featherbottom. Then Tyreservski. He came in around 5:30 and then left around 6 pm. Then we have nothing until around 10 pm when Mrs. Whiteman got home. The chef and maid got home about the same time. They're married. The butler, Snively Blackman, got home later. All of them have more or less alibis for where they were."

"So how did Whiteman get in the concrete panel? He would have to be at the plant wouldn't he?" asked Lohman.

"I don't think they came up there and poured him," said Bongwad. "Yeah, he was probably down at the plant to get poured into the concrete. He may even have been killed there. We don't have it figured out yet."

Bongwad got a notebook out of his chest pocket and looked at it. "Here's what we know. At that Calumet plant they check people in and out after the day shift which ends at four. Mrs. Whiteman was down at the plant. She left and was checked out around 4:15. About that time one of the Whiteman Panel Company vans left the plant. This was just after she left. One of the bodies in the Pedway was the panel company driver driving that van. No one at the plant said they saw him after Whiteman disappeared. The van checked back in at around 8:30 pm. The driver's car was still there that night, but was gone on the next day.

THE DEAD ONE PROTRUDES

It was eventually found out on the West Side near that Salerno contractor place and towed away as an abandoned vehicle."

Bongwad looked over his notes. "Mrs. Whiteman says she was going to a movie she wanted to see and which her husband didn't want to see. She said the only place it was playing was at a mall theater not too far from the plant. She says she got there early and ate and shopped, but didn't buy anything, until the show started. She doesn't have a receipt for her meal. Who keeps those things anyway? After that she says she drove home."

Bongwad looked at the notes again. "The chef and maid said they were at dinner in a family gathering at a family member's house. The family members confirm this. They say they got home about 10 pm and they and Mrs. Whiteman say they saw each other coming in. Tyreservski says that after he left Whiteman, he and his wife were at home eating dinner with her parents. They confirm this. Blackman says he had a date and went to a show in the River North area just north of the Loop. He had two reserved tickets for the show and the box office records show they were used. He got the tickets from a ticket broker who confirms that he sold them to Blackman. He says they got there in his car around 5:30. The theater has a parking lot and the attendant remembers Blackman. Blackman pulled up in an Audi and gave the attendant a big tip and when the show was over he gave the attendant another big tip to pick up the car. Now, I don't know what a butler is doing with an Audi and giving big tips, but he says Whiteman gave him the car and he often chauffeured him in it. Other than that, we couldn't pin down Blackman's alibi. The woman he said he was with was killed about a year ago. She was shot in a car on the Dan Ryan expressway on the South Side. One thing - we asked Blackman what the show was and

THE DEAD ONE PROTRUDES

he told us it was a musical about a love triangle. He even had a brochure for it. He looked at it."

Bongwad paused and then said, "That's something we want to go into further. We found out the show ran from 6 pm to 8 pm, but it was actually about something else than what the brochure described. The brochure had the right name and characters and actors, but a different sort of plot was described. When we mentioned this to Eddie Whiteman he told us that the theater had printed up the wrong brochure for the opening. Blackman had gone to the opening. Eddie said it was in the news at the time. He remembered reading about it. A big thing. We checked it out and that was true. When we asked Blackman why he told us the wrong thing, he said he couldn't remember that far back and had just used the brochure to remember it. He says he was collecting show brochures. It's a good thing for him that the parking attendant can alibi him."

Bongwad then paused. He continued. "Eddie Whiteman. Now he told us he and his wife went to a party at a hotel after he left his father. We checked that out with a few people he said saw him there. He left his father about 4:30 in the afternoon and he met his wife at the hotel around five. it was at the Swifton Palace Hotel downtown. He says he got there about five and that he took an Uber car. We were able to get the Uber charge records and that checks out. The people he said saw him there confirmed his attendance. One couple says they met him there soon after five and another couple says they sat at his table at dinner. After the dinner there was a presentation and everyone sat at the dinner tables for that. It was a reception for some construction industry big shot. Eddie and his wife say they got home around ten. After that we can't confirm where they were."

THE DEAD ONE PROTRUDES

"So could he have gone back to his father's place?" asked McClurg.

"Sure," said Bongwad. "He could have come back and killed his father. There is no record of his checking into the plant that night. Of course he could have killed his father and had others getting the body and disposing of it just like the others, but unless all the others are lying, Avon Whiteman was not at home by around ten."

"His car was still there, wasn't it?" asked McClurg.

"Yes," answered Bongwad. "So he probably didn't get himself down to the plant. He was probably killed at home, but that's just a guess. He could have got down there some way and have been killed there. That doesn't make too much sense though." Bongwad looked at his notes again. "Then he looked up and said, "There's one thing. The name of the woman Blackman gave us as his date that night led us to finding out that she had died in an expressway shooting. However, her description in the records did not match the description we got from the parking attendant of the woman Blackman was with that night. The woman killed in the shooting was a tall black woman. The woman the attendant said he saw was a tall white blonde. We asked the attendant if he could be mistaken and showed him pictures of the woman shot on the expressway. He seemed less sure after that. What he was sure of was that it was Blackman who gave him the tips. He was positive when we showed him pictures of Blackman."

"So why would he lie?" asked McClurg.

"Who says he lied?" said Bongwad. "It sounds more like a mistake. We asked other people about this to see if anyone saw his date. No one said they did, but Mrs. Whiteman said she had seen Blackman with

THE DEAD ONE PROTRUDES

another woman around that time who he identified as someone he was dating. She said the woman was a tall black woman."

"Did you hear about the panel company van that was there that night?" asked Lohman.

Bongwad said, "Tyreservski mentioned it." He told Lohman what they had heard and then Lohman told them about what the Ambassador Hotel doorman had told him about it. "Bongwad said, "We're trying to check that out. We'll talk to that guy. We'll also follow up on what anyone in the neighborhood saw. We can't hear from everyone, but so far the only people we have been able to find out who were there then and have been able to talk to say they didn't see anything. All we can find out so far is that a van left the plant around 4:15 and got back there around 8:30. The driver was listed in the check in and checkout records and the van number was recorded. It was the same van and the driver was the guy found in the Pedway. They record the license numbers and all occupants of the vehicle. Nobody was listed as being in the van with the driver. Neither the panel company nor the art panel company had any records of who was driving it, though. The art panel company doesn't have any vehicles. They sell the panels to Whiteman Panel Co. and that company sells the art panels to the contractors and delivers them. We asked around at the plant and found out what I told you. People never saw him around there after that night and, as I told you, his car never left the plant that night, although it was gone the next day, Saturday. Several weeks later it was found abandoned on the West Side near the Salerno contractor yard. It was towed to the pound and no one claimed it. And that Delez guy who runs the art panel company – he checked out around five."

THE DEAD ONE PROTRUDES

"So maybe the van picked up Avon Whiteman or his body?" asked Lohman.

"Could be," said Bongwad, "But who killed the driver? We're still looking into this."

Bongwad looked at his notes again and then added, "When it got to the plant the van went to the loading dock for the panel company. That's out of sight of the parking lot attendant. The only other people working there that night were the security crew and an art panel company pour crew. The security guys are three guys who work out of a separate little building. They mostly work outside. Everything is locked up. They didn't notice anything. There weren't any jobs coming up on Saturday so no big morning crew came in. The art panel people probably came in from the door between Streets & San and the panel company. There was no check in record for them in the Whiteman lot. That's unfortunate because that art panel company doesn't keep records of who they were and the temp agency they worked through is defunct."

Lohman asked, "What about the door to the Streets & San yard next door?"

Bongwad answered, "We checked on that. It is kept locked. You have to ring to get in that way. We don't know what its status was that night. There isn't any record if anyone came in or when or if the door was locked or unlocked or open or shut. We were just told that it is always kept locked and you have to ring to get in. And we don't know if anyone did that night."

Lohman then remembered what Cass had told him. "One other thing. Cass Tyreservski, that friend of Whiteman's who was at his house the

THE DEAD ONE PROTRUDES

night he disappeared. He told me he went there because someone called him to come over. He said he didn't know who it was, but it was a woman. He said the voice sounded strange. Did you guys find out who made the call?"

Bongwad said, "We haven't been able to find out who made that call. We asked all the secretaries and other people in the company who might have made the call and the house servants. No one says they made the call. Mrs. Whiteman too. She says she didn't do it. And no one was there with him that we know of. We're still trying to find out."

"And I heard something else," added Lohman. "I heard that about when D'Gregor disappeared a D'Gregor Temple Deacon was brought back here for burial. He had died in Mexico where he was working, but he came from here so they buried him here. D'Gregor was at the guy's burial, but no one ever saw him after that."

"Where did you hear that?" asked Bongwad.

Lohman said, "Bungus LaRue. He's a Deacon of the Temple too. Did he tell you?"

Bongwad said, "We haven't talked to him yet, at least not much. We'll follow up on it. Thanks for telling me."

Not much else was discussed and the police left. McClurg and Lohman got back to work.

At lunch time Lohman was due to go over to the Normal Club with Cohenstein to meet with one of Cohenstein's clients who they both knew. As they were walking over there Lohman told Cohenstein about what he had learned from the police. Cohenstein picked up on the

THE DEAD ONE PROTRUDES

show Blackman went to. He said he had gone to the show too and the same night, the opening night, that Blackman went there. He said, "I got the brochure for the show at a hotel lunch. They had brochures for all sorts of events there and while I was waiting for someone I picked it up and read it. Seemed like a great show so we went. Zelda and I went." Zelda was his wife. "Turned out the show wasn't what was described in the brochure."

"What was it about?" asked Lohman.

"Crud!" exclaimed Cohenstein as he dodged a pigeon that was strutting straight at him. "I thought these birds kept away from us"

"This one must be different," said Lohman.

"What," said Cohenstein. "They have individual personalities?"

"Maybe," said Lohman. "They probably do, just like us, but we can't tell the difference. Like ants. We can't tell the difference. What about the show?"

Cohenstein said, "The brochure said it was some kind of love story, a musical, but it turned out to be some kind of comedy horror show with music. Whatever it was, it was good. We liked it."

They came to a street with stop light for pedestrian traffic and stopped for a bit. The cross street was a one way street, but it had dual bike lanes along their side of the street for bike traffic in both directions. The green walk sign came on and as they started to move off the curb into the bike lanes two bikes came zooming along. One, in the lane nearest them, was trying to beat the car traffic about to cross in front

THE DEAD ONE PROTRUDES

of him at the intersection. The other, in the lane going the other way, had just sped through the intersection. They almost got hit.

"Christ!" said Lohman.

"Yeah, he's the one who does these things," said Cohenstein.

Lohman said, "Well he was Jewish, you know. The Christians started up way after he died."

Cohenstein said, "Yeah, I know, but it's fun to blame everything on you guys."

Then a car turning into the street almost hit them. "Crap!" said Cohenstein who was the one nearest the car. "This is the same thing that happened to me yesterday on the way to the Club. I almost got hit then too."

"Me too. Yesterday when I was going over to the College Club. What kind of car was it that almost did it to you yesterday? I wonder if we're dealing with the same guy here?" asked Lohman.

"A Ford," said Cohenstein.

"What kind?" asked Lohman.

"A Fucus," said Cohenstein.

"You mean Focus?" asked Lohman.

"Yeah. That one. And it was bright orange. And it had a yellow top. Like that one."

THE DEAD ONE PROTRUDES

"That's the same one that almost hit me. And here it is today going after both of us," remarked Lohman. "It's got to be the same guy. Look - it has the yellow top - and the plates - same ones I saw yesterday - "HUMP2016" - and that sign on the door - 'Hump For President! Same car. How many of those are? Did you see the driver?"

"How?" asked Cohenstein. "It's got those smoked glass windows. Who can see? Maybe it's one of those autocars."

"You mean self-driving?" asked Lohman.

"Yeah, one of those," said Cohenstein. "Maybe no one's in there. After all, with Hump on the outside there probably isn't anyone on the inside, especially up front."

Right away Cohenstein changed the subject. He was looking at an attractive young woman coming towards them. "Look! What a nice goylie," he said.

"Girlie," corrected Lohman.

Cohenstein replied, "No. She's for sure not a princess."

As they went on, Cohenstein's attention shifted to a young man standing at another one of the corners, waiting for his light to change. He looked to be just out of his teens. He had on a light blue suit with an extremely tight and short jacket with hardly visible lapels, tight pants which ended well above his shoes, bright red and yellow patterned socks and very light brown shoes with toes that extended far beyond the end of this feet. He was wearing sun glasses and had a shoulder bag that looked like a purse. He was vaping and talking on his cell phone. "Look," he said. "There's one of those wadda-ya-callems."

THE DEAD ONE PROTRUDES

Lohman said, "Generation Z, I think."

"Yeah," said Cohenstein. "Aren't we starting to get some associates like that? He's not one of ours is he?"

"Well, we have some," said Lohman. "He's not one of ours I don't think. At least I don't recognize him. You know, the way they dress offends some of our people. Some of the clients too. I try to get them to tone it down. I hate policing the joint"

"Gotta keep the customers happy," remarked Cohenstein. "Myself, I don't care. It's all about changing everything. How can you sell more of a good product that lasts forever when everyone has it already? You have to change things. Clothes used to be an easy one. You just tell them the old stuff is out of fashion. Just look at men's clothes while I've been around. They just keep changing all the details. Tight, loose. Width of lapels. Pleated pants. Un-pleated. Cuffs, no cuffs. Long jackets and pants, short ones. The number of buttons. Same thing with other products. Keep changing it. And now they have a new tool. Make it so it doesn't last. Not only does it go out of fashion quick, it doesn't last very long. You have to get a new one. Change everything! The biggest sales tool there is."

"We do it too," said Lohman. "Or at least we benefit from it too. It's called changes in the law."

"Thank God for that," said Cohenstein. "Everything changes. Everyone wants change. Look at that," he said as he pointed to an old building that they were approaching. "See above the entrance where it says MDCCCXCII?" He spelled it out. "It's one of those anal dominant numbers. Who even knows what that is. What year is that?"

THE DEAD ONE PROTRUDES

Lohman said, "I think it's just called Roman numerals. You're thinking of when a date says 1892 AD. AD means anno domini or Latin for year of the Lord. That date there is 1892."

"So who needs it?" remarked Cohenstein. "Five hundred years from now we're just going to use a string of dots and dashes. That's why we don't live five hundred years. We couldn't stand all the changes if we did."

They finally got to the Normal Club and went on in, met the client, and ate.

After that Lohman got back to the office and just as he was getting set up at his desk Tete rang him. "It's the Saint," she said, meaning St. Charles.

Lohman picked up the phone and greeted him. St. Charles said," Bumper, I've been thinking about all this time the police have been taking around the firm. Talking to people, taking their time, getting records. Some of the partners have complained about it. And with the unfortunate incidents we have had in the past, every year it seems, they have been taking up a lot of our time for some years. What are we going to do about billing this time? How will we add it to our bills? Put that down on the agenda for the next Management Committee meeting will you."

Lohman paused to caution himself. Then he said, "Perhaps that could be an ethical problem We can't bill clients for time not spent on their matters."

"Well we should see how we can recover our costs," responded St. Charles.

THE DEAD ONE PROTRUDES

"The only thing I can think of," said Lohman, "is to increase our hourly rates in general. Although if the police time we spend is directly attributable to what a specific client has done, then maybe we could bill it. Anyway, if we increase rates in general then we in effect have a price increase and you know large firms at the top like us only do that in tandem, except for the top billers."

St. Charles said, "Well, don't bother me with the details. You handle those. Put it on the agenda."

"Of course," said Lohman.

THE DEAD ONE PROTRUDES

22 MORE OF THE PRACTICE OF LAW

Early on Monday, August 14th Lohman and McClurg met with Trulia and Eddie Whiteman to review progress on the loan renewal and possible acquisitions. Lohman brought up the subject of the panels containing the bodies in the Pedway and Riverwalk. Neither Eddie nor Trulia knew anything about them before they came out of the panels. They said they never heard anything about bodies being put in the panels until they heard the news and then they had not specifically remembered that they had done those jobs. Lohman also asked them if they knew who called Cass to come in and see Avon the night he disappeared, but neither knew anything about that and neither could even guess who it was. They did say no one else was in the house that they knew of and that he did not ordinarily have a secretary on call when he was home, much less on Friday nights.

Lohman asked about the van driver too. What did they know about him? Did they notice his absence? Once again, they knew nothing. Trulia said, "We have a lot of employees and we, Eddie and I, we don't deal with them directly on day to day matters. He had a supervisor. He didn't say there was any problem, did he Eddie?"

Eddie said, "No. Nothing I heard of. I left scheduling to him. Anyhow he could have had some time off. I usually hear about it if someone doesn't show up for several days. He could have been fired or quit or something."

Trulia then said, "Well anyway, I am just here to help Eddie. I don't run the company now. That is, I never did. Anyway, I need something to

THE DEAD ONE PROTRUDES

keep me busy so I want to buy the bagged cement operation. How about that?"

Eddie gave her a surprised look.

"Oh don't worry sweetie," she said to him, "I'll give you a commission on sales."

McClurg chimed in at this stage. "We can't do that. That is, our firm. We can't represent you both in this. It's a conflict of interest and the type of conflict that cannot be waived even if you both agree to the waiver."

Lohman added, "I think we have gone over everything we need to at this stage so we should end this meeting. Now, I am going to say something that is required just because of the conflicts of interest in the situation. This is not because of any lack of cooperation or unpleasantness, but just because of the legal technicalities. We want to meet with Eddie alone at this stage. We have to discuss with him what just came up. And Trulia, it would be advisable for you to get your own lawyer if you want to follow up on this. Please understand. We hate to say these things. It sounds so – well – who wants to hear this. But the legal technicalities require it."

He went on further with this kind of nonsense and he finally managed to get Trulia out of there without further incident. He and McClurg then found out that Eddie had never heard anything about this before and that he did not know what to think of it. They discussed the pros and cons of it and what Eddie could do and they all agreed that basically he would stall her if she followed up on it by saying he was studying the matter and that he would report any further efforts by

THE DEAD ONE PROTRUDES

Trulia to pursue the matter to them. In the meantime he would consult his accounting firm about what form and pricing a sale should take. Since Eddie was not eager to sell what he called a profitable business, he was not enthusiastic about all this, but he agreed to look into it.

After Eddie left, Lohman asked McClurg if he had heard anything about Trulia's proposal before. He hadn't. It was news to him too.

Later, around lunch time, there was one of the events the firm sometimes hosted. They had their own food service and lots of meeting areas so sometimes they let organizations related to the practice of law meet there. Today was one of those days. The organization having a luncheon meeting there was OGSBAC, the Open Gender and Sexuality Bar Association of Chicago, which was having one of its monthly meetings. Most of the attendees were of ordinary appearance and behavior, but some were very interesting. The meeting went on till one thirty when it ended and the members started to leave.

About this time Lohman was sitting in his office when he got a call from one of the partners, Moira Weiner (pronounced Whiner) who was always quick to bring matters of immense complaint to the attention of Lohman. She had a nickname. She was called, but not to her face, The Weiner (pronounced Whiner). She loved to be offended. She couldn't wait to be so treated. And she loved to complain. Complaints required offenses. So she was constantly on the lookout for good ones. Today she had a good one. She had left one of the conference rooms on the floor where OGSBAC was meeting to go to the women's room. What horror should she find there? A drag queen. No doubt about it. A huge three hundred or so pounder. Despite his extravagant dress and jewelry, her instant wrong doing radar was confirmed when he spoke

THE DEAD ONE PROTRUDES

to her and he asked her where the urinal was. She told him in no uncertain terms where it was and kicked him out. He had a friend with him too and she told that one to get out too. The friend said, "No. I don't go. I belong here. I'm Tran."

The Weiner was so pleased by this offense that she almost fainted on the spot. She could hardly contain her outrage when she called Lohman to complain, which she did often. And, as he did quite often, Lohman listened to her patiently and then told her he would look into it and see that the situation was rectified. Then he forgot about the matter. But not after reflecting on how odd the situation was. He was one of the few people in the firm who knew that Weiner had once had a sex change operation herself to become a male and then decided that she didn't like it and had another sex change operation to become a female again.

Lohman had just terminated his call with Weiner when he got another call from a lawyer in the firm who represented a large insurance company. Insurance companies have a lot of litigation involving whether or not the people they insure are liable for something. In essence their customers are being sued and they get the lawyers for the customers. The greatest quantity of this legal work is for auto and homeowners' insurance and is done at low rates. It is the type of business which F, P & C didn't touch. However, these insurance companies did have high end legal business in dealing with their investments and corporate matters. There were also insurance companies that had clients with large liability business matters and these matters were billed at high rates by the law firms that had the companies as clients. F, P & C had some of these high rate insurance clients and the lawyer calling represented one.

THE DEAD ONE PROTRUDES

He explained to Lohman that he might have a conflict of interest problem and asked Lohman what he should do. The client insurance company insured a major business against general liability matters. The business rented the Hump name for its line of financial products and Hump had filed suit against them for defaming his name and devaluing it by doing bad business deals. The insured business wanted to file a counter claim against Hump claiming it was he who devalued the name and the business wanted to recover everything it had paid him and damages to boot. The lawyer had heard that the Conflicts Committee had been discussing a matter involving Hump so he wanted to clear the matter. Lohman told him he would consult the committee and get back to him. He then referred the matter to the Business Manger to run through the Committee members

Lohman then got back to the business of his own clients and finished up the day's work and went home where he did outrageous things to his innocent wife Gloria.

THE DEAD ONE PROTRUDES

23 WORLD AND LOCAL AFFAIRS ARE BUTT CRAZY

Tuesday, August 15th was a big news day. First thing in the morning all the media outlets were featuring stories about a tweet released by Hump at three in the morning and follow up interviews around the world which were continuing throughout the morning confirming what Hump had tweeted. Hump proclaimed that he had formed OWEP, the Organization for World Everlasting Peace. The previous day he had secretly met with the Heads of State of the following countries at an undisclosed location: the President of the Philippines (Querty Werty), the Supreme Leader of North Korea (Ping Pong Poo), the Supreme Leader of Iran (Watwa Falamumbhi), the President of Turkey (Taptoe Gerdogan), the King of Saudi Arabia (Ibo Fado), and the President of Zimbabwe (Candy Apple). News organizations throughout the world were hard at work to find out and report what was going on and in the meantime to display themselves, not the subjects of their reports, as the great attention getters of society.

Throughout the morning the details of OWEP dribbled out, one by one, but overall the only specifics that emerged were that they confirmed that they had met and that they had formed the organization and that they were going to work for peace. The specifics of how and who was running the organization or how it would work were not revealed, except for one thing — all the members were going to dye their hair yellow, except for Hump.

Flinton was asked about all this and all she had to say was that she heartily approved of it and that Hump was just the right person to deal with these people.

THE DEAD ONE PROTRUDES

While all this was going on Lohman had business to attend to. The grand and wonderful Graybourne St. Charles, Chairman of the firm, had been approached by a client who wanted to expand into a new business area by getting government contracts throughout the country to rebuild the "infrastructure". That was the popular new term for roads, bridges, dams and other public works, which was the old term used when they were built by our forefathers. Flinton had persuaded Congress to appropriate several trillion dollars for this purpose and the new boondoggle was beginning.

Buying government contracts was easy enough. You just made massive campaign contributions to the politicians who controlled the money. In this case though, there had been a lot of public attention focused on this process so Congress had adopted a system to insure this did not happen. They created an Ethics Board composed of civil service employees who would be responsible for supervising the contracting process to see there was no improper offering of money. Even though most of the contracts would be made by state and local governments, this Board would have jurisdiction because Federal money was to be used.

The head of the client company was the person who St. Charles dealt with. He was a person of immense eminence and superior social standing. To confirm the old saw that our most prominent people have the dirtiest underwear, he had informed St. Charles that he wanted to buy the contracts from local officials throughout the country. St. Charles never met with anyone alone. The more subordinates you have, the more superior you are so he always had other lawyers with him when he met clients. In this case, he had called Lohman and explained the situation to him and asked him to come to the meeting

THE DEAD ONE PROTRUDES

and to bring LaRue, the Governmental Affairs partner, and other lawyers "in suitable areas of expertise" to the meeting and "associates as needed". Needed for what? How can you tell what is needed before hearing what is going on? Lohman knew what. To fill up the room (and the bill).

Everybody was going to meet in St. Charles' conference room. Lohman got on an elevator to go up to St. Charles' floor and LaRue was on it. They started to talk about the morning's news. After a while Lohman said, "What do you think? Maybe next thing we'll hear is that Hump formed a new religion where he'll be the grand holy one?"

LaRue said, "No. I don't think so. God wouldn't like the competition."

They soon reached the 55th floor where St. Charles had his offices and went on in to the conference room. Most of the other lawyers were there, but not St. Charles or the client. They were in his private office and would not come in until his secretary informed him that everyone else was there. One of Lohman's major jobs for the meeting was to tell her when this happened, which he did. Then the grand entrance took place and everyone was introduced and the discussion started. The situation was discussed and "What to do, what to do?" was gone over. Finally there came a time when Lohman had to get out of there and he motioned to LaRue who then came up with a potential solution. He suggested that the client, through his lackeys of course, should get the local officials responsible for entering the contracts to run for office of some kind. Then he could make campaign contributions to them. So what if they lost. They would have the money. And if they won, they had a good new job. Several of the people present were assigned to look into this and report back to St. Charles. The meeting then broke up and everyone went back to work.

THE DEAD ONE PROTRUDES

Why didn't Lohman just have LaRue throw out this idea right up front? That would have cut the meeting, and the billing short, and St. Charles would have had a fit. As it was, he caused the meeting to end far sooner than St. Charles would have liked. But on the other hand, St. Charles could take credit for his supremely brilliant solution.

Lohman had to get back to his office to meet with a potential new client of his own. The client had been referred by an accounting firm and was being prosecuted for violation of the interest disclosure laws on consumer loans. Among other things the Truth in Lending Act was involved. "Truth" is a bad word to use in a law office so the politicians must have come up with the name for this on their own. The client had a string of mattress stores in the Midwest. They engaged in massive advertising campaigns to sell their wares. They were in competition with the other mattress chains who did likewise and the lot of them had stores all over – almost one store for each mattress.

The common pitch to the customer was zero percent financing and no money down and no payments for a while. So how does anyone make money this way? Simply by hiking up the price of the mattress. If I can sell you a two hundred dollar mattress for fifteen hundred dollars, I don't mind letting you pay for it with no interest for several years.

Competition is tough when selling for free. The potential client had come up with a new pitch. It was going to offer negative interest rates, not just zero rates. The fifteen hundred dollar mattress would be paid for over time with payments that added up to less than fifteen hundred dollars. The disclosure here would be as truthful as the zero percent interest disclosure. However, this went too far for the Federal Trade Commission (FTC) which enforced the Act. It decided to take a new approach. The mattress companies were no different from other

THE DEAD ONE PROTRUDES

businesses. They had to pay their bills. The no money down and deferred payment scheme left them without any money coming in to pay the bills. Therefore they sold the loans. The agreement to pay the fifteen hundred dollars over time was sold to a finance company. But the finance company was not going to pay fifteen hundred dollars for a no interest loan in that amount, especially if the borrower had a dubious credit rating or a rating that had never been checked. They paid far less. The FTC had decided to compute the actual interest rate in the loan by comparing the price the mattress company sold the loan to the finance company for to the payments made by the mattress buyer. This produced a whopping rate of interest which had not been disclosed.

Lohman did not have much sympathy for the client, but he took the matter on and told the client he would look into it and get back to them. After the client left he called Sean to see if he was in. Sean was a CPA besides being a lawyer and Lohman thought that might be helpful. Sean was in so Lohman went to his office to get him started on the matter. He also called DiBello and asked him to come to Sean's office. Lohman wanted him to get to work on the regulatory aspects of dealing with the FTC. Then Lohman went to the Business Manager's office to get him started on a conflicts check.

When Lohman got back to his office one of the partners was waiting for him. The guy was one of the older partners who had come from the St. Charles side of the firm before Cohenstein brought his crew around. He was an old line "conservative" who was still outraged that Hump had lost the election. He had a black eye.

What he wanted to see Lohman about was Sean. He never had much to do with Sean. To begin with he never wanted Sean assigned to his

THE DEAD ONE PROTRUDES

matters. However, Sean could be seen here and there around the firm and several times he had been sent to this guy's office by someone else. The last time was earlier that day. He was in his office with a client of similar sentiments and Sean had showed up with some documents for him from another partner in the firm. His secretary had sent Sean in. The partner explained to Lohman in outraged terms that his client did not like fags and was very upset, as was he. He described Sean's dress and his "hands on hip style" and blond hair. He explained how he grabbed Sean and threatened to hit him if Sean ever came near him or any of his clients again. Then he got to the outrageous point of his visit. He explained how Sean punched him and flattened him right in front of his client.

Lohman's job as the Managing Partner involved dealing with matters such as this. So he did. He told the guy, "I'll tell you what the Queen told her gardener — keep your hands off the pansies."

The other partner gave him a look indicating he did not comprehend what Lohman had just said.

Lohman followed up with, "I'll bring it up with the Management Committee. And I'll talk to Sean."

"Fire him!" the partner demanded.

"For self defense?" said Lohman. "You physically attacked someone. What do you expect?"

The partner stomped off in a huff.

Lohman then called Sean again about the partner. "Sean, he told me you flattened him. What happened?"

THE DEAD ONE PROTRUDES

Sean said, "Well, Mr. Lohman, he grabbed me. He doesn't like me. I think it's because I'm gay. So he got up and grabbed me and pushed me around and I could see his other hand coming so I hit him. I know some self defense tactics, you know. I didn't do the big hit, but he stopped. I just left."

"So why didn't you tell me about it?" asked Lohman. "We have a procedure for that. Everyone knows."

"Well, it's no big deal. I don't want to go around complaining about it. I just give them tit for tat when that happens," said Sean.

Lohman put the matter in the agenda for the next Management Committee meeting. Cohenstein would probably like hearing about it. Fluffy strikes again.

THE DEAD ONE PROTRUDES

24 ASS PISS MEETING

Saturday August 18th was when the great quarterly meeting of the American Serenity Providers Society was to be held. One would ordinarily refer to this organization as ASPS, not an easily pronounceable abbreviation. Accordingly some blasphemous sinners referred to it as Ass Piss. Hell hath no gates or fences and there they will run free.

Ass Piss (dear reader, I like heat better than cold) was an organization of all the religious organizations in town and was formed to further the word of God and to raise money for that purpose. The religions shared in the funds raised according to their relative membership. The organization was formed and run by The Prophet Andy who had formed the worldwide rapidly growing Gabriellian Faith, the Evangelical Congregation of The Angel Gabriel or ECOTAG. The Prophet Andy was the Angellic Leader. He took a management fee of twenty percent of the gross from Ass Piss as well as two percent of the net plus ECOTAG's share of the proceeds. Today the quarterly meeting of Ass Piss was to be held at The Aspire, ECOTAG's 2500 foot tall building near the mouth of the Chicago River.

The main money raising mechanism of Ass Piss was The List. This was a list of all donors by name and amount given. It was equivalent to the social register of old and if you were not in it you were a nobody and if the amount you gave was low, you were still a nobody. It had turned into quite a profitable venture, especially since the donors included large businesses as well as individuals. Naturally F, P & C was in The List as well as many of its partners. The meetings were usually large affairs

THE DEAD ONE PROTRUDES

where the donors and associated people came to network and display their prominence.

Of course the heads of all the religions were there, along with many of their associates. The Prophet was there as was Cardinal Brandon Samuel, the Cardinal Sammy. The local heads of the other religions were there too. Naturally quite a few people from F, P & C were there as well as people from numerous other law and non-religious organizations. F, P & C was high in the List, as of course was St. Charles himself. Lohman was one of the nobody donors, but he and his wife Gloria were there too. While he was a low amount donor, he was familiar with The Prophet and some of the other religious leaders from their having consulted the firm from time to time about legal matters. Now, you would think it is God who makes the law as he pleases, but it seems he has apparently been out to lunch lately.

Anyhow, it was a grand occasion. It had the usual convention, big group, meeting format. First the cocktails and mingling. Then the dinner. Then the presentations from the dias. After that more mingling and some dancing.

The Lohmans were there. They moved through the crowd meeting and talking to people they knew and meeting people they had not known before. Soon they came across Cohenstein and his wife Zelda. They had just broken away from a group and were looking around. "Zenon," said Lohman. "And Zelda. How are you?"

"Good, good," said Cohenstein. "I think I picked up some business. I'll tell you later."

THE DEAD ONE PROTRUDES

Zelda looked at Gloria and said, "What a marvelous dress. Where did you get it?"

Gloria couldn't help it. She said, "Sears. I always wanted one of their dresses so finally I went in there and got one before they went under. A lot of people tell me they like it. I think it's so different from the high end stuff that they think it's the latest new thing that came from some exotic designer."

Zelda looked contemplative and then said, "That's where Zenon gets his suits. Same reaction from the fashion crowd. Don't tell anyone. And don't even ask where I got my clothing."

"I won't," said Gloria. "Looks good though."

As they were talking The Prophet had come up to them. They noticed him and they all greeted each other. They talked a bit and then The Prophet asked, "You people represent the Whiteman firm, don't you?"

"Yes," said Cohenstein. "I'm not their lead counsel and I don't do much of the work, but Bumper here has been working for them. Right Bumper?"

Lohman said, "Yes, but I am not their lead counsel either. I just help out."

"So what I want to know," said The Prophet, "is what is going on there. One of our organizations is involved. That D'Gregor Temple. Now I know Trulia Whiteman and their butler, a fellow named Blackman, are among the leaders of the Temple. And so was Avon Whiteman. Then we hear that the Whiteman company delivered a concrete panel containing the body of Avon Whiteman and then another panel

THE DEAD ONE PROTRUDES

containing the body of D'Gregor. What was going on there? And the butler seems to be running the dining room. Several people here tonight have told me he is running around soliciting donations to the Temple."

Cohenstein looked at Lohman. Lohman said, "Well, we can't talk about our clients' affairs. You understand, having been a client of ours from time to time. Anyway, we don't know what was involved there. The police have been talking to us too and they don't seem to know either."

The Prophet continued. "That D'Gregor was something else. You know that at one time he was an atheist? He told me. He was very devout in his early years. Then he said that one day when he was meditating and praying to know God's will for him he made conscious contact with God. He asked what was God's will for him and you know what he told me?"

Cohenstein said, "Are you serious?"

"Yes," said The Prophet. "Yes. He said he heard God say, 'Go fuck yourself'. So he became an atheist. Then he claims he got reconverted and learned that the answer was to start his own religion. I think he was just trying to make money for himself. He was a very crude guy. He may even have been and agent of the Devil. I'll say one thing for him though and I have said it before. When I have been told that he had character defects I have always pointed out that he had no character, so how could he have character defects. Character defects would have been an improvement for him."

THE DEAD ONE PROTRUDES

The Cohensteins and the Lohmans looked at each other. Cohenstein decided to joke it out. "I got character defects. I'm OK."

The Prophet ignored this. He evidently had not liked D'Gregor. "And that Temple of his. I realize it is being run by Mrs. Whiteman and that butler of hers now, but it still isn't a real church. I think it's a scam. They are flexible when it comes to the principles of God. And then there are all those big cash donations and all those politicians on the payroll. And he told me once they had some police on the payroll too. I don't know, but I have heard rumors that they somehow are involved with drugs. Maybe that relates to the drug and alcohol clinics they run. Yes, I know about that too. Anyhow, he's gone so I hope the Temple can improve."

At this stage the Cardinal came by with some of his aides. They all greeted each other and then the Cardinal brought up another subject. "Andy, did you hear about Hump? He wants to build mosques. I was just talking to Akmud over there. He told me." Akumd was Akmud Mahmood, the leader of the Chicago Muslims. The Cardinal continued. "Akmud says Hump is trying to make a deal with the governments of some Muslim countries to publicize how nice Muslims are and then Hump will build mosques around the world and rent them or sell them to Muslims and he will rent his name to them to put on the mosques. His Vice Presidential candidate was a Muslim. Akhmed Faruqe. He's handling the project."

"Oh really!" exclaimed The Prophet. "I have to hear about this. Where is Akmud?"

The Cardinal pointed him out and The Prophet bid everyone good bye and left

THE DEAD ONE PROTRUDES

At this stage several of the top F, P & C partners and their wives came by. They greeted everyone and started schmoozing up the Cardinal. They started telling the Cardinal how devout they were and how they especially appreciated his messages of humility in the face of God and how he made them realize that they were nobodies. They were trustees of a legal services charity and they had one of the staff lawyers with them. That nobody started saying how he appreciated the Cardinal's message too. He said it was important for him to be humble and realize that in the great scheme of things he was a nobody.

The two partners who came with him looked at each other and then looked at their wives. One said to the other, "So look who says he's a nobody."

The Cardinal and his crew bid them all goodbye and the group all broke up and went on to more of an evening of delightful networking.

THE DEAD ONE PROTRUDES

25 HUMP DELUXE GOES DOWN

Sunday, August 20th was a pleasant, but overcast, day so many Chicago residents were lolling around in their air conditioned homes hooked into their "devices" or, in the old folks' homes, watching TV. Needless to say the devices and TV did not disappoint. Hump operated an international airline under the name of Hump Deluxe Air. Early in the morning one of its flights from Bogota in Colombia to a vacation area near the Humpy Cement plant near Cancun in Mexico crashed in the area near the airport. This was nothing special. Airplanes crash all the time. However, the baggage area of the plane was ripped open and in working on the crash the authorities found massive amounts of cocaine and heroin. Hump was usually up early in the morning so the news people had been able to contact him about it. He claimed he knew nothing about the drugs and he said they must have been checked on by a passenger. When asked how the bags could escape detection by airport security he said security is awful in Colombia. He also indicated that it might well be that the Mexican authorities, who he said were notoriously corrupt, were perhaps trying to falsely implicate him. The show was on all morning and the end result was that no one knew anything about how the drugs got on the plane or, indeed, if they were planted there after the crash to cast aspersions on Hump or his airline. Hump did indicate that the Central and South American airlines were envious of his success. The Mexican authorities were continuing their investigation, but so far, no results.

Lohman had been relaxing at home and was exposed to all this periodically throughout the morning. He and Gloria skipped their church attendance since, being Presbyterians, they were the

THE DEAD ONE PROTRUDES

beneficiaries of "predestination", meaning that they were going to Heaven no matter what they did. Not predestined to go to church, however.

Monday morning Lohman rang up Wiggy, the firm investigator. "Wiggy," he said, "did you hear about that Hump Air crash this weekend. I have a hunch or question or whatever. How did the Mexican guy found in the Pedway panel get to Chicago? He might have got here on a plane right?"

Wiggy said, "Mr. Lohman, I do not know. It would have been hard for him to come here as a passenger since he was a prison escapee. Going through security would have been too risky. On the other hand one of my contacts out at O'Hare tells me the police have been nosing around there about a body Hump Air brought to Chicago shortly before the bodies were found in the panels. I'll get in touch with her and see if I can find out anything else."

"Thanks," said Lohman. "Let me know what you find out."

THE DEAD ONE PROTRUDES

26 THE RING

Lohman managed to get some work done for his clients the rest of Monday morning. After that he went over to the College Club to meet Cohenstein and Sweeny for lunch. For once there were no pressing client matters to discuss and they did not do so. They were enjoying their lunch and conversation when Cohenstein spotted something that caused him to stop speaking in mid sentence. It was the Weiner. Moira Weiner, the partner who loved to complain. And she saw them. What an opportunity! The co-chair of the firm and the managing partner. Right there, set to hear her out.

Lohman and Sweeney noticed her too. They all stopped talking. She was by herself and there was an extra seat at their table so she headed straight for them. She got there and they all greeted each other. She sat down and got to work. "Thank Heaven I found you. I want to tell you about that Sean Featherbottom. That little sticker is something else!"

Sweeney said, "I think he's the stickee."

"Stickee?" exclaimed The Weiner. "What's stickee? I meant stinker. Stinker. He stinks. That cologne is terrible."

"Oh, forget it," said Sweeney.

"I won't forget it," she said. "His cologne stinks. It's terrible."

"Yours stinks more," said Sweeney.

"It's relative, relative. Take it easy," said Cohenstein. "One man's fart is another man's perfume."

THE DEAD ONE PROTRUDES

That sort of stopped the conversation.

The Weiner started up again. "Gay is one thing, but what about our clients having to deal with people like that? It's enough they took over half the North Side for their own area. What is the world coming to?"

"You mean that Pansyland?" asked Cohenstein.

"What is that?" asked the Weiner. "Is that some new kind of Disney theme park"

Cohenstein said, "Fruit. Gay. That kind of pansy. You never know what to call anyone these days. Oh, I remember. It's called Boystown."

Sweeney chimed in. "Dude! Where's girlstown?"

This was too much for The Weiner. She was going to scream and start ripping out her hair so, just in time, she got up and said as she was leaving, "I forgot. I have to see someone." As soon as she had appeared she disappeared.

Sweeney said, "Thank God. You know guys, I think she's at the top of the list by far."

"What list?" asked Lohman.

"The shit bag list," said Sweeney.

"it's a good thing Graybourne isn't here," said Lohman.

"Oh that's OK," said Cohenstein. He added, "He wouldn't know what we were talking about anyway. And if he did he wouldn't listen. So," he asked Sweeney, "where's this girlstown?"

THE DEAD ONE PROTRUDES

"All over," said Sweeney.

"Mostly wherever you are," said Lohman dryly while looking at Sweeney.

After lunch they went back to the office and went on their separate ways. No sooner did Lohman get back in his office when McClurg phoned him and told him that they had found a document in Avon Whiteman's tax files. It was a tax letter given to him by the D'Gregor Temple resale shop charity where Sean had bought Avon's ring. It acknowledged a contribution by Avon and described his distinctive ring. McClurg mentioned that It gave a date for the contribution which was after Avon's date of death. McClurg did not know how it came to be dated that way. Lohman asked him to ask the family and whoever he could about it. They discussed who they could ask and, besides the family, McClurg said he would ask the people who prepared the return. McClurg said he would have a copy of the letter delivered to Lohman.

Lohman had to talk to Sean Featherbottom about a matter Sean was working on for him and he wanted to find out what Sean could say about this too. So he got up and went to Sean's office without calling him first to see if he was in. When he got there the door was partially open so he gave a knock and walked in. What he observed was not the usual sort of thing. Sean had his pants down and Tambola Cook, the associate who had a thing for Sean, was messaging his buns.

Lohman asked, "What's going on here?"

Tambola said, "Oh, Sean has a rash and I bought some ointment for him to try."

"Oh Christ!" said Lohman. "Can it. And why is the door open?"

THE DEAD ONE PROTRUDES

Sean just gave him a caught in the headlights look. Tambola did the silent pout.

He told Tambola to get back to work and then asked Sean about the tax letter. Sean had never seen it and of course Lohman didn't yet have it with him. They went over what Sean could remember about when he got the ring which was after he delivered papers to Whiteman, although he couldn't remember exactly when. He could tell Lohman, though, that it was a lot more than a few weeks. Lohman said that regardless of how the ring got to the resale shop, the tax letter would clear up questions about when he got the ring and about where he got it. He told Sean he was going to tell the police about it and they might demand the original, but he would see Sean got a copy.

At this stage Sean said, "There's a problem, Mr. Lohman." Sean had some experience in preparing tax returns, although he was not in the tax department. "Tax letters usually don't give the date of the contribution. They give the year, but not the date within the year. At least usually. I've seen ones with the exact date, but it isn't usual. And how could he have given the ring after he died?"

Lohman said, "Ah, now I remember." He didn't usually do any tax returns, but he got a lot of tax letters from charities acknowledging his contributions. "Yes, there's usually no exact date for the contribution on the ones I get. But someone else could have brought it in for Whiteman."

Sean said, "He was dead. People do things like that, but technically if the contribution was made after death his estate or trust would usually take the deduction to begin with. And it may have been that he or his estate had excess deductions and no one used it."

THE DEAD ONE PROTRUDES

"So now you're telling me this doesn't clear you, right?" asked Lohman. "On the other hand," he added, "it says that either someone made a mistake or someone was trying to hide the actual date of death."

Sean just looked at him and gave a wiggly shoulder shrug.

After this Lohman and Sean went over the client matter Lohman had assigned to him and Lohman left. When he got back to his office he found an envelope with a copy of the tax letter. He had Tete send a copy of it to Sean and then he called Det. Bongwad and told about the tax letter. He told Bongwad the details and Bongwad wanted to get the original so Lohman had McClurg arrange to deliver it to him.

What with all the documents Lohman was working with on this and other matters, Lohman was going in and out of his office and in an out of the reception area where Tete was. He was due to see McClurg and LaRue about a client of LaRue's that needed some non-political legal work done that afternoon and both showed up while he was talking to Tete at her desk. Lohman was asking Tete about the tax letter and copies being sent here and there. LaRue could hear all this and when the name of the D'Gregor Temple was mentioned he asked what was going on. McClurg spoke up first and explained it to him.

Lohman said, "Bungus, you're a Deacon there or some sort of officer, aren't you?"

"Yes," said LaRue.

He turned to Tete. "Give him a copy of that letter." Then he turned to LaRue. "Bungus, see what you can find out about that. It's got a date for a contribution by Avon Whiteman after he died. It's signed by someone at the resale shop. Maybe you can find them and see what

THE DEAD ONE PROTRUDES

they know about it. Maybe you can get into their records to find something out."

"I'll try," said LaRue, not sounding too encouraging. "I'll ask Trulia and that Blackman fellow too. They seem to run the place now. I was down in Aruba recently, that place just off the coast of Venezuela. You know, it's amazing all those little islands and strange little countries I have to go to to meet up with a lot of politicians. So I'm there and she and Blackman show up too. She was going to confer with the same people. We were all together for part of the time. I don't know why Blackman was with her. He wasn't doing any butler work. Maybe because their business involved the Temple. But I hadn't heard anything about that. I think they have something going on together."

At this stage Tete spoke up. "There's a rumor going around about that. I heard it at the salon." Tete had her hair done at one of the most wonderful salons in Richtown, even though she didn't live anywhere near there. It was not too far from the office, but the main reason she went there was for the gossip, which in other contexts is called "intelligence".

"You heard that!" McClurg exclaimed.

"Yes I did," said Tete, "but I hear a lot of things like that. That's what you hear in those places. The last time I was there, just a week ago, I heard that Flinton wants to attack Russia because Russia is attacking ISIS warriors in the Middle East and we created ISIS and Al Qaeda to make war and a market for our war goods and to get higher political donations. Do you believe that?"

"Some of it," said LaRue.

THE DEAD ONE PROTRUDES

Tete went on. "And you can never tell if any of it is true or which part of it. It's just like that Hump guy we keep hearing about all the time here. Now there's a guy. He'd make a great circus clown. He wouldn't even need make up. He gets in the news all the time with statements about this and that. The other day I heard someone say, 'Why does he lie about everything?' Her friend said, 'Because his mouth is open. He's camel shit crazy!' Everyone's crazy these days. At least it's interesting."

Tete looked at a lit up light on her phone and then continued. "Talking about crazy, you know the firm psychiatrist? That Dr. Van Gubbie we tell people to go see sometimes. I hear he was advised by his psychiatrist to quit because we are so stressful. Now who knows if that's true."

McClurg, LaRue and Lohman of course wanted to hear more of this, but they had to get to work and went on into Lohman's office.

THE DEAD ONE PROTRUDES

27 MORE OF THE COPS

Wednesday morning, August 23rd, Lohman was sitting in his office when he did hear more. Tete, who had been listening to the news on the radio, came in to tell him the cops were coming to talk to him about the tax letter. She then filled him on the morning's news which was that Hump was going to open an international string of hair salons, starting in Mexico. There was to be massive advertising and he was going to star in the ads. She then went back out and soon Bongwad and Gilbert, or is it Wilbert, showed up. They had been busy.

They had already got a copy of the tax letter from Tete and the original and had talked to the manager of the resale store about it. He had identified the signature as his and had shown them a copy of the letter they had in their files. He said he couldn't remember any of the details and he himself did not man the store to receive the actual donations. He had given them the names of the people who did and they still worked there. Bongwad and Gilbert had not talked to them yet, but were going to. The files did not identify who had brought the ring in.

They asked Lohman what he knew about the tax letter and he told them what he had heard. It didn't seem any news to them and they had heard that tax letters usually did not show the exact date of the contribution, although some did. They said the store manager said that sometimes they did give the exact date and sometimes they did not. He said they had no set policy. If the donor wanted the exact date they could get it in their letter.

Then Bongwad said, "We learned some interesting things. You know that the Guzalemonez body, the Mexican drug lord's body that was in a

THE DEAD ONE PROTRUDES

concrete panel that was delivered to the Pedway on September 22nd, 2014. Now it may be a coincidence, but a body was delivered to O'Hare Airport on September 19th. That was a Friday. It was delivered on a Hump Deluxe flight. This was the Mexican Deacon that D'Gregor Temple was having a service for here. There isn't any record of another body being on the flight and there isn't any other record of a body from Mexico being delivered to Chicago by air in that period – from when the drug lord disappeared in Mexico to when the panel was delivered to the Pedway here. The Deacon was being buried here because he originally came from here, although none of his family was left."

"We tracked him down in Mexico. There was such a guy there. He was like a reclusive monk. Mrs. Whiteman and Blackman say they knew him and he was trying to organize a monastery there. All you need to bring a body into this country is a death certificate and compliance with some sanitation laws. The body was picked up at O'Hare by a Salerno Funeral Home hearse and taken to the Home for burial preparations. After that the body was taken to the D'Gregor Temple building for a service and then on to the cemetery for burial. It was all closed coffin. I guess he wasn't in too good a shape. The pastor, Hevencent, presided over all this. Everyone interested was at the D'Gregor service and the cemetery. Even some people from Whiteman it appears. We don't know who, but one of the cemetery workers saw one of the Whiteman vans there."

Bongwad continued. "D'Gregor had come to the cemetery with Mrs. Whiteman, but he was not going back with her because she had to go direct to another appointment so he left the cemetery in the hearse. We can't find the hearse driver. He retired. Salerno says the driver of the hearse took D'Gregor back to the Temple where he lived. No one

THE DEAD ONE PROTRUDES

saw him there and after that he disappeared. We found a gas station near the Temple and they remembered the hearse stopping in for a fill-up. They often get hearses involved in services at the Temple. The gas was charged and they got the receipt records for us which show that was just after the time of the burial so this was after the hearse had gone to the cemetery and come back."

Bongwad then paused and continued. "We found out something else interesting. Real interesting. We found the gun that killed D'Gregor and the panel company van driver. It was in the Pedway panel with the driver. It wasn't easy for them to get everything out of the concrete, but an x-ray showed a gun and they got it out. It killed both of those guys. It wasn't the gun that killed the drug lord, the other guy in the Pedway. Remember that D'Gregor was found in another panel in the Riverwalk that was delivered later. On the other hand, both the driver and D'Gregor had the broken thumbs. So, if the gun that killed D'Gregor was in the Pedway, even though his body was not, he was killed before September 22nd when the Pedway panel was delivered, even though the panel with him in it was not delivered October 31st. That would account for why he was missing during that period."

Bongwad the said, "Now something else. We got the body of the Mexican Deacon exhumed. We got a court order and got the grave opened. No body. Nothing. Just an empty fancy coffin. We checked with Mexico. There was such a person there. The death certificate was based on information given to the local authorities by the local D'Gregor outfit and so far as anyone there can tell the guy did die then."

Lohman listened to all this. "So what now?" he asked.

THE DEAD ONE PROTRUDES

Gilbert, who had been standing at attention through all this, said, "Featherbottom. We want him."

Lohman said, "But you have the tax letter showing the resale shop didn't even get the ring, much less sell it to him after the death."

"Not so fast," said Bongwad. It had bogus date on it. He even could have brought it in himself and said it was for Whiteman. Then he could have come back and bought it."

"So why was the original letter in Whiteman's tax file?" asked Lohman.

"He works here sir," said Gilbert.

Lohman said, "He's also a CPA with some tax experience and he would know that an after death contribution cannot be deducted on a decedent's final tax return." Then he remembered that at that time no one knew Avon was dead, but he did not mention that.

Bongwad said, "The whole thing could have been arranged to throw us off the course. The point is not legal correctness, but the dating. Where is he?"

Lohman said, "I don't know. I'll try and find him and have him contact you."

"Do that," said Bongwad and they said goodbye and left.

Soon after they left Tete told Lohman that Sean was in the outer office waiting to see him. Lohman went out and brought him in. He then told Sean what the police had to say about the ring and the tax letter.

Sean looked disappointed. "I thought I was in the clear, Mr. Lohman. I got my receipt for the ring. I found it. That's why I came down here.

THE DEAD ONE PROTRUDES

Here's a copy of the credit card receipt from the resale shop, and I have the written receipt describing the ring too. Or at least a ring. Here's a copy. This is dated way after the tax letter. Way after he was killed."

Lohman looked at the papers. "This probably won't do it with them. You would need someone to personally identify the person who brought in the ring. Well, at least the law requires proof beyond a reasonable doubt."

Sean was devastated by this. Lohman consoled him and sent him back to work.

THE DEAD ONE PROTRUDES

28 FIRE!

The next day was Thursday, August 24th. It was getting to the point where each day began with startling news about world events involving our magnificent and benevolent world leaders. Such news was a blessing for all troubled souls who had run out of anything else approaching interesting to occupy their attention. Without the new normal of everyday bombshells, they might have to go back to work and play computer games all day. Today they did not have to do this.

By this time the U.S. had paid its defense suppliers. Both the U.S. and Russia had gotten rid of the hacks in their defense systems. Missiles galore were at the ready. You got 'em, sooner or later you use 'em and that is what Russia did this morning. They launched missiles to the east and the west towards the U.S. What they did not realize though, was that North Korea and Iran had missiles of their own which were activated and blew the evil Russia's missiles to bits in the skies. The internet, the news givers, everyone, went crazy. It was the best morning show for some time.

Flinton had conferred with her military advisers and they advised her that they had not figured on North Korea and Iran having missiles either so in the midst of this war even bigger news emerged which was that Sillary and Vlad, The Putin, had declared peace and negotiations to combine the two countries as one were commencing.

Hardly anyone went to work. Amazon sold out. Peaceful serenity and Glory was spreading all over the world.

THE DEAD ONE PROTRUDES

Soon Hump appeared at a press conference with other representatives of OWEP and claimed credit for preventing world war and creating world peace. A little difficulty here was that the aide leading him to the podium stumbled and Hump fired him on camera, but what the Hell, that had been at the heart of the popularity of one of his TV shows.

Amidst all this big time news there was of course small time, everyday news. One of these tidbits was that both Hump and Flinton had filed for divorce, not from each other of course. When this came online Lohman got a call from Bungus LaRue, the Governmental Affairs partner. "Bumper," he said, "did you hear about the Flinton and Hump divorces?"

Lohman had been viewing the news on a TV in his conference room. He said, "Yes. Can we as a nation divorce them too?"

Bungus said, "Oh come on! They're good for business. We're lawyers. No problems, no business. Anyhow, I just want to inform you about some of the rumors going around D.C. because I don't know but what they might affect the Conflicts Committee investigation of the matters involving Hump."

Lohman sighed. "What now? Couldn't you just tell me they died?"

"Now Bumper," said LaRue, "when one of 'em goes away another just takes their place. Anyhow, they aren't going away. The rumors are that Hump is doing Sillary and Bill is doing Hump's wife."

"Christ!" said Lohman. "Is any of this going on in the Oval Office? Talk about conflicts! This would mean that the President and Vice President who live and work in the same place are suing each other for divorce. That's a new situation."

THE DEAD ONE PROTRUDES

LaRue said, "The only new part is the divorce proceeding. The activity isn't."

"Ok. Thanks for telling me," said Lohman. "I'll bring it up at the next meeting."

Lohman had to get back to work, but as he was getting up to turn off the TV smaller time news was being reported. Large fires of any size are much more unusual these days than in the past and one was being reported. What caught Lohman's attention was that it was at the Salerno Contractors and Salerno Funeral Home on the West Side. The fire had been put out, but they were showing some video scenes. Along with this the commentary stated that drugs had been found on the premises in an open Excelente Cemento bag. There were bags within it containing the drugs and they were buried in the cement. This had been discovered by the investigation started after the fire was put out to find out how it started. The cause had not yet been determined. The guy who owned the business could not be found for comment.

Later in the day McClurg came in to see Lohman about the fire. "Bumper," he said, "did you hear about the fire at that Salerno place?"

"Yes," said Lohman. "I saw it on TV this morning."

"And you heard about the drugs in the Excelente Cemento bag?"

"Yes," said Lohman. "That's sold by Whiteman, right?"

"Right," said McClurg. "That's what I want to talk to you about

"Drugs!" said Lohman. "I keep hearing about drugs when there is talk about Whiteman and what is happening with these bodies in their panels. Are they the only ones who sell that cement?"

THE DEAD ONE PROTRUDES

"Yes," said McClurg. "Eddie and Trulia have been contacted by the police and they are worried about what this might lead to. They said they told the police all they knew."

"Which is what?" asked Lohman.

"Nothing," said McClurg. "They never heard of drugs in the cement bags. Trulia is outraged. Eddie is kind of just amazed by it all. They want to know what to do."

Lohman asked, "Is that all they said?"

'That's about it," said McClurg. "Trulia keeps emphasizing that the cement bag the fire investigators found was open. Someone could have just stored the drugs in there. Now the police want to search the plant and the cement bags there."

"That could be a problem if there are more drugs there, couldn't it?" said Lohman.

"Except that there aren't any more Excelente bags there. They ran out. They already had ordered more before that Hump Deluxe plane went down and the shipment is on the way. There was one bag there and Trulia opened that and said there were no drugs in it. She put the cement in the cement bin with the regular cement for mixing with the aggregates to make the ready-mix stuff they truck to various construction sites." McClurg paused, then continued. "I asked her how often they run out of the Excelente cement. She said it has happened once or twice, but not often. So the police aren't going to find any Excelente bags to search."

THE DEAD ONE PROTRUDES

"So what if the Excelente bags do contain drugs? That might account for the high price and why they are locked up. What do you think?" asked Lohman.

"I hope not," said McClurg. "Anyway both Eddie and Trulia say they don't know anything about drugs. If something like that were going on at the plant it would be hard to hide it from them. So what do I do?"

"There I don't have any idea," said Lohman. "Maybe we could talk to Zenon about the publicity aspects."

"I called him," said McClurg. He's tied up today."

"In a dungeon?" asked Lohman.

"Nah," said McClurg. "He'd talk his way out if he was."

They bid each other goodbye and Lohman turned his attention to the events coming up the following weekend and what would occur on the Labor Day weekend. On the last Saturday before Labor Day the firm had its annual golf event. This was a tournament where the participants gave to charity in inverse proportion to their scores. The lower their score, the more they paid. The highest scorer paid $10 per stroke. Each stroke less resulted in a gift of $10 more for each stroke less. So if the high score was 90 strokes, that golfer paid $900. If the lowest score was 70 strokes, that golfer paid $21 per stroke or $14,700. This was an event of note amongst those who wanted the publicity and of course the firm got great publicity for sponsoring the charitable event. The participants were mainly clients of the firm and other persons of prominence and the firm lawyers who used the event to network with the clients and prospective victims. There were firm lawyers hosting every foursome and naturally they made sure they lost,

THE DEAD ONE PROTRUDES

both by having more strokes than the winner on the low end and less strokes than the winner on the other end. The firm paid their contributions.

The golf tournament came and went and everyone was very satisfied with the publicity. Lohman had trouble scoring higher than any of his clients, but to prevent this from happening firm members were prevented from winning at either end by adjustments to their scores. This was no secret. So what have we got here? Lawyers cheating? Right. And the persons affected did not view themselves as victims, but as beneficiaries. Lohman had fun at the outing and took the rest of the weekend off to recover.

Over the weekend between the golf tournament on September 1st and Labor Day on September 4th, the firm had to prepare for its next major event. This was one of the spectacular parties it often held for some made up reason. This party was to be held at the exclusive Squash Club in the middle of the Gold Coast. This was located a few blocks south of Lohman's home on the same street and not far away from the Nudie Mansion and the Ambassador Hotels which were on the next street over and down one block further south. The Club, needless to say, had a lot of squash courts.

Preparations for the party were proceeding well. Everything was in order so the powers that be gave everyone news of more disorder. When Hump and Flinton are the lead characters in the news show, there is always a new episode. Late on Saturday, September 2nd the new episode hit the news. It turns out that Will Flinton had been involved in an auto accident in the back woods of Tennessee. He had to be taken to a local hospital which was practically full because of some local epidemic of some kind. On top of that they did not really have

THE DEAD ONE PROTRUDES

facilities suitable for occupancy by a Vice President. No one had known Flinton was there, including his secret service detail which was not with him. He was alone, except for a woman in the car who claimed she was his temporary secretary. Because of the overcrowded state of the hospital, the only place they had to place Will Flinton was in the psycho ward, which is where he was put. He got the only private room. Of course this had an automatic lock on it, as did the ward, so there he was, locked up in the psycho ward.

When the White House got word of this Sillary Flinton decided to go there for the publicity value. She had come out of her usual weekend hiding and had been meeting with Hump so he went with her. They had been meeting at Camp David on some unspecified matter. They flew to the nearest airport on Air Force One and went to the hospital with the secret service crew and the presidential limousine and other equipment and personnel that went in accompanying planes. The hospital was in a southern backwater and they were not really familiar with Hump or Flinton because they were more interested in possum, hunting than what was going on elsewhere. At first they would not allow them in. They already had people in the psycho ward who claimed to be the President and Vice President. However, the secret service threatened to use force so the hospital administrators let them in to the psycho ward. Unfortunately the whole ward had automatic locks and, since the administrators were convinced they were nuts, the door was not unlocked. After all, when you already have people in the ward who claim to be the President and Vice President as well as occupants of other high positions around the world, what are a few more?

THE DEAD ONE PROTRUDES

The Presidential party of course had their own communication devices so soon the local National Guard was called out and sent to the hospital. Unfortunately the commander and the head of the hospital were good friends and the commander accepted the fact that they were dealing with a bunch of nuts and left. Naturally there was valid evidence upon which this conclusion was based.

At this stage the secret service got in touch with the head of the Joint Chiefs of Staff, but he would not act without a confirmed direct order from the President and he would not believe someone calling from a psycho ward. At this stage the Secret Service got in touch with the Speaker of the House to take action as the next person in line when both the President and Vice President are out of action.

In the end a kid, who was another resident of the psycho ward, escaped and let them all out. So all was well.

Not quite. Later in the day news came that a ship belonging to Wao Tang Nu, the shipping company that hauled Humpy Cement from the Humpy Cement plant in Mexico to Whiteman in Chicago, had disappeared. There were reports that a nearby ship had seen it explode and go under. The news included a statement that the ship was bringing a load of cement to the Whiteman operation in Chicago.

THE DEAD ONE PROTRUDES

29 FIRM PARTY AT THE SQUASH CLUB

By the time everyone had calmed down from this the firm party was starting. It was Monday, September, 4th. The party was to be held at the Squash Club, one of the most exclusive old line clubs in Chicago. Besides just being a party at which many of the leading members of life on earth would be present, the firm always had a theme for its parties. This time it was to honor and give awards to the leading charitable donors in Chicago in the past year. Rich people. Who else? St. Charles loved these parties. He could be with the outstanding nobles of the American upper class. Cohenstein loved them too. He could schmooze up the potential clients. All the people there loved each other too and loved to be there, although usually not only because the leading donors were honored. They had combinations of the St. Charles/Cohenstein reasons too.

Because of the prominent participants the press was there too. The participants loved the publicity too.

The party was held in all the public rooms of the Club with the stage set up in the Grand Ballroom which was where dinner was to be served. After all, who has balls these days? Other rooms held the cocktail and dance areas which were the socialization areas before the dinner and show. The guests started streaming in and Glory was present again!

The dais was set up with a podium and seats for the major firm leaders. St. Charles was to give the awards. Cohenstein did his work in the crowd, so he would just be introduced as a big shot and then just be on display. Lohman was to be the Master of Ceremonies so to speak. The only other person to be seated on the podium was the Mayor, Toby

THE DEAD ONE PROTRUDES

Rich. He liked to mingle with the other rich ones and he had clout so he was up there.

Lohman and Gloria arrived as people were still coming in and started the mingle. They soon came upon John Sweeney and his pop star client, Trisha DeLang. They were talking to St. Charles and his wife Faith. Alone. No one else was with them. Lohman cringed when he saw this. He could hear Sweeney saying, "I was washing the dishes when the phone rang so - ."

At this St. Charles exclaimed, "What! What did you say?"

Sweeney continued. "I was gonna say, I answered the phone."

"No. Before that," said St. Charles.

Lohman intervened. "He said he was washing the dishes."

"What!" exclaimed St. Charles. "No respectable lawyer does that! Not in this firm. It's demeaning."

Sweeney said, "OK. My bad Dude. I meant I was sitting around contemplating what a prestigious big deal I am and it was so awesome that I shit my panties and I was washing them out in the sink when the phone rang."

"What! What!" St. Charles almost shouted.

Lohman said, "He didn't take his meds today."

"Remove him from my presence," ordered St. Charles.

THE DEAD ONE PROTRUDES

That is exactly what Lohman did. He got Sweeney and Trisha over on the other side of the room and then on into another room. On the way he said to Sweeney, "Christ! He was a bit discommoded by that."

Sweeney said, "Nah Dude. He wasn't sitting on the toilet. How could he be knocked off?"

Lohman just blew air in exasperation. Gloria and Trisha giggled.

Trisha added, "He's gonna go to Hell anyway."

"No doll," said Sweeney, "he already went. He's just out on work release. Anyhow, Heaven or Hell, either place would have to quarantine him."

Just then Trisha spotted Rajah Philestina. "Talk about Heaven and Hell, look." She pointed at Rajah, an old guy with a walker. "There's that guy who hangs around with The Prophet and the Cardinal. He's got one of those religions too. I hear he claims to be one hundred and five and that his religious status with God got him there. Watch out, though. He got ahold of me once and gave me a lecture on how sinful my act is. He's such an asshole! How did he get to be one hundred and five? I think he's lying. I was going past that burger joint the other day that advertises, 'Home of the Whopper'. I thought for a moment that was his house. I think he's probably forty or something like that and he just smokes and drinks a lot. Probably does blow too. Maybe he's just losing it though."

"Losing it?" said Sweeney, "He never had it. I've had it in with him too."

"Yeah," said Trisha, "well maybe he got to be one hundred and five just because he's such an asshole. He's such a prick that he can't get into

THE DEAD ONE PROTRUDES

Heaven and I don't think the Devil would take him either so we're stuck with him. I think God must have been throwing out the trash when he was born."

Lohman refrained from confirming this and, since he noticed that Rajah was coming their way, led them on into another room where they split up and went on their separate ways meeting others. On the way Gloria said, "I don't think the highbrows are ready for them yet."

Lohman said, "But they are ready for the fact that Trisha brings in millions."

They went on about their socializing until dinner time and then took their seats for the meal. After dinner the show began so Lohman left Gloria at the table and went up to the podium to do his business. He introduced himself and St. Charles and Cohenstein, who were seated on the dais alongside a chair waiting for Lohman. Cohenstein made short remarks of his own and then made a special effort to be praise-worthingly glorious when introducing the Mayor, Toby Rich, who he invited to come to the podium and speak. The mayor did just that and as he got to the podium a group of his intimates stood and shouted "Heil Rich!"

St. Charles took this to mean that were praising the rich and he remarked, "Hear, hear."

After his blabber, in which he proclaimed that he had created every job in Chicago, Rich went back to his own seat on the dais. Lohman then turned the podium over to St. Charles to present the awards. Naturally he needed prompting so the podium contained a little computer screen into which had been fed the script. The firm's IT guy, Henner

THE DEAD ONE PROTRUDES

Pigman, was behind the podium to feed it. In case of trouble, he would be nearby to consult with Lohman.

Everything was going well when, all of a sudden, all the doors busted open and a police SWAT team with automatic rifles out busted in, followed by Bongwad and Sergeant Gilbert and a crew from the Federal ATF (Alcohol, Tobacco and Firearms), the drug guys. The SWAT team went to the outskirts of the room and Bongwad and Gilbert looked around until they saw Sean Featherbottom seated at one of the tables.

Gilbert went over and grabbed him while Bongwad went up to the podium. He went to the podium, pushed St. Charles aside and took over the microphone. "Nobody move! Stay where you are! We're just here to take that Featherbottom kid. He's under arrest and he's going in. He murdered Avon Whiteman. Just relax and stay where you are and there will be no trouble."

Lohman wasn't going to put up with this. Had he left it to Bongwad and Gilbert, Featherbottom would have been long gone. He got up and approached the podium and said, "Hold on. He didn't do it. Let me tell you who did and what Hump and Flinton had to do with it."

At this Toby Rich, who was owed money by Hump, stood up and said to Bongwad, "Just hold on officer. Let's hear what Lohman has to say."

Bongwad looked at him as if he wasn't going to hold off and Rich said, "Remember, I'm your boss. Hold it."

Bongwad gave him another dissatisfied look, but looked out at the audience and over to Gilbert who had grabbed Sean and had him standing up and handcuffed and said, "OK, wait."

THE DEAD ONE PROTRUDES

There was silence in the room. As when the crowd at the symphony finally realizes that the concert is going to begin and the conductor will not come out until they are quiet. Lohman came to the podium and said, "This matter has involved our firm in a variety of ways. First, the person killed was a client of ours and a friend of mine. Secondly, Avon and three other people were in concrete panels sold and delivered by Avon's company Whiteman Materials, another of our clients. And thirdly, the police have been making it clear that they were after Sean Featherbottom, one of our lawyers. Because of this and some curious matters that have come to light I have been going over what happened repeatedly to figure out what was happening here. I was going to contact the police to go over these matters so I am glad they are here. Let me tell you what I have found."

As Lohman paused to collect his thoughts there was total silence in the room. Lohman pulled a little note book out of his coat pocket and put it down on the podium. Total silence. He got a pen out of another pocket and brought it down to the podium like the conductor making his first move of the baton. He began.

"Whiteman Materials makes concrete for construction projects and sells cement and materials for use with cement to contractors, mostly in bags. Most of the concrete is made from cement and other materials like what we would call gravel or crushed stone. They call that aggregate. They are put together at a Whiteman plant and mixed with water and then put in trucks and delivered to the construction sites where they are poured into forms and left to set and cure and become hard. The material is usually poured over steel bars set in the forms. This steel is called rebar and strengthens the concrete. Whiteman also sells precast or panel concrete. These are panels or other formats of

THE DEAD ONE PROTRUDES

concrete which are poured at the Whiteman plant and set and hardened there and then the finished panels are delivered to a construction site. There is also a company that uses the Whiteman panel concrete area to make panels with art moldings on them. This amounts to decoration on the panel instead of the flat surface. This is a separate company and Whiteman does not own it. However, Whiteman sells the art panels and delivers them."

Lohman gave a look at his notebook and continued. "The bagged cement is sold to smaller contractors for smaller jobs. There are two types. There is the regular grade of cement in bags and then there is a special high grade cement that is sold in bags and for a much higher price. That is branded as Excelente Cemento. It is kept in a locked area of the plant, as opposed to the other bags which are in the open area. All the cement Whiteman sells or uses comes from Humpy Cement on the East Coast of Mexico near Cancun. It is owned by Ronald Hump. The cement is shipped over the Atlantic Ocean to the St. Lawrence Seaway. The Seaway starts in Eastern Canada and comes down the St. Lawrence river into Lake Ontario and gives access to the Great Lakes from the Ocean. The ships come down to the Calumet River which enters the Lake around 95th Street and then down the River to the main Whiteman plant. Whiteman has other plants, but all the cement goes there to begin with."

Lohman paused and looked around to collect his thoughts. "The same shipping company brings in all the cement, both the bulk cement and the bags. Ownership of the shipping company is unclear, but both the Hump and Flinton foundations have interests in it and it also gives large donations to those foundations. Congress found these things out. This in itself is a curious thing, which would make anyone wonder what is

THE DEAD ONE PROTRUDES

going on with that arrangement. The bulk cement goes to other plants after it has been delivered to the Calumet plant, but the Excelente bagged cement is sold only at the Calumet plant."

Lohman then looked at this notebook again. "The art panel company is called Chicago Art Panel Company. It uses the panel company facilities when they are not being used, usually at night. The manager of the company says he does not know who owns it. Its owner so far as we can determine is one of those trust companies in the Caribbean where you can't find out who the beneficial owner of the trust is. We have found this out when we have been looking into the matter. The Whitemans don't know either. One thing we did find was that the manager of the company takes orders from a lawyer who got the company registered in Illinois who says he is the agent for the owner."

Lohman paused again to decide what to go into next. "Now here we start with Sean Featherbottom. He used to work at Whiteman at the Calumet plant. This was while he was in school which was some time before Avon disappeared. He was fired. This was after he complained that locking up the Excelente bags made it difficult to deal with them. Now I don't know if complained is the right word. It sounds to me from what I have heard that he just mentioned the problem. Soon after that he was fired and told it was because he was gay. He was fired by Eddie Whiteman, son of Avon, who handled the day to day physical aspects of the business and the plant. An interesting thing is that he was told by Eddie a short while before that that he was doing a good job. In this regard, let me tell you something else about Sean and the company. Lately, after Avon's body was found, at Hump Tower as you recall, our firm has had occasion to review the financial statements of the company in connection with some matters that required due diligence,

THE DEAD ONE PROTRUDES

which is a legal term for what those people involved in certain business matters involving a company do to see that the financials and other information given about the company to others are accurate and do not contain any misrepresentations. Sean was involved in this. He is a CPA as well as a lawyer and he also had experience working at the company, although he was just a general plant employee then. He has stated that he thinks the sales listed in the financial statements far exceed the physical capacity of the Whiteman plants. This is a conclusion based on the financial statements that a variety of other companies and individuals have and the actual plant facilities so it is not secret information for anyone who cares to look into it. By the way, the company operates in other cities, but the locations in other cities are subsidiaries and they all have separate financial statements as well as the overall consolidated statement and what Sean was saying just applies to the Chicago operation."

Lohman went on, "Anyhow, Avon bought all his cement from Humpy and his body was found in a panel delivered by his own company to Hump Tower. That is a little curious. Humpy Cement operates in the U.S. through an agent company here in the Chicago area run by Jared Bannon. The agent company is Humpy Materials. This was set up in Illinois by the same law firm that worked on the art panel company. This law firm also set up a construction company in Illinois for Hump who wants to be the concrete contractor for the walled off safe community Flinton wants to build here."

Then Lohman talked about control. "So who is in charge of this Whiteman Company that delivers concrete panels with bodies in them? While he was around Avon was. He owned the entire interest. His son Eddie handled the day to day business, but not the finances,

THE DEAD ONE PROTRUDES

and he took orders from Avon. When Avon disappeared someone had to be put in charge and his wife, Trulia, was appointed by the court to be in charge of Avon's affairs until he showed up or until a seven year period expired, after which he would be presumed dead. That seven year period was cut short earlier this year when it was discovered that he was dead. Now, according to the way Avon set up his estate plan, Eddie is in control. Trulia continues to be active in the business as she always was, both before and after Avon disappeared."

"Now," said Lohman, "what went on when discussing an estate plan with a client would ordinarily be privileged and I couldn't tell you about it, but this had been disclosed by Avon to others. He was going to change his estate plan to give more to Trulia, but shortly before he died he changed his mind. Both Eddie and Trulia knew this."

"Contractors in various businesses have minority requirements that have to be met for them to get the contracts. Construction is one of these areas because so much business comes from jobs paid for, at least in part, by government money or otherwise subject to government control." Lohman sensed that he could not control himself when he added, "Soon, when the robots take over, one of the minorities will be humans. But so far it is only certain human minorities that are required to get some of the business from the humans who control the business. Whiteman had a good supply of the minority firms. Avon, of course was black. So that was the majority here. However, sometimes white was needed so his wife, Trulia, who was white, had her own subcontractor. Another subcontractor was owned by their butler, Snively Blackman, who was also white. Another subcontractor was owned by their chef and maid, a married couple who were Hispanic. Then there was a firm named Whiteman

THE DEAD ONE PROTRUDES

Consulting. Its ownership was unknown. Our firm did not set it up. What it was used for was unclear, but Blackman evidently had said it was to be used for whatever minority was needed at the time. Presumably he got this from Avon. And as to what a butler was doing in the business matters I will touch on later."

Lohman looked around the room and then said, "So this is the general background of Avon's affairs. Now let's go through what happened that led up to the police coming in here tonight. To begin with there is this Mexican drug lord who popped out of the panel in the Pedway. He had been arrested in Mexico and was in prison. In early September 2014 he escaped and was never heard from again until his body was found here this year. Then, after the drug lord disappeared, on September 12th of that year Avon disappeared. That was a Friday. The next Monday a panel containing his body was delivered to Hump Tower here in Chicago. The panel was made by the Chicago Art Panel Company in the Whiteman panel company's space that Friday night. The art panel outfit was usually staffed by Streets & San workers who also worked at the Streets & San yard and plant next to the panel company. They usually came in through a door in the panel company building that led out to the Streets & San property. The door is usually kept locked and there is no record of who the workers were."

"So," said Lohman, "Avon was poured into the panel that Friday night. He disappeared from his home, right on this block, but the panel was poured way down at the plant. The panels take some time to dry out and start curing before they can be delivered."

Lohman looked at his notes again for a while and then looked up and continued. "Now, Avon disappeared from his home. He, as I told you, lived over there in the Nudie Mansion on State Street on this block and

THE DEAD ONE PROTRUDES

he was seen there by several people before he disappeared. First his son Eddie was there talking to him. This was around 4pm. He was there until about 4:30 when he left. As he left Sean was coming in to see Avon and Eddie let him in. Sean had been sent there by one of our partners to deliver papers to Avon and explain them. I don't think that lawyer, our Shannon McClurg, knew that Sean had been fired by Whiteman. Anyway, Eddie left. As he let Sean in, he remembered him and greeted him and welcomed him. Later we found out from Eddie that he did tell Sean he was fired because he was gay, but that Avon had told him to do that and give that reason after he found out that Sean had said locking up the Excelente bags made it difficult to serve the customers. He acknowledges he had told Sean he was doing a good job just before that."

Lohman paused again. "Here, I might mention something that did not happen that night. Avon had a distinctive ring which he often played with and took off and put on. Any conversation with him involved watching him play with that thing. Eddie says Avon had it on that night. After Avon disappeared Eddie and Trulia were in a conference with some of our lawyers, including Sean, and they saw Avon's ring on Sean. In other words Avon had a ring that night and after he disappeared, Sean had that ring. So Avon ran the company that fired Sean and Avon disappeared and was killed and Sean has his ring. Open and shut according to the police. Tell the penitentiary to get ready for another murderer. Tell them he is a lawyer so they better strap his mouth shut before he foments riots amongst the other prisoners." At this everyone turned and looked over at the table where Sean was being restrained by Gilbert. Sean had an open mouthed look of desperateness on his face.

THE DEAD ONE PROTRUDES

"But all is not so clear," continued Lohman. "He kills Avon and openly wears his ring in front of the family? And this was after Avon's body was found. I might also mention one thing that is fairly clear. Avon did not kill himself and pour himself into concrete. He could have killed himself with the drug that was in him, but for sure he did not do the pour."

Lohman went on. "So what happened next? Avon's wife, Trulia, had been at home and Avon was there when she left. She was going to the plant and got there around 4 pm. She left around 4:15 pm. She was then going to meet Avon at home later, but not until a good time later, she says. In the meantime she says she went to a movie at a mall down there. About when she checked out a Whiteman Panel Company van left the plant. The driver was identified at checkout. It is the same guy who was found in the Pedway panel with the Mexican drug lord."

"So Trulia is at the plant and leaves. Then Eddie leaves Avon around 4:30 that afternoon, just as Sean is coming in with the papers. He lets Sean in as he is leaving. Eddie says he then went to an event downtown with his wife. When Sean came in no one was around. Remember, Avon was not the one who let him in. Sean came in and he looked around and wound up in Avon's office off the reception area by himself until Avon showed up. He delivered the papers to Avon, who apparently did not recognize him, and left to deliver papers to another client. Then he went home and changed for an affair at the Artists' Club and was seen there later. He says he doesn't remember if Avon had the ring on that night. From what he has said about the meeting and his interest in things like art, china, crystal and jewelry, I think he was very interested in the drink container on the chest behind Avon. Sean says Avon was not using it or drinking when he was there. Anyway, Avon

THE DEAD ONE PROTRUDES

was very attached to that ring and Sean would have had to resort to magic to get it off him while he was still alive. And he was alive when Sean left because a friend of Avon's came in later and chatted with him."

"After this the manager of the art panel company left the plant. Around 5. Then after that the next thing involving these people was the butler, Snively Blackman, arriving at a show in the River North area. The show went on from 6 to 8 pm and he got there in his car around 5:30 pm. The theater had its own parking lot and he left the car there with an attendant. The attendant remembers him because he received a large tip. By the way, Blackman also left a large tip after the show when he picked up the car. The attendant says he was with a tall blonde. A white woman."

Lohman paused to look at his notes again and continued. "About the same time Blackman got to the show parking lot a friend of Avon's came in to see him. The friend is Cass Tyreservski. He says a woman called him and said Avon wanted to see him. Who this woman was we don't know, but he said she seemed to be using what he called a funny voice. There was not any woman there. Avon said he was alone. They didn't talk about the call and the two just had a friendly talk. Avon usually had a drink as part of his evening routine and as Cass was leaving he had poured himself a drink from the container he had on the cabinet behind his desk. I've been there around the same time myself. He liked to have a drink around then and kept it in a crystal decanter on his desk. It was kind of fancy. Anyway, Avon offered Cass a drink, but he didn't want any and left. While Cass was there he did not notice if Avon had his ring on or around him. He left about 6. His car had been in the driveway between Cass's car and the street. As he was leaving he

THE DEAD ONE PROTRUDES

saw a Whiteman Panel van going north on State Street and slowing and starting to turn towards the driveway, but it straightened out and went on North. Remember that a van left the plant earlier around 4:15 pm. Those of you who have driven between that area and here can tell you it takes about an hour at that time of day, unless there is some unusual blockage of traffic. So if this was the same van it was doing something more than driving straight to the Nudie Mansion. All this was right over there on this same block, but over on State." Lohman then pointed in the direction of the Nudie Mansion. "It's the Nudie Mansion, for those of you who don't know exactly which house I am referring to. And that van, or at least a Whiteman van, was seen about that time by the doorman at the Ambassador West Hotel over there. The Hotel is just a few buildings south of the Mansion. south of the mansion. He saw the van coming south on State and it pulled into the Hotel's driveway and turned around and went north on the street."

"So," said Lohman, "Cass was the last person we know of who saw Avon alive. And Avon was alive when he left. Whether or not Avon had his ring at that time, we don't know. Avon was about to have a drink when Cass left. Whether or not all this happened as I am telling you, of course depends on the truth of what the various people involved have been telling us and the police so far."

"The next thing we have an indication of is that the Whiteman van that left the plant earlier checked back in to the plant around – ", here Lohman looked at his notes, "around 8:30 pm and it had the same driver. The one who was found in the Pedway panel. No other occupants were noted in the check in records. It went to the panel company loading dock which is out of sight of the check in station and the various security officers who were there. There was an art panel

THE DEAD ONE PROTRUDES

pour going on that night and it was being done by a crew from Streets & San who got in through the back door between the Whiteman property and the city property. It was usually kept locked and someone has to let the people in when they come through there. There isn't any check in for that door apparently. Anyway, it is not known exactly who was there and the security people do not have a view of that side of the plant. The people from Streets & San who did the art pours were not on the art panel company payroll. They were on the payroll of a temp service company which has gone out of business so that's probably why there are no records of who they were."

"The driver did not checkout that night or on Saturday before work hours and no one saw him after that. His car, which had been in the Whiteman lot that night, was found several weeks later on the West Side near a Salerno Contractor yard. Salerno is a small contractor who buys the expensive Excelente cement from Whiteman. Salerno also operated a funeral home next to its contractor yard."

"Then," said Lohman, "the show Blackman drove to ended around 8 pm. Blackman picked up his car around 8:30, and later, around 10, Trulia Whiteman came home. Their chef and maid came home at the same time and they all confirm each other's arrival times. The house was locked and Avon was gone. His car was still there. Blackman got there later." Lohman glanced at his notes again and turned another page and the said, "The other thing I noted is that Sean Featherbottom got home around midnight."

"So, after that –," Lohman went through his notes again, "after that we have Saturday. Trulia says she found an unopened letter from our firm on Avon's desk. The maid says she found the drink container from Avon's office emptied out in the pantry sink and washed out. She is not

THE DEAD ONE PROTRUDES

sure of the date, but she thinks that happened on that day. She did not put it there and she is the one who usually handled it. She would make sure it was filled each day and it was in the office when she did this. Not much of note happened after that until Monday when the panel containing Avon was delivered to the Hump Tower. So – ," Lohman looked around the room, "Hump again. As we go through all these facts we find Hump here and Hump there and Flinton too. That Hump Tower panel was delivered on September 15th of that year, 2014. Then on Friday, September 19th Hump Air delivered a body to O'Hare airport here. It was identified on the death certificate as a Deacon of the D'Gregor Temple who was working for the Temple in Mexico. He had apparently died here and the body was shipped back here for burial because he had grown up here. Other people working for the Temple in Mexico had given the Mexican authorities the information for the death certificate. A death certificate and compliance with certain sanitary laws is all that is required to get a dead body into this country. You don't need a passport or any other elaborate identification. No other bodies came into O'Hare or Midway or any other airport around here during that period. One could have come in by land and we can't rule that out, but you will see why the other facts make that not too relevant. The body was picked up in a Salerno Funeral Home hearse which took the body to the funeral home on the West Side next to Salerno Contractors. A few days later the body was taken to the D'Gregor Temple for a closed coffin service and burial. The service was – let's see," Lohman turned a page in his notes, "it was on September 20th. Then the body was driven to the cemetery by Salerno. A Whiteman van was at the cemetery and D'Gregor was there. He was driven there by Trulia Whiteman, but he left in the Salerno hearse because she was going elsewhere. They were going to take him back to

THE DEAD ONE PROTRUDES

the Temple. A gas station near the Temple issued a gas receipt to Salerno soon after the funeral."

"Now, the Pedway panel with the Mexican drug lord and the Whiteman driver was delivered to the Pedway on September 22nd. Both were shot, but with different guns. The gun that shot the driver was found in the panel with him. Remember, that gun was not the one that shot the drug lord. Then on, let me see, - " Lohman looked at his notes, "on October 31st the panel containing D'Gregor was delivered to the Riverwalk. He had been shot by the same gun that shot the driver in the Pedway panel, but not the drug lord. Something else to note was that both the driver in the Pedway and D'Gregor had broken thumbs in each hand. Another thing to note here is that after all this started being investigated by the police they exhumed the grave of the Mexican Deacon and found that the coffin was empty."

Lohman then looked around and said that what he had related was substantially what happened up to earlier this year when Avon's body popped out of Hump Tower and the other bodies were exposed later. "I'm not surprised at Avon's body popping out. He was a big guy, maybe too big for the panel. He was over three hundred pounds. I don't know about D'Gregor and the drug lord, but the van driver was supposed to be smaller. A lot smaller. I remember Eddie telling me that in one of our meetings. And just the other day we found out that a Hump Air plane flying from Bogota in Columbia to Cancun in Mexico, which is near the Humpy Cement plant there, crashed and was full of drugs. Then there was a fire at the Salerno Contractor plant and they found an open Excelente bag there that had smaller bags of drugs in it. The authorities then wanted to checkout the Excelente bags at the Whiteman plant, but they said they had run out, except for one bag

THE DEAD ONE PROTRUDES

which Trulia said she checked on and found nothing in. She says she put the cement in with their bulk supplies. In the meantime Whiteman had new supplies on order and they were supposedly out at sea in a ship belonging to the shipping company that usually brought them in. After all this news came out, the ship blew up out in the Atlantic and no trace of it has been found. In the meantime I hear Salerno can't be found."

At this stage Rich said loud enough for everyone to hear him, "So what does all this have to do with Hump and Flinton?"

Cohenstein added, "Yeah, let's get to the good stuff."

Lohman turned and looked at them and then turned his view back to the crowd "Drugs. It's pretty clear that Whiteman was distributing drugs to dealers here and that the drugs were in the Excelente bags and that the source of the drugs was Humpy Cement which Hump owns and that the drugs came here by ships owned by a company that both the Hump and Flinton foundations have interests in. They personally may be the majority owners, but who has that interest is not known. Their foundations have similar interests in Progressive Pharma which is a drug company making drugs for medical use. Among these drugs happen to be things like fentanyl, which killed Avon, and methadone and amphetamines. D'Gregor Temple owned a national string of drug abuse treatment centers and they are a major user of these drugs to help with withdrawal and maintenance therapy. I also suspect that they have a customer list, so to speak, which includes many addicts still using drugs who would make a good market for the illegal drugs. There is no hint of that, though, in the facts we know of. So there you know what Hump and Flinton have to do with it. And you should also know that it is rumored around Washington that Hump

THE DEAD ONE PROTRUDES

acted crazy and lost to Flinton on purpose and that they are old friends. In fact Congress found that their foundations had made major gifts to each other's foundations."

"There is also the fact that the Whiteman company appears to be taking in a lot more money that its production capacity would produce products for and it has a lot of cash receipts. Drugs are sold for cash."

"Then," added Lohman, "there is this D'Gregor Temple with its drug treatment business. Both Avon and Trulia and also Blackman were Deacons of that organization. Since D'Gregor and Avon disappeared those familiar with the Temple say that Trulia and Blackman seem to be running it. In addition it has many politicians on its payroll which is a convenient way of bribing them. You can't ordinarily pay a politician straight out with no one asking why. The Temple is a church and churches don't have to file the same tax returns as other not for profit organizations so the payroll payments are not going to become public to begin with. Also, when a politician converts campaign funds to personal use there are laws which are violated. I know that here in Illinois they say this is OK so long as you declare it as income and pay tax on it, but nationally that doesn't go. So instead of taking outright bribes or campaign contributions they can be on a payroll somewhere which you fund."

"Finally," said Lohman, "there is something else you should know about drugs here. Avon and D'Gregor were going to start their own drug company to supply the Temple drug addiction centers. Then, after Avon was found to be dead, Trulia wanted to buy the Excelente bagged cement business from the Whiteman company which she no longer controlled. She had control as administrator, but only while Avon was missing. And one other thing. Salerno was known to be a dealer. Other

THE DEAD ONE PROTRUDES

people who were known to be dealers were seen at the plant buying Excelente bagged cement. Salerno could have got the drugs elsewhere and hid them in the Excelente bag but the buying of Excelente bags by known dealers suggests otherwise. Also remember that Sean Featherbottom was fired after he complained or mentioned, if you will, that locking up the bags made it difficult to serve the customers."

"Now some Chicago and gang history," said Lohman. "Broken thumbs in each hand were a mark of a Syndicate kill, meant to give a message. If you know about crime in Chicago through the years you remember that organized crime here was run by Al Capone at one time. The organization he headed was eventually called the Syndicate or the Outfit. In other cities it was called the Mafia, but not here. It made money off prostitution and gambling and, starting with Prohibition, off alcohol. After Prohibition ended it still sold alcohol through its own companies, but it was not any good at legitimate businesses and sold the stuff mainly with threats of violence directed at the bar owners to get them to buy it. They still continued to operate fairly open gambling and prostitution operations, but in time the corruption necessary to get away with this was no longer accepted and the population was getting, let's say, able to get sex without paying for it. So what did they do? They concentrated on legal gambling, mainly through Las Vegas and other such places and they had a way, called the skim, of avoiding the taxes. Anyhow, gambling eventually became legal in more and more forms and in more and more places and that ruined their business. They had never gone into drugs and that did them in. It's the big illegal business now. The drug business is now supposedly in the hands of numerous street gangs who sell the drugs supplied by the Mexican and other drug people. So the Syndicate has ceased to exist? Maybe and maybe not. Those who are close to the drug world say the

THE DEAD ONE PROTRUDES

business is run by a big guy. It is rumored that someone with the nickname of Fat Tuna is in charge. So it could be that the Syndicate still is in business because it got into the drug business and the way it did so was not to be the retail sellers, but to be the suppliers. In effect the wholesalers. And who is Fat Tuna? There is a rumor that it is the Bannon fellow who is the agent for Humpy Cement here in the U.S. At least some one has said they heard him referred to that way."

Lohman thought more about this and then said, "All this might explain why the Mexican drug lord was killed and found here. He was a competing supplier."

Rich then spoke up again. "Ok on the drugs, but who killed those people?"

Then Bongwad spoke up. "Yes, stop the blabber. You said you were going to tell us who did it. You're just trying to confuse things. Featherbottom did it. So let's go." He motioned to Gilbert who was still holding onto Sean.

"No!" said Lohman. "All the blabber is just informing you and everyone here of what happened so we can put two and two together, or in this case, fifty eight and ninety three. It's complicated. There is no smoking gun that will reveal the guilty ones. But when all the facts are reviewed, they emerge." Lohman hoped that the crowd would not realize that he was reviewing the facts as he spoke and still did not know who did it. In other words, he was figuring it out in front of them.

Rich added, "Hold it officer. We don't want another one of those ten million dollar law suits for false arrest. That kid doesn't look like he's worth that much, but you never can tell with these lawyers."

THE DEAD ONE PROTRUDES

Lohman said, "Look at who had access to Avon. That we know of that Friday when he disappeared, only a few people from the afternoon on. First, someone we do not know of could have been at his house and put the fentanyl in his drink container and that includes Trulia, Blackman and the chef and maid and anyone else who could have been there earlier that day. And it does look like he got it in the drink, unless he committed suicide, in which case how did his body get to the plant? Eddie was there, his son. Then Sean was there. Then Cass saw him. All say he was alive. Then we do not have any record of anyone there until about ten when Trulia and the chef and maid got home. Blackman came home later. The only one we know to have been around the drink container alone, without Avon there, was Sean when he first came in. Eddie had let him in so Avon did not let him in. He was elsewhere and Sean was in the office with the drink container alone for a while."

At this time Lohman looked over at Shannon McClurg, the primary Whiteman Material lawyer. "Shannon over there is the lawyer who sent Sean there. Shannon, what time did you send Sean there? Do you remember?"

"McClurg stood up and said, "I went over that when we started finding out about all this. It was late that afternoon. I had been hurrying to get the papers done. Sean knew what they were about so I got him and sent him and told him to get them over there right away. He had been working on the matter for a while, but I never heard that he had worked for Whiteman before or that he had been fired. Maybe he didn't want his boss to know that he had been fired by the client. I don't know. He was pretty new at the firm."

"So," Lohman said, "on short notice Sean is told to go over there. Now if he wanted to kill the guy why hadn't he done it before? He had three

THE DEAD ONE PROTRUDES

years or more. Remember again that Avon was not the one who fired him. Eddie did and he didn't tell Sean it was on Avon's orders or that Avon told him what reason to give. And, since he didn't know he was going there, how did he get the drug? Did he stop on the way to buy some? Maybe. But how did he know he could get it into Avon? He hadn't been there before and he wouldn't know about the drink container. And then he wound up with Avon's ring. How could he have got that? The idea is that he took it off Avon when he killed him. I can tell you he collects things like that. But he says he bought it from a resale shop at the D'Gregor Temple and he has a receipt from them saying he bought a ring there after Avon disappeared. It doesn't describe the particular ring, Just a ring. Before that the resale shop gave a donation letter to Avon showing a contribution date after his death which did describe the ring accurately. Now that donation letter was found in Avon's income tax file here in the firm. However, a decedent's final tax return cannot deduct a donation supposedly made by the decedent after death. But then, it was not then known that Avon had died. So how did it get into the tax file? The police point out that Sean had access to our files."

"What does this show?" asked Lohman. "Avon was not around to make the donation. But a donation can be made by someone through an agent. So the donation letter would show that Avon was still alive after the day on which he disappeared. The killer may have done this to show that Avon was still alive then. Clever. And since the resale shop did not pay for the ring, the killer was not trying to get money out of it. It is the date that is the thing. The resale shop has no record of who actually brought the ring in. The police claim it was Sean and that he was just trying to cover his tracks as to the killing and keeping the ring which he wanted. Fine. So why did he wear it

THE DEAD ONE PROTRUDES

openly here in a conference in the firm with Trulia and Eddie, which is where it was discovered that he had the ring?

"There is a thing the law requires," continued Lohman. That is proof beyond a reasonable doubt. These facts do not prove beyond a reasonable doubt that Sean brought the ring in or that he brought fentanyl with him when he went to see Avon or at any other time. After leaving Avon he went to a conference with another client which is confirmed and then says he went home and changed and went to a party, which is confirmed. He would have trouble coming back to see Avon after Cass left and before getting to the party in the time available. Remember that Avon or his body got to the plant that night. I will explain how that probably occurred around eight thirty which doesn't leave much time for Sean to come back and kill Avon, especially since it takes time to get from the Nudie Mansion to the plant. And how did Sean get Avon or his body to the plant? There is no record of his being there. And why would he come back? Only to plant the fentanyl if he had not done it before. Would Avon let him be alone to do that? Or Sean could have come back to wash out the drink container and leave it in the sink? But why? Remember it was in the office when he left earlier because Cass saw it there. So to hide the form of the killing he could come back and wash out the container. If Sean was not known to be the killer, why would he come back to hide the form of murder? That would just give anyone an additional chance to place him there? And how would he know that no one else would be there? Furthermore, why would Sean kill the van driver and D'Gregor? And when and how? Of course he could just have killed Avon and not them, but that is unlikely as I have explained."

THE DEAD ONE PROTRUDES

At this Cohenstein rose and said out towards the floor to Sean, "Take it easy Fluffbottom. You're in the clear." Fluffbottom was his nickname for Sean because, as he once explained, he was sure Sean got his bottom feathers fluffed a lot.

Lohman had a little time to think while this was going on. He then continued. "Someone could have come in there and given the drug to Avon. But how? If Avon was in their presence he would see it. They could have forcibly administered it, but who was there who was big enough to do it? And who was there at all? On the other hand, if they knew Avon and knew his habits they knew he had an evening drink and they could have put the drug in his drink container earlier in the day when Avon was not watching them. The fact that the container was left in the sink washed out, which was not the usual way it was handled, indicates that this, the container, was the way the drug was administered. Of course the date this happened is not absolutely attested to by the maid, but she thinks the container was found in the sink the day after he disappeared. If putting the drug in the container was the way the drug was administered then someone could have put the drug there before hand, knowing that Avon would take it later. He didn't die the day before so it was probably done sometime after his drink time then and before Eddie was there. Unless Eddie or Cass or Sean did it while they were there on Friday. Eddie and Cass were always in Avon's presence while they were there, at least according to them, so that rules them out, unless they had come in before on that day. Whether or not they did, we don't know. Sean, on the other hand was alone with the drink container, but once again, he does not seem likely to have known in advance that the opportunity would be available. At least not long enough in advance to plan the murder and get the drug. And he is not an addict. I can tell you that and I doubt he

THE DEAD ONE PROTRUDES

would know where to get the drug. And how, once again, how would he know he would be alone with the opportunity to plant it in with the booze?"

"Of course, Avon could have committed suicide, but how did he get his dead body down to the plant and how did he pour himself in concrete? He could have arranged for someone to do this for him, for instance the van driver, but it would take more than one person to move his dead body around. And why would he want his body disposed of that way?

"So this narrows the field down to someone who put the drug in the container before Eddie got there, knowing that Avon would soon take it. This means we look for someone with access to the container. There is no indication that Eddie or Cass was there earlier in the day. So who had access? The place was not open to strangers to get in and there is no indication of a break in. No one suggests that while they were there some person who was not a regular was there. This leaves Trulia, Blackman and the chef and maid. They had all been there earlier in the day. There is no indication of any other people there, such as people coming in to see him. It is highly probable that Avon, even if he was there all day, was not in his office all the time. I do not know if he was there all the time, but I suspect the police have found out where he was that day. At any rate he could not have got the drug in him elsewhere because it kills quickly. He would have died where he took it. By the way, I knew Avon personally as a friend. I can tell you he was not an alcoholic or drug addict and no one thinks or claims that he was."

Lohman then sighed and took another look at his notes. He was also wondering when people would start yelling at him to shut up or get to

THE DEAD ONE PROTRUDES

the point. However, the audience was really interested. This was a way better show than they had signed up for. Even better than the daily Hump and Flinton show. It was as good as the old radio and TV mysteries, even as good as the Shadow – "Who knows what evil lurks in the hearts of men? The Shadow does." With relief, though, Lohman realized that he was getting to the point where he could actually point to the likely suspects.

He went on. "So who are we talking about? We know who had access and opportunity and knew Avon's habit of an evening drink. What about their possible motives? What about their alibis?"

"The chef and maid had been out at a family event and that was confirmed. They got nothing out of Avon's death. They had a minority contractor, but it wasn't netting much, either before or after Avon disappeared. And how did they get the body to the plant? They could have help, but from whom? Were they in league with the driver? The driver couldn't move the body alone so were they there to help? No, their alibi is confirmed."

"Cass is ruled out as I have said because of lack of opportunity to put the drug in the drink, unless he is lying about what happened while he was there. Or unless he came back later. But there are the same questions about how he got the body to the plant. His alibi confirms that he did not come back later and he would have the same problem moving the body as anyone else. But most importantly, what possible motive did he have? He got nothing out of the death and he was a friend. There is no indication he had developed some sort of dispute with Avon. And Avon had to let him in."

THE DEAD ONE PROTRUDES

"Let's also consider who could get in if Avon was dead and the place kept locked? Another resident who had a key. The chef and maid are ruled out. That leaves Trulia and Blackman. But they have alibis. And neither one checked into the plant that night or through the morning hours until the checkout stopped at 8 am. 8 am through 4 pm were the working hours and people were not checked in or out. However, the employees had to check in before their shift so there was a separate check in gate for that where they could get admitted before the shift started. Trulia or Blackman could have come in after 8 am without the check in, but by then the concrete pour had been done."

"So where were they? Remember, we are not talking now about when the drug was put in the booze. They had access to that, along with others. We are talking about how and when the body got to the plant. And did they stand to get anything if Avon died? Or was Avon doing anything they did not want done? Let's look at Blackman. First there are the rumors that he and Trulia were romantically involved. Eddie says Avon suspected this, but also that he was always suspecting her of involvement with other men. Then Blackman is the one who has connections with all the others we have talked about. First he is seen at Bannon's house. Bannon is the agent for Humpy Cement. Drugs are coming from Humpy Cement to Whiteman Materials. There is a rumor the drug trade is headed here by a big guy and Bannon apparently has a nickname of Fat Tuna. Blackman is always telling Avon what to do about business matters in the presence of others. He is seen at the plant and nearby with Streets & San workers. The D'Gregor Temple is running a substance abuse recovery business which uses drugs and gets them from a drug company in which Hump and Flinton have interests. And the illegal drugs coming here are shipped in ships belonging to a company in which both Hump and Flinton have

THE DEAD ONE PROTRUDES

interests. And Trulia and Blackman are Deacons of the Temple, as was Avon, and are rumored to be in control of it now. This all smacks of either Bannon or Blackman being the big guy in the drug trade here. And remember that Blackman was getting a lot of money out of all this, not just a butler's pay. Probably Bannon was the boss and Blackman was the one carrying out the orders and delivering them which was an Outfit method of separating the big guy from his underlings so no one could say who the orders came from with proof to back it up.

"Now there is Trulia. Once again there are the rumors about her and Blackman and she got large sums of money out of the company. These sums going to her and Blackman increased a lot after Avon disappeared. Avon also had been thinking of giving her more of his estate in his estate plan, but had changed his mind shortly before his death and she knew this. Furthermore, Eddie would be in control of the company when Avon died. He didn't handle the finances when Avon was alive, but if he was in charge he would have to and he might ask why Trulia and Blackman were bleeding all the money out."

"Now," continued Lohman, "Avon and D'Gregor wanted to start their own drug company. In other words he wanted to move in on the drug business. No wonder the drug people wanted him and D'Gregor gotten rid of. So kill him and D'Gregor and the drug business stays in the right hands. But if Avon was killed and also D'Gregor who would be in control? Eddie would be in control of Whiteman Materials, not Trulia. She and Blackman could take over the Temple and its substance abuse business, but the main distribution mechanism of the illegal drugs was the company. So to avoid this, they wouldn't just kill Avon, they would hide the killing. That way he was a missing person and an administrator had to be appointed by the court to handle all his assets until either he

THE DEAD ONE PROTRUDES

reappeared, was found to be dead, or seven years passed, at which time he would be presumed to be dead. During those seven years they could figure some way to get the drug business out of the Company. But Avon was discovered to be dead well before the seven years ran and they had not got the business out of the Company. This could account for Trulia all of a sudden wanting to buy the Excelente bagged cement side of the business. They, Trulia and Blackman, seem to be the ones who stood to gain by his murder and by covering up the fact that he was dead. Too bad the concrete didn't hold. They were also the ones to benefit from the disappearance of D'Gregor. Bannon, and Hump too would benefit."

Lohman looked around the room. Then he said, "So they had the motive and opportunity, but so far all we know is that Avon was dead there in his house on Friday night. Somehow his body got to the plant that night for the pour. Now the Syndicate way of ordering someone killed operated through intermediaries. The big guy did not tell the killer to do it. He had the message delivered through someone else so the actual killer could not testify that he gave the order. If the actual killer did know who did give the order, any testimony by him to that effect would be hearsay and not admissible at trial. So think of this. Let's say the van driver came there to get the body and take it to the plant. Let's say he picked up Trulia and Blackman on the way and they all helped get the body in the van, perhaps with something like one of those big wheeled garbage or material bins. Then the van driver took Trulia and Blackman back to their cars and then went on to the plant with the body. No one there would know from direct observation who gave the orders or killed Avon or how or any of the details. Someone had to give them orders to put the body in the pour, but that could have come through other intermediaries. Only the driver would know

THE DEAD ONE PROTRUDES

that Blackman and Trulia were involved from direct observation. That would indicate why he was killed, probably by someone else in the plant through other orders. Remember he disappeared after that, although he was poured into a panel later. His car was found near the Salerno Funeral Home and perhaps he was preserved there until the time for his pour. And a Salerno hearse was the last place D'Gregor was seen and that was before Avon disappeared, even though his panel was delivered later. Remember that the gun that killed him and the driver was found in the driver's panel so they both had to be killed by the time the panel with the driver in it was delivered. Salerno was probably keeping the bodies around until the time for the pours. Remember drugs were found at his place in an Excelente bag and that he has disappeared. By the way, I would not be surprised to hear that Blackman and Bannon have disappeared too. By the way, Bannon was invited here tonight, but I have noticed he is not here."

"Fine you may say. That's a nice story, but when you say Blackman and Trulia and the van driver went to pick up Avon, they were elsewhere. Blackman was at a show and Trulia went to a shopping mall and a movie. But did they? Is that where they were? Their alibis are not confirmed. In fact they seem to be contrived and made up. First Trulia. There is no witness or other evidence placing her at the show or the mall. She could have driven up north, parked her car somewhere, and been picked up and dropped off by the van up there. Or she could have been picked up by Blackman and then gone with him to the theater parking lot."

"Now," Lohman went on, "Blackman. At this stage we might say the butler did it. Where was he? At a show in River North. We have a confirmed sighting of him there by a parking lot attendant. Both before

THE DEAD ONE PROTRUDES

and after the show. Why did the attendant remember all this about one of many customers? Because Blackman gave him big tips, both when parking and when picking up his car. And Blackman was there with a date. Blackman identified her and we find that the woman he identified was a black woman who was shot in a drive by shooting on an expressway on the South Side some time later. There is no such woman alive to confirm his story, or I might say to disagree with it. However, the attendant told the police that he was with a tall white blonde, which describes Trulia. When shown pictures though, the attendant couldn't confirm this. What this means is that Blackman was there. It appears that he over tipped to get the attendant to remember this. And why would he tip both before and after parking? Then he had tickets for the show and the records show that they were used. But by who? Who used those tickets? Nothing shows that he is the one. It was an opening and usually there are people waiting around asking people for tickets. He could have given them to such a person or he could have sold them or disposed of them to someone else in advance."

"Now, what was this show? When asked Blackman referred to a brochure for the show and told the police the plot of the show from that. He said he couldn't remember, but he said he collected brochures. However the brochure was wrong. Apparently it was something that was reported in the news at the time. Even Eddie, who was not at the show, had heard of it. Our Vice Chairman, Zenon here, went to the show too and he was surprised at the difference from the brochure which he had also read. You would think Blackman would have remembered something about the show. So, not only do we not have proof he went to the show and used the tickets, we seem to have an indication of a made up alibi and an attendant who may have seen Trulia there with him. The van driver could have picked them up during

THE DEAD ONE PROTRUDES

that period and drove them to get Avon. Or Blackman could have gone to get Trulia wherever she left her can and then they both could have gone to the theater parking lot and then been picked up by the van." All of a sudden Lohman realized what he had said. He thought of the old song, "Hey lady, stick out your can, here comes the garbage man." He wanted to make some crack referring to that, but instead he said, "Sorry, I meant pick up her car." Then he continued, "Later the van driver would have dropped them back at their cars or both at the show, leaving Blackman to drive Trulia to her car. Then they could have come home at different times so no one would think they were together that night. They would not have gone to the plant or else the people there would know from direct evidence that they were involved with the body. Only the driver would and he apparently was shot soon thereafter by someone else. So there you are Detective Bongwad. Blackman and Trulia did it and the drug lord was thrown in by someone in the drug trade who wanted his business." He pointed at Trulia who was in the audience.

"She was running towards a door without a SWAT officer directly in front of it screaming, "You're crazy!"

Bongwad motioned to the officers and some of them grabbed her and brought her to the front of the room. By this time she had decided to make a deal. "I didn't do it," she screamed. "Snively did. He gave the orders. He was the one who put the drug in. He got it from the Temple's clinics. He made the plan. We had to get rid of Avon. He wanted to take over. Snively told me what to do and gave me the alibi. He told the driver what to do. That's why he had the driver killed. He gave the orders for that to someone else to pass on. I went along just because he thought they may need help. We did have the materials bin

THE DEAD ONE PROTRUDES

in the van, just like you said. I don't know how you figured that out. I think he wanted me along just to implicate me though and keep me quiet. But it was all his work, his orders, his actions. I didn't do it. He did. And listening to you I think I may be next."

"So where is he now?" asked Lohman, looking down at her. "Blackman. Where is he?"

"Who knows," said Trulia. "He's gone. He took off. I don't know where he is. He took off when the drugs were found. He's the one who told me to destroy the Excelente bags we had left. I don't know where he is."

Eddie shouted out, "Bannon's gone. We usually have frequent business contacts because he is our supplier and we haven't been able to contact him in the last few days."

Lohman looked out at Gilbert who was still restraining Sean who looked like he was waiting for the guillotine blade to drop. "So let him go. Maybe I am not correct, but you have no proof beyond a reasonable doubt that he did anything and you do have a confession here." Bongwad waived at Gilbert who then released Sean. The audience broke out in cheers and applause. Great show. No advertisements. No ticket charge. Justice prevails once again.

Trulia was hauled away by the cops and the firm got on with their awards and then everyone went on home or to other events.

THE DEAD ONE PROTRUDES

30 NEWS OF THE WORLD

While the firm party was going on the messy stuff was hitting the fan in Washington. This began to hit the news early the next morning when it was revealed throughout the world that that the entire security forces available in Washington had been called to the White House when someone in the oval office had accidentally hit the emergency button indicating that an attack was going on there. The Marine officers on duty rushed in. The hit on the button also independently activated all the other security forces which were mobilized and sent to the White House. An attack on the President or Vice President is an event the security forces had prepared for and they descended on the White House en mass to protect the Head of State. Unfortunately this massive concentration of manpower on the White House prevented total secrecy as to what was going on and before it could be suppressed the story came out. Ronald Hump and his wife Salmania Hump and Sillary Flinton and her husband Will Flinton had been caught having a four-way orgy in the oval office. When the Marines had rushed in they were found engaging in acts which are too shocking to tell you about dear reader and each was with the spouse of the other. This was reported throughout the world before the news could be suppressed. All Flinton and Hump had to say about it was that the Russians had hacked the system and they had recently converted to nudism. As to what they were doing in the nude – they claimed that the Marines rushing in were so busy and panicked to notice what was really going on - which was a reading of one of the books on the nudist philosophy.

THE DEAD ONE PROTRUDES

At this the entire world just got fed up and stopped listening to or reading the news any further. And so dear reader, it is time for you to stop reading too.

THE DEAD ONE PROTRUDES

NEVER TELL YOUR PARENTS YOU READ ABOUT THIS. YOU'LL

GET WHACKED. THEY VOTED FOR

ONE OR THE OTHER OF THESE CLOWNS.

For more trash like this see

Donniesyellowballbooks.com

THE DEAD ONE PROTRUDES

Made in the USA
Middletown, DE
13 May 2021